NANTUCKET ROSE

By the Author

Stick McLaughlin: The Prohibition Years

Exchange

Night Voice

Nantucket Rose

Visit us at www.boldstrokesbooks.com

NANTUCKET ROSE

by
CF Frizzell

2017

NANTUCKET ROSE

ISBN 13: 978-1-63555-056-6

THIS TRADE PAPERBACK ORIGINAL IS PUBLISHED BY
BOLD STROKES BOOKS, INC.
P.O. BOX 249
VALLEY FALLS, NY 12185

FIRST EDITION: NOVEMBER 2017

CREDITS
EDITOR: CINDY CRESAP
PRODUCTION DESIGN: STACIA SEAMAN
COVER DESIGN BY SHERI (GRAPHICARTIST2020@HOTMAIL.COM)

Acknowledgments

For me, writing a novel set on the island of Nantucket brought back a myriad of fond memories. Commuting there from Hyannis Harbor, now many years ago, always had me marveling at the daunting Atlantic, enjoying the ferry rides as much as days spent working on the *Grey Lady* itself.

You can't see the island from the dock in Hyannis, but beyond the horizon some thirty miles out sits a quaint, historic Massachusetts community once known around the world for the courage and success of its valiant whalers. The Atlantic Ocean is no less a part of daily island life today, but time does move on, and I'm grateful that generations of Nantucketters have persevered, protecting treasured elements of the past in the face of ever-changing times. There are no McDonald's restaurants on Nantucket; camping is not allowed; bringing your car to the island costs a small fortune. But there's that Charles Dickens feel to tree-lined Main Street, with its cobblestones and street lamps; shop owners selling the work of island artisans—who all know you by name; and a whole town's worth of support for the high school varsity team. Treasured elements like individuality and community. A settlement that's pushing four hundred years old knows what matters most.

I credit my late father for my love of the ocean, which led to writing *Nantucket Rose*. He was a sailor before, during, and after WWII and would have lived his entire life aboard any ship, if my mother had let him. How he gloried in our last excursion together, standing at the bow of the ferry *Eagle* as we crossed Nantucket Sound, silently adrift in his memories. I know he would be pleased to visit Nantucket again through this novel.

And I'm most thankful for my wife Kathy and her love, support, and creative inspiration. Writing a novel without her is inconceivable to me.

I've written a locale full of memories in *Nantucket Rose*, and appreciate every reader who comes aboard to visit. I hope you make fond memories here, too.

To Kathy
for making every dream come true

Chapter One

The ornery Atlantic Ocean landed another jab to the ferry's ribs, determined to pound the ship back to the mainland. Maggie Jordan and fellow passengers swayed with the broadside blow, wincing like the audience in a prize fight as the hardy ship heaved to one side and absorbed the hit. She clamped both hands around her cardboard cup to keep it on the table. Gyroscopic, she thought, watching the scalding coffee remain perfectly level while the world tilted around it. Heat seared into her fingers and she withdrew them only slightly, and risked letting the cup sit unaided while the ferry hammered through the angry sea.

The clock on the lounge wall said she had another hour to go before reaching the island, reminding her she sat directly in the middle of busy Nantucket Sound where there was no land to be seen—if she could have seen anything through the sheets of rain outside.

She counted on the snack bar coffee to keep her queasiness in check. Her stomach rolled as much as the Steamship Authority's beefy ferry, the M/V *Eagle*, and had never been this upset on previous trips to Nantucket. Wishing her appointment with the general contractor had fallen on a nicer day, Maggie marveled at how most passengers took this rough ride in stride. Granted, a few looked a little green, but most calmly sat, reading or chatting as children played in their seats and dogs on leashes slept soundly. For a moment, she envisioned her own dog, Retta, testing her patience, eager to play, and Maggie knew that challenge would come soon enough.

She returned to her iPad and details of the work ahead. The last phase of her biggest turnaround project to date beckoned loudly. She couldn't wait to be hands-on and settled in to bring her vision of

Nantucket's newest B&B to life. Months of sketching and planning, hours of phone calls, mountains of regulations and forms, and too many hurried—and not always pleasant—trips to the island were all in their final stages now, and she itched like a child at Christmas to see them all to fruition.

She scrolled down the list of tasks yet to be done, noted their impact on her budget, and the timetable involved. She sighed and stared off into space, hoping the B&B's opening was still on schedule. Less than three months to go. She nodded at her list. Still doable.

"Pardon me, dear. Would you mind terribly sharing your booth?" Wearing tweed blazer and slacks, a woman with an extraordinarily long silver braid stood holding a Bloody Mary and gripping the seat back for balance. "I don't mean to disturb your work." Her assorted bracelets jangled when she gestured to the table.

"Oh, no. Not at all." Maggie quickly moved her things aside. "Please have a seat."

The stranger put the cocktail down and folded her long camel hair coat into a neat bundle on the bench beside her. "A full house on the boat today." She loosened the cashmere scarf at her throat and drew her drink close. "I'm Julia. What's your name, dear?"

"Maggie Jordan." She offered a smile, more intrigued than upset by the interruption. "Nice to meet you, Julia. Looks like we've picked a terrible day for a crossing."

"Indeed. My travel itinerary forced me out of lovely South Carolinian sunshine yesterday and into a homecoming with this ghastly weather. What's your excuse for enduring such a ride?"

"A business meeting, completing renovations on my B&B. I hope to open on Memorial Day weekend."

"Oh, my. Now that's exciting." She drank heavily through a straw. "Are you local?"

"I'm a Philly girl, but I spend so much time working away from home, I probably qualify as a nomad."

"You don't say. And where is your B&B?"

Amused by the questions, Maggie handed her a business card from a leather portfolio, and Julia riffled through her huge straw tote bag until she produced reading glasses. "My Tuck'r Inn is the former Captain Joshua Pratt House on Davis Street."

Julia's head popped up, eyes wide and crinkled with focus. "I've always loved the Pratt House, and now you own it? Or, should I say," she glanced at the card, "Valentin Enterprises owns it?"

"Yes." Maggie smiled at Julia's innocent mispronunciation. "I am Valen*teen* Enterprises. My grandfather was a Slovak, my biggest supporter growing up, so I named my one-woman corporation after him. I like to think he brings me luck." She stopped short of revealing that Valentin's luck had extended for the past nine years—and included no less than eleven turnaround projects like Tuck'r.

"Lucky to land the Pratt House, truly," Julia said. "A prestigious home in its day. Such a tragedy, I must say, that it fell to foreclosure some years ago and didn't stay in the family."

Glad it hadn't, Maggie nodded. "I was fortunate to buy it as soon as it went back on the market, and couldn't bypass the opportunity to name it myself."

"You're not using the Pratt name. You're calling it Tuck'r Inn?"

"Well, the Pratt name, literally, has been missing from the building for some time now. Besides, I've had the Tuck'r name in mind from the moment I decided on Nantucket. There'll be plenty of history inside, of course, but that name was just too perfect."

"So." Julia sighed. "Valentin will be adding to our island's charming attractions." She drank absently, but the keen look in her eyes said the observation begged for more detail.

Maggie took a guarded approach to the subject of her work, ever since locals violently opposed her Lake Tahoe condo turnaround several years ago. That fire and rebuild cost her far more than insurance covered and set her back eighteen months before she could secure a buyer. The siphoning of her bankroll jeopardized her entire business and cast a long shadow over her future, and the unexpected level of opposition left a deep emotional scar. Could she win a community's approval? *Must* she choose this site and stir up such dangerous negativity? Did she dare appreciate her opponents' position? Confident she always did her best to accommodate, she countered her personal and professional doubts with a show of faith in herself—and a vow *not* to disclose Valentin's renovate-and-sell mission.

And Nantucketters, in particular, as she'd learned at the start of this project, didn't warm easily to outsiders tampering with their territory or their history. "I hope Tuck'r will become part of the community, make a statement for many years to come," Maggie offered, "and that islanders as well as visitors will cherish it."

"I see. Well, I'll grant you that the Pratt House deserves to flourish." She set her empty plastic glass down with finality. "I'm sure the task has made you a veteran traveler by now."

Maggie sent her a skeptical eye as she rose from the table. "Thank you, but I'm not too sure I'm—"

As if on cue, the *Eagle* tilted so far off-center, Maggie slapped a palm to the wall to avoid toppling against it. Her view out the rain-lashed window swung from sky to ocean, both nearly identical in color and demeanor, and she wondered if Julia had conjured a taste of nature's wrath to discourage her. Just as quickly, the ship leveled off, in time to be slammed by another robust wave. Everything shuddered, and Maggie grabbed the fiberglass tabletop for stability.

"Frankly, I can't imagine ever getting used to this." She gulped the remains of her coffee, eyeing the trash bin at the end of her aisle of booths. Hand extended, ready to grip anything secure en route, she staggered along the rolling deck to the trash, deposited her cup, and staggered back to where Julia now sat reading, remarkably oblivious to the ride. Maggie dropped into her seat in time to stop her iPad from sliding off the table.

"So you think I'll get used to this?"

"Yes, dear." Julia didn't look up and Maggie couldn't tell if Julia simply took these two-hour mini-cruises for granted or no longer cared to prolong their conversation.

"Well, this is my worst trip so far. They *do* stop runs to the island at some point, don't they?"

"Yes, they do, when the sea gets too rough."

Maggie almost laughed. At the far end of the lounge, a businessman with a hand to his mouth hurried into the rest room. The ship rolled again and a toddler crawling across a bench banged his head on the seat back. He cried loudly, disrupting nearby readers.

"Rougher than this will get messy," Maggie said. "Does it have to be a hurricane before the Steamship Authority cancels trips?"

"Are you afraid?" Julia frowned over her tinted lenses. "This isn't uncommon for the Authority, and certainly nothing a stout and sturdy ship like the *Eagle* hasn't handled a thousand times." She closed her novel and leveled her gaze, as steely gray as the clouds and ocean Maggie tried to ignore. "I'm sure you're aware, hurricanes come in summer and fall. This time of year, it would be a blizzard."

"Lovely thought."

"Might you be entertaining regrets about your project?" The wistful lilt in Julia's question sounded like a challenge or hope. "This is part of New England's island life," Julia added, "a part to which you'll become accustomed—rather quickly, I trust."

Maggie hardly saw herself becoming much of an islander in just the short time required to sell the property. In fact, with luck, she might be off the island by the time hurricane season picked up in August.

"No regrets. Actually, I couldn't be more excited. I think Nantucket is enchanting." Julia took the compliment with a gracious smile. "You're a native islander?"

"Oh, no, dear. We retired here almost twenty years ago, but my husband and I are as integrated into the life as we can be. Are you married?" She immediately held up a hand. "No. Pardon me for—"

"It's okay," Maggie said. The subject wasn't as painful as it was last summer when she and Stephanie parted ways. "I'm single. I've created quite the demanding job for myself." *And that's my top priority.*

The *Eagle* rocked again and Maggie slid her iPad back from the table's edge. "I do love being up in New England. I enjoy the antiquity, the success so many of the towns have had preserving their character."

Already, Maggie could see herself and Retta, headed north to this full-time adventure in early May. The ocean would be considerably more agreeable than today; she'd really rather not confront the Atlantic's March madness again.

"Sounds like you're determined to succeed." Julia removed her glasses and sat back. "Your appreciation of history and aesthetics should serve you well here."

"That's very nice of you to say. Thank you. I have a feeling the hardest work is ahead of me, though."

"Whatever made you choose to settle on Nantucket?"

"The charm won me over. It's so unique and teeming with history. A temptation I just couldn't resist."

She didn't want to get into it any further. Besides, it wasn't appropriate, not with a stranger. Self-examination, airing her dreams and desires were things she once shared with Steph, and sometimes with her sister Rachel over many glasses of wine. And launching herself into *this* project had required considerable calculation and introspection.

Maybe she did it because it took her thirty miles off the coast of Cape Cod and removed her from everything routine, or maybe it was the prospect of a big-money payoff, or the experience of island living and a summer on the beach, or the triumph of scoring a historic whaling captain's home. She couldn't pinpoint the reason but knew this job had her more emotionally invested than any challenge she'd met. In less than two months, she would sublet her condo in Philadelphia and take up island residence to establish a saleable property. With a prospective buyer already awaiting her finished product, it wouldn't be a drawn-out process, and then she'd be free to move on to a new challenge.

The ship dipped and heaved, and Maggie's stomach protested. She pressed a hand to the wall again. Julia braced herself on the seat and didn't miss a beat.

"Residents—particularly the native islanders—they take immense pride in that history," Julia stated. "The few islanders left now are madly protective of their heritage." She tapped a bejeweled finger on the table. "No doubt you've encountered our extreme building restrictions with your renovation work."

"Oh, I certainly have." Maggie nearly winced, remembering the endless budget revisions she'd made to accommodate Nantucket's demanding building code.

"Well, that's just one example of how highly we value preservation." She again dove into her tote bag and pulled out a change purse. "I hate to impose, but would you be a love and get me another Bloody Mary?"

The *Eagle* rolled again just as Maggie stood. Stumbling, she grabbed the table, swiped at the passing iPad and missed, and watched it hit the floor.

"Damn." One hand still clinging to the table, she edged into the aisle and stooped to retrieve it.

"Got it." A long arm in charcoal gray canvas reached the iPad first, and Maggie straightened just inches from a uniformed *Eagle* crewman. *Woman.* Their proximity briefly unnerved her, and she froze in the grip of bright, electric blue eyes beneath the brim of the sailor's ball cap, the austere expression across slim lips and angular jaw.

Wow. Do you light up the night with those eyes? An extra beat passed before she realized the sailor held up her iPad.

"Oh. Thank you." A few inches taller than Maggie, the woman stood formidable and thickset around the shoulders of her jacket, athletic and steady.

"Y'welcome," she said, her voice just above a mumble.

Then the ship ducked out from under Maggie's feet and her knees buckled. Instantly, the sailor cupped her elbow, the hold expansive and firm, and Maggie regained her posture just as the boat shuddered again.

"Whoa," she gasped. "Thank you. Again."

The sailor stepped back, assumed a slightly spread stance, unfazed by the *Eagle*'s motion. "Best to stay seated."

Maggie sat quickly.

"Ah, y-yes. You're right."

The seaman touched a finger to her cap and spun away. Maggie watched her stride the length of the deck to the stairwell, grip the railings in each hand, and swing down, out of sight.

How have I never noticed you before?

❖

The overcast afternoon made Ellis Chilton shrug deeper into her jacket as she walked up to Main Street from the waterfront. So typical of Nantucket, the westerly breezes had shifted to northerly, pushing the April morning's pleasant temperature down to chilly, and she was tempted to turn around and spend the rest of her day off at home with a good book.

It had been a long while since she'd given herself a "free day." Home renovations were always her main focus, hard labor alone, which she preferred, and time-consuming, especially when she had precious little to spare. After several years of part-time Steamship Authority service, the promotion to chief mate four years ago commandeered the bulk of her waking hours; work at home ate up the rest—and she liked it that way. Today, with renovations nearly complete, she treated herself to this escape.

She paused on the corner and looked up the length of Main at its centuries-old intersections with other cobblestone streets, the brick sidewalks and their benches, the rugged oaks whose long reaches promised shelter once buds blossomed. The setting, its character and atmosphere, could be traced back to Nantucket's glory days of whaling, and nostalgia and respect for that era always drew Ellis to a stop.

The historic horse trough that centered the street lacked its seasonal floral display at the moment, but she looked forward to seeing it overflow with flowers when Nantucket's annual Daffodil Festival began next weekend. She warmed at the prospect of sunny, colorful planters and window boxes again lining every street, insistent in their brilliance and brightening everyone's spirit. She knew boatloads of tourists and seemingly every resident would descend on this quaint downtown district to celebrate spring with parades, exhibits, and picnics. Ferry work would double, and pushy off-islanders would irritate her, but the festival had been putting smiles on faces for nearly fifty years. Distinctively Nantucket, it drew residents out of hibernation, sent the green light to tourists, and basically opened the isolated community's windows to another refreshing season. Ellis counted on that optimism as much as the island did.

Her friend Jeannie, a dispatcher for the Authority, trotted across the street, waving. "I'm amazed you actually showed," she said as they turned down South Water Street. "It's about time you took some R&R."

Ellis couldn't remember the last time she'd spent a Sunday afternoon in a bar with a friend. Jeannie probably couldn't either, bubbling like the occasional tourist she was. Shorter than Ellis and hefty in build, she beamed up at her from behind unnecessary black sunglasses. Ellis shortened her stride so Jeannie could keep up.

"I figured I'd take the afternoon. I have to hit the supermarket later, anyway."

"Right. Best not to food shop on an empty stomach, so we'll get lunch. I love the massive sandwiches at Dell's, and we can sample a bunch of their microbrews. Not bad for a little place on the wharf."

At the real estate office ahead, an older woman working on a window box paused at their approach and pushed up the sleeves of her bulky sweater. She waved an empty flowerpot at them. "Ellis Chilton. When's this weather going to turn?" She pointed to the sky. "Afternoon's turned into November, for heaven's sake. How can I put my arrangements out here in this?"

"Your shop will be gorgeous as always, Abbey," Ellis said as they passed, "and I'm sure you'll win this year. Just don't put the snow shovel away yet."

"Oh, pooh!" Abbey tossed a hand at her and returned to work.

"The forecast is calling for a sunny weekend, at least," Jeannie said, and they turned the corner toward the waterfront.

Cold gusts off the ocean roared up Broad Street, and Ellis and Jeannie dipped their heads into the wind. They made room on the sidewalk for a well-dressed couple strolling in the opposite direction.

The man nodded at Ellis and she nodded back. "Mr. and Mrs. Bergstrom."

Four paces later, Jeannie spoke. "He didn't seem too friendly."

"Decent guy. Banker."

"Ah."

She said no more, and Ellis knew Jeannie was putting together pieces Ellis didn't care to discuss. Ellis's past experiences with the bank hadn't been pleasant and, Nantucket being a small, close-knit community, everyone knew it but never broached the subject with her. Those painful times had led her to find work with the Authority and turn her life around. As much as Jeannie loved to gab, she knew not to pry, and Ellis was grateful, but that didn't mean Jeannie fell silent for any length of time.

"I don't think I could've hung around here all my life like you. Everyone on this rock knows you. I'd have been a paranoid, claustrophobic basket case by high school."

Ellis snickered. "High school just got in my way. I never wanted to come off the ocean to sit in a room all day, but you do what you're told."

"But you did leave for college."

"Dad always said it was Mom's dream for me to go, plus, I figured it would benefit the business." She shrugged. "I picked Suffolk in Boston on purpose, spent as much time racing back here as I did in classes."

"For your dad."

"Yeah. He'd only hire a helper when he absolutely had to, and made me crazy, worrying."

They crossed to Dell's bar on Easy Street and Ellis looked ahead, down Steamship Wharf to the sea beyond. They'd had a good thing going, she and her father, running freight to and from the mainland and the Vineyard, rugged but exhilarating work that had been in her blood since she was a little girl. Generations of salt water, not blood in their veins, Dad always said.

Jeannie nudged her as they entered the small, softly lit bar. "I still can't believe I got you to join me here." She removed her sunglasses and led them to a pair of stools opposite the television hanging behind the bar. "Yankees are in town," she said, studying the screen. "When's the last time you went to Fenway?"

"Two thousand four," Ellis promptly answered, knowing Jeannie would be surprised.

"When they broke the curse?" Incredulous, Jeannie made the bartender wait for her order. "No way."

"Twice. Regular season and playoffs." Ellis ordered a beer and a pastrami sandwich as Jeannie continued to stare at her. "Order, will you?"

Jeannie rattled off what she wanted and spun back to her. "You, who never leaves your precious Gray Lady, the land of foggy bliss? How'd that happen?"

"The tickets were gifts from a friend."

"I went just last year. My luck, the Royals kicked our ass."

A patron two stools away leaned in their direction. "At least you both got to see Big Papi play."

Ellis and Jeannie turned and agreed readily, but beyond him, an attractive woman paying for a takeout order at the end of the bar caught Ellis's eye. Dressed in a fitted forest green leather blazer, jeans, and knee-high cowhide boots, she slung her bag over her shoulder and laughed with the bartender as she prepared to leave. Her bright, sincere sound easily carried over Jeannie's conversation with the man nearby. A sense of familiarity struck Ellis, especially when the woman turned toward the door, a small wheeled suitcase in tow.

The wind no doubt had mussed those auburn waves free of their clip and brought a rosiness to her cheeks, and those dark eyes seemed to dance beneath slim, slightly arched brows. Ellis tried not to stare as she struggled to recall if they'd ever met.

The woman walked with a poised authority that commanded the door to open, but of course it didn't. With food in one hand, she released her luggage to shove the door open, then grabbed the suitcase handle again and tried to slip out before the door closed.

Ellis suddenly found herself holding the door open, close enough to see exasperation turn to surprise on the woman's face, just before a blast of ocean air made them both blink.

"Thanks so much." The woman hauled her suitcase across the threshold.

"Y'welcome. You had your hands full."

"I should've backed out." She let go of the handle to swipe hair from her face. "I wasn't"—she looked directly at Ellis and her eyes widened—"thinking. Hello."

The chilly wind found its way inside Ellis's collar, and she blamed it for the tremor in her chest and completely forgot she still held the door. Delivered softly with a warm smile, the single word carried a hint of recognition, but as much as Ellis wanted to solve the mystery, she was too lost in the winsome face before her.

"Hello," she managed.

A patron inside yelled at her. "Hey, shut the door, will ya?"

Jolted from her haze, Ellis stepped out to let the door swing shut and inadvertently closed the distance between them.

The attractive stranger edged back, fumbling for her luggage handle.

"Sorry to keep you," she said and promptly moved out to the

sidewalk. "Thank you for the assist. Again. It was nice seeing you." She flashed a smile and walked away.

Ellis stared after her, taken by the definitive, feminine lines of her jacket, the way they hugged her shoulders and back, the way the wind tossed her hair. She walked confidently, as if daring the bricks and cobblestones to twist an ankle. The suitcase bobbled along behind her and drew Ellis's attention to the slight sway of her hips. She could only shake her head. *So we* have *met.*

Jeannie banged through the door and stopped short when she found Ellis still looking down the street. "You let her leave? Shit, El. When are you going to stop gawking at them and make a move?" She punched her arm playfully. "Jeez, she was hot." Ellis looked at her blankly as a memory fought to take shape. Jeannie tugged her back inside. "Come on. The Sox have bases loaded with no outs."

CHAPTER TWO

Retta, no!" Maggie flung aside her copy of *Coastal Living* and sprinted after the ever-ready athlete that was her chocolate Labrador retriever. "Retta, come!" Retta and her selective hearing were on a mission: a toddler's pink rubber baseball rolled up the ferry deck's main aisle.

But then the door to the snack bar opened into that aisle and hit the ball back. It bounced over Retta's head and she jumped for it, oblivious to forward momentum that sent all her sixty-two pounds into the legs of the sailor who'd just emerged. Both seaman and dog tumbled to the deck.

"Oh, my God! I'm *so* sorry!" Maggie snatched up Retta's rainbow-colored leash and urged her back, away from licking the sailor's face. "Retta, behave." Recognition suddenly made it difficult to speak. *As if I need to keep bumping into you.* "This is so embarrassing." *Did I just say that out loud?* "Um…Hello. Again. Are you all right? Really, I'm awfully sorry."

"It's okay. No harm done." The seaman straightened her lanky frame, but not before Retta could lick her cheek one more time. The woman scruffed the fur between Retta's ears good-naturedly and scooped her cap off the floor.

Maggie watched her resettle it over short coal-black hair, and took note of the name "Chilton" engraved on the brass name tag clipped to her uniform shirt, the very sharp, form-fitting uniform shirt. *Damn.* Now even more uncomfortable, she resorted to familiarity to ease the awkwardness of the moment.

"Hello again."

"Good morning."

"Um…This is on me, my bad. It's Retta's first Nantucket ferry, so she's excited—plus she loves people and playing catch." Chilton appeared to listen carefully, her steady look unreadable and dangerously consuming. "Well…I mean…" Maggie stumbled on, "she'd been good for the first half hour, but I should've known she wouldn't contain that energy for the whole trip. I'm really sorry. I'll be more careful."

She held her breath, awaiting the response, truly apologetic and not wanting anything to spoil this big day. Until now, everything had gone according to her meticulously organized schedule, even this morning, when she'd awakened before dawn at her sister's home in Hyannis to catch this first boat out. Her adventure had officially begun. She didn't need *this* added excitement. *Of all the crew members, at least Retta picked the hot one.*

Retta pressed forward and Chilton stroked her head. "You have her on a leash and that's good," she said, her rich tone full of official directive, "because we have strict rules about pets on board."

"Yes, I know. I'm very sorry." *God, you have such gorgeous eyes.*

"And you know that leashes work best when someone's on the other end."

Excuse me?

"Oh. Well, of course—"

"Shipboard safety is paramount. It could have been a child, another passenger knocked to—"

"I'm quite aware, thank you." Irritation flared, compounding the embarrassment of being scolded in front of dozens of passengers. Adding insult to injury, Retta insisted on getting closer to Chilton, eating up the attention to her ears. The damn dog's eyes were closing in blissful contentment beneath the broad, deeply tanned hand.

"Please be cautious if you take her out for a stroll on the promenade deck. Labs love the water."

I know my dog.

"Yes. We're inside on this level for a reason."

"Very good." Chilton gently lifted Retta's muzzle and spoke into attentive amber eyes. "Nice meeting you, Retta." To Maggie, she added a simple, "Enjoy your trip," before walking away.

Swell meeting you, too.

Retta stared after Chilton, squirming where she sat, her wet ultra-sensitive nose pulsing and tail relentlessly swishing.

"Come on, traitor. She could've been nicer to Mama, you know." Maggie had to tug a bit, but Retta eventually followed her back to their seats, where she obediently sat at Maggie's feet, still focused on the last spot she'd seen Chilton. "Hey. We'll walk around in a little bit, but you have to behave for the next hour or so." Maggie leaned down and whispered to the top of her head. "There'll be other attractive women on Nantucket for you to swoon over, and hopefully they'll be as friendly to your mama as they'll be to you, but we've got to get there first."

Retta spared a look over her shoulder, the pleading look with tilted eyebrows and half-moon eyes that said "But I want to play with her" and went back to studying Chilton's exit. Maggie chuckled. *You're a sucker for a gentle touch, too. She's certainly nice to look at, but not much personality.* She scratched Retta's head, winning only a two-stroke tail wag.

Maggie flipped the pages of her magazine, but the windows framing the main lounge drew her attention to the view and the miles of ocean that surrounded them. Hardly a trace of Hyannis Harbor remained now, and she looked ahead for a thickening of the horizon, where Nantucket magically rose from the hazy edge of the world.

Maggie knew her family still worried about her success at this venture, so removed from "civilization." But this wasn't *escaping* to a new life, as she'd told herself a thousand times. This wasn't *avoidance* either, despite how her friends had lectured for the past year. This was all about a new beginning, leaving the past where it belonged, and concentrating on the future. *Being single, successful, and moving forward.*

Lost in the ocean view, Maggie hoped to find "civilization" far more real *on* the island, closer-knit, fundamental, and rejuvenating. She believed the ocean to be the key, predictably unpredictable, vital and ever-changing. She'd already learned that the ocean and the weather it carried ashore dictated practically every aspect of daily life, and had been gifted due respect from all islanders since the original Native Americans inhabited this place. She tried conveying such newly acquired revelations to family and friends, but doubted she'd been convincing. *It's my life, my dream, and I intend to keep at it.*

Once again, everywhere around her, around the *Eagle* and its load of passengers, cars, and trucks, there was nothing but water, this time a mature, rich blue, majestic, imposing, and still damn cold in early May. The wind had been brisk when they boarded, and she now knew that "chilly and brisk" at the dock meant "cut through your jacket" out in Nantucket Sound. The millions of tiny white caps that randomly speckled the surface could just as easily be splashes of frost. Eyeing the promenade deck almost made her shiver.

After all those bitter, stomach-lurching trips of the past eight months, she yearned to lounge on the open deck, work on her tan a little, and enjoy summer breezes. There was a method to her madness in taking the Authority "slow boats" instead of the "fast ferry." These two-hour trips provided just the right excuse to relax and think, luxuriate in the view, catch up on paperwork, even though foul weather sometimes tested her love of the ocean. She only reverted to the pricier hour-long catamaran ride—or the twenty-minute plane jump—when expediency warranted.

Today, spring was hard at work, battling to pull the Atlantic out of its notorious "off-season" mode, and Maggie found it hard to resist the temptation to join that effort, stroll the deck and withstand the buffeting chill. A blue-sky morning like this felt like a test she desperately wanted to pass. But she was a newcomer to this change-of-season stuff on the ocean, and doubted she'd ever achieve "veteran traveler" status like that held by islanders she'd come to know, like that Julia woman she'd met last month, like seamen aboard ferries like this.

"I've been through far worse already, haven't I, sweetie?" She rubbed Retta's side and then her belly when Retta lazily rolled over. "My good girl. I promise we'll go to the beach later and you can check out how cold the water is. And, if you must, you can go swimming."

That word set Retta on high alert, back on her feet in readiness, ears perked.

"Not now, Retta." Maggie regretted uttering the "S" word. "Chill, baby. Later, I promise." She found a chew toy in her hefty shoulder bag and grinned at Retta's happy acceptance. A handful of treats and another chewy just *might* keep Retta content until they docked, as long as an excited voice or the whiff of something delicious or the appearance of a certain handsome sailor didn't throw decorum overboard in an instant.

❖

Shaking her head at Nantucket's chilly air, Maggie blasted her heater and spared a glance into her rearview mirror. Retta looked every bit the sightseeing tourist, gawking out the Rav4's open rear driver's side window as they drove off the *Eagle* and onto Nantucket soil, a family of two. Hopefully, they'd be happy here for a while and make this work.

"Deadline's in about a month, Retta. We'll make it." The car bounced over the cobblestones, and she smiled as she passed the

Easy Street sign. "We have to work our butts off, but we've got four bookings already. Not bad, huh?" She glanced in the mirror again and watched Retta's head turn with the passing of a German shepherd on the sidewalk. "He was a good-looking boy, I know, but listen. We'll be at our new home in a few minutes, and you'll have plenty to do."

Retta looked back at Maggie in the mirror and readjusted her footing on the seat. She had her niche in the back, surrounded by boxes, bags, bins, suitcases, lamps, two chairs, and a small secretary's desk. From front passenger seat to rear windshield, the car was full to the ceiling, as was the large carrier on the roof. Everything jiggled and creaked as they cautiously traversed the uneven, lumpy road, and Maggie rocked from side to side as much as Retta did.

"God, driving on these is evil. Imagine horses and wagon wheels dealing with this? Some are the size of footballs. How did they do it, way back then?" Maggie turned off Main Street, thankful to see asphalt ahead. "Almost there. See the hedges? Those are ours." She pulled up in front of the ten-foot-tall privet hedge that shielded the property from the sidewalk, and stopped where the greenery arched over a tiny gate. "See, Retta? We're home!"

Both of them stared through the white picket gate and up the narrow walkway, a herringbone pattern of dusty gray paving bricks that led to the slate patio and a wide, wooden screen door. Shoulder-high shrubs channeled the path, as ragged and unkempt as the battered weeds growing between the pavers, and Maggie mentally added yard maintenance to her already lengthy list of chores.

"Give me a minute, Retta," she said, getting out. "I'll be right back. You stay."

Holding open the gate as she stood beneath the hedge arch, she took a moment to size up work done to the mid-nineteenth-century house in her absence, and nodded at the completion of the exterior project that had eaten a sizeable chunk of her budget. Totally re-shingled in unstained cedar from the ground to the second-story roof, the building stood welcoming and warm, a honey-brown in the morning sunshine, and she saw it as a house reborn, eager to match its weathered gray neighbors. The scent of fresh cedar on the salty breeze was invigorating. Tall grids of wooden lattice encased the four pillars that supported the porch roof, and she envisioned columns of pink roses offering a picturesque, aromatic greeting to guests.

She strolled the lengthy walkway and circled the house, inspecting the new windows and shutters, the sealing and painting of the foundation, so pleased with the finished work she didn't mind the construction disaster in the yard. Scraps of lumber, strapping, paper and plastic labels, discarded coffee cups, and miscellaneous debris littered the grounds all around the house. Both narrow side yards, the compact backyard, and even the white shell lot that *might* accommodate three cars were a slum-like disaster all the way to the bordering hedges.

Nevertheless, Maggie smiled. Cleanup was the least of her worries. If the flowers and shrubs flourished the way she'd seen in old photos, the property would dazzle, and guests would marvel at the landscaping as they lounged in cozy little sitting areas throughout the yard.

She led Retta on a repeat of her stroll and pointed out the property boundaries, including the gated rear driveway area, and hoped Retta wouldn't dig her way out to introduce herself to the neighborhood.

"You promised to be good, remember," she said, as Retta stopped for the hundredth time to sniff hedges. "This *back*yard is for you to do your business. And this gate here is for cars to go through—*not you.* This is your yard now. And no digging." She led them back to the front of the house. "Time to park the car. Let's go."

She curled the Rav4 around her privet hedge and down the narrow lane beyond, then jumped out to open the driveway gate at the rear of her property. Retta eyed her every move, excited when Maggie returned behind the wheel. She leaned out the window and looked down toward the foreign sound of tires crunching over seashells.

"Yup. We're here, sweetie." Maggie patted her head as she trotted back to close the gate. The span of white pickets complained and wobbled as it swung, and it, too, went on Maggie's list of "eventual to-dos." She dug house keys from her purse and opened Retta's door. "We're home, Retta. Check it out."

Retta bounded from the car and romped across the sparse backyard lawn, picking up speed and racing in delirious ovals from side hedge to side hedge like an Indy car driver. Maggie stopped at the top of the four back steps and laughed. "Are you coming or what?"

Retta ran toward the car, stopped on a dime, and cautiously sniffed her way onto the seashells. Apparently satisfied they wouldn't attack, she approached the Rav4's front bumper and marked her territory with a sizable puddle.

"Good girl, Retta!" Maggie said brightly, hoping Retta made a habit of going on the driveway instead of ruining the lawn Maggie hoped to grow. Retta rocketed back across the yard and up the stairs, eager for the door to open to further exploration.

Maggie gave her a substantial hug. "Such a good girl. You ready?" Retta only briefly broke her stare at the door to send Maggie an answer. "Okay. Let's go."

She opened the storm door, unlocked the interior wooden one, and swung it wide. Retta loped in, nose to the floor, and was off, investigating.

Maggie crossed the little mudroom, entered the spacious kitchen, and her heart sank.

Spacious it *should have been.* Appliances she'd ordered months ago, an array she admittedly would like in her own home someday, sat still crated. They crowded the wide room, scattered over the torn and stained linoleum flooring. Refrigerator, dishwasher, freezer, washer and dryer, the stainless steel stove of her dreams, and the soapstone farmer's sink were nowhere near ready for installation. The room itself sported new drywall and plumbing, but that was all.

So much for cooking our first meal here tonight. And why is no one working today?

"Damn it." She pulled out her iPad and started making notes. All the big pieces seemed to be accounted for, she thought, checking crate labels for accuracy, but the refinished wood flooring, all the restored original cabinetry, the butcher block countertops…She sighed heavily and moved on, now leery of what she'd find.

Off the kitchen, the three small rooms she'd had converted to two for the proprietor's residence glistened. Old hardwood flooring and trim glowed warmly, and the wall colors she'd selected proved ideal. Her bedroom set and a small table with chairs would fit perfectly, once the moving truck arrived on the midday ferry. And her little desk would be right at home in the sunny nook beneath the side window.

A small en suite bathroom had been completed as well, and she was never more thankful to find it ready. Stepping in, she flicked the light switch and nodded approvingly, then flushed the toilet and ran hot and cold water in the sink, tub, and shower.

"Thank God."

She jerked around at the sound of the front screen door slapping shut. Retta rang her own doorbell, barking ferociously in another room.

Maggie hurried to the opposite end of the suite. "Retta?" She threw open the door and looked through an anteroom to the vast common room. "What—Oh. Hi, Bud."

A short, chunky man in coveralls stood with his back against the screen door, looking from Retta to her as the barking persisted.

"Hi. She friendly?" He pointed at Retta.

"Yes. This is all pretty exciting for her—and me." Maggie soothed Retta's raised hackles with several long strokes of her palm. "You can say hi now, Retta. Bud's a good guy. He's in charge of all the work we need." Retta approached him slowly, nose to his work boots. Her tail only began wagging when he gave a friendly rub to her head. "Come in, please. We just arrived, actually, but I'm really glad you're here. There's a lot to talk about."

"That there is." He stepped up beside her as she perused the room. "Under all this paper, the floors came out great," he said, shuffling his feet. "And the built-ins, we just finished staining two days ago. Room's pretty much ready to go. You check out your office?"

Maggie looked to the anteroom she'd rushed through moments earlier. "Not really." She went back to the open Dutch door in the corner that separated the common room from what she'd planned as the office. Sunshine, despite the unwashed new window, lit the room brightly, and the woodwork glowed.

"It's perfect." She stepped in and turned around. "Plenty of room for a real desk and filing cabinets. Plus, I can see everything out to the front door—and access it from the residence, which is gorgeous, by the way." She beamed at Bud, and a proud smile added more wrinkles to his weathered face.

"All this covering on the floor can come up now, I suppose," he said, walking back out to the common room. "Your furniture still coming today?"

"It better be or I'll be sleeping on the floor."

He waved a dismissive hand. "Not to worry. Those guys are used to this. Deliver all over the island all the time. You can count on them." He rubbed his chin as he surveyed the space. "Need a lot of stuff for this room. It's the whole width of the house."

"Well, I have enough for now, but I'll add pieces as my budget permits." She tipped her head toward the doorway that led back toward the kitchen. "There's still a lot to be done, however."

"The kitchen, yup. Sent my crew over to an emergency in 'Sconset this morning, but they'll be here in about an hour. Every week, something messes up my Monday schedule. But your cabinets are already on the truck, and all the butcher block is due this afternoon, so we're hoping to have the cabinets and countertops done today. It'll go quick. You'll see."

"It has to, Bud. It seems I'll be eating out for a while."

"Well...yup. My floor guys should be done by the end of the week. The plumber will be finishing her thing, too, and we'll get the backsplashes up. Hey, we could plug in the fridge for now, if you'd like."

"I'd appreciate that." She wandered to the large antique wood stove, now situated at the stone fireplace opposite the front door. "I know this was quite a project. It's usable now, I hope? I just love it."

"Yup." A lock of his fluffy silver hair fell into his eyes when he nodded. He swiped it away. "A pretty big expense, but it's a beauty."

"I'm counting on not having to sleep in front of it tonight."

He chuckled at that but shook his head. "No worries there. Heat works just fine. Furnace overhaul is good for another fifteen years, and the tank is new and full. Got your first oil delivery last Thursday."

"Yes." She grimaced. "The bill was emailed to me immediately. At least prices are better off-season." Thankful she wouldn't have to worry about those cold, raw months, she headed for the stairs at the far wall. "Okay, Bud. Now, take me through the progress up here."

Happy to see a polished sheen on the old banister and a paper runner rising to the second floor, Maggie started up the newly stained steps, their edges rounded smooth from generations of use. Thoughts of previous residents' foot traffic nearly distracted her, the history of the place so compelling, but a brush of Retta's strong shoulder against her leg kept her on track.

"The downstairs was a picnic compared to up here," Bud said, trailing after them. "*Really* old houses like this come with their own unique nightmares. Configuring nine rooms, plus two suites and ten baths took us since Christmas. Hell, it *felt* like Christmas when we finished."

Maggie reached the landing with a bounce in her step and noted the refurbished hardwood floor also mostly covered by protective paper.

"It's all done? Really? What I can see of the flooring looks amazing."

"We had to match a board here and there, but overall they turned out great. So...let's see. The plumber's still waiting on a few more sink fixtures, I'm afraid, but the shipment of air conditioners came in. They're at my place, and I can bring them over any time now. And the electrician finished putting up all the ceiling fans last week."

Maggie couldn't stop smiling as they checked the two suites at the front of the house, nor as they traveled the hallway back and stopped in the other rooms. It was easier than ever now to picture them with beds and furniture, curtains and scatter rugs, bathrooms with coordinated towels and shower curtains, fresh flowers in vases throughout...Her heart beat joyfully as her long-held vision began to materialize.

"You've done an incredible job, Bud. I'm *so* pleased."

He shrugged modestly. "Can't do the slap-it-together kind of work. It's not how I do business. Around here, it's done right. Expensive, I'll grant you, but this *is* an island, and the town's pretty darn fussy about everything."

"Oh, believe me. I know everything's pricey here and the Historic District Commission is ridiculously particular, although that's not necessarily a bad thing. But competition for Nantucket accommodations is strong, and I intend to make Tuck'r Inn the cutest little sanctuary possible. Top-quality work is worth the investment. That's how *I* do business. So I thank you."

"You're welcome. Hey, I got one more thing for you. Let's go back downstairs."

In the oversized closet in the common room, he stepped around Retta to pull a long, narrow object off the shelf. Maggie watched, curious, as he removed the bubble wrap and held out a piece of wood in both hands.

"I remembered the sketch you sent me, way back in the fall when we first hooked up," he said, "how you wrote about having the Tuck'r Inn name on a quarter board someday, just like all Nantucket houses have. So..."

Maggie's eyes had already gone wide. With plump clusters of roses etched into each end, the wood had been intricately carved, its entire outline routed, gilded in gold leaf, as were the letters, all against a background of dusky gray, the future accent color of the house. Displaying a ship's quarter board bearing the house or family name was a Nantucket tradition, and Maggie couldn't have felt more humbled, more honored, if she'd been planning to make Tuck'r her permanent home. The welcome was genuine and touching.

"Oh, Bud. It's absolutely beautiful. I don't believe you did this. Thank you *so* much."

"The least I could do for you, trusting my outfit with a job this big."

Maggie lifted the board from his hands and examined it from end to end, ran her fingers over the woodwork. Something about touching it lent more substance, more reality to her project, and she was surprised to feel so moved. Her eyes filled, and Retta wandered to her side and sat against her leg. Maggie acknowledged her with a stroke of her head and chuckled at herself. "This makes it official."

"That's for sure," he said. "It's mahogany, and sealed so it'll last. Had a woodcarver friend do it. He's got a shop on Straight Wharf."

"I'll look him up. This is just gorgeous, such incredible detail. Could you hang it for me?"

"Not till we're done. I'm not superstitious about most things, but that I am. When your inn is ready, it'll be the finishing touch. Should probably go between the second-floor windows. That's where the old Pratt quarter board used to hang. Don't know what happened to that, though. Maybe the Whaling Museum ended up with it when the bank took the house, back before your previous owners. Pratt was a big-time whaler."

"My attorney's given me a pile of title research to look at, once I have time, but she did tell me the basics."

"Well, it's yours now, Maggie. And you'll be up and running in no time."

"Thank you again. What a precious surprise."

Maggie couldn't believe her good fortune. What a day this turned out to be, she thought, how lucky she was to have hired Bud.

Tuck'r Inn would indeed open for business on Memorial Day weekend. Her timetable to receive her first guests still looked solid; even the prospect of the summer roses framing the entryway seemed realistic. Some three weeks remained to square away all the projects on Bud's list, then dress up the place. Not for the first time, however, she prayed for the stamina to do the interior design and prep herself. And that would just be the beginning.

CHAPTER THREE

Ellis tossed her hammer into the open toolbox and stretched her back, stiff and sore from the day's work, but she was pleased with the outcome. The last item on her modifications list could be crossed off, and she considered celebrating. Finally, she had an interior wall separating her bedroom from her kitchen—actually, her forward berth from her galley. Chores at home always brought a satisfaction she seldom achieved elsewhere, and since her fifty-two-foot *Nantucket Rose* became "home" more than ten years ago, she often found herself thanking the boat as she would a friend.

"What would I do without you?" she mumbled and pulled a beer from a cooler in the galley before climbing the steps to the main deck. *First week of May is never too chilly for a beer on the water*, she mused, *especially when you've worked up a sweat all day*. She zipped a windbreaker over her sweater and drank greedily.

Several years of saving every last cent had rejuvenated the *Rose*, and now light shone on a future that had loomed dark for far too long. She knew she was back in decent financial shape at last, had a steady, albeit average income, and had a substantial roof over her head again.

"Lots of banging going on down there, Ellis. What're you up to now?"

She squinted through the late afternoon sun to see the harbormaster standing on the dock alongside, hands in his jacket pockets, his head wagging at her in disbelief.

"Should have put up the partition way back when. Would've kept my electric bill down."

"You're one tough woman. Stubborn as your old man."

She usually didn't take well to comments about her father—his death at sea years ago still pained her—but this man had been his friend.

"You go and build a bulkhead," he added, "and now you'll roast in the summer."

"Just a wall, Sam, and come summer, I usually sleep out here anyway."

"Yeah, yeah. Pretty soon you'll have condos and a pool on that old barge."

Ellis offered a salute with her beer can as he strolled away. Only he, out of respect to her father, could tease her that way. A barge, the *Rose* obviously was not. The beefy, broad-beamed vessel, a sizeable fixture in this harbor even by Nantucket's often glamorous standards, boasted a hard-worked history worthy of respect and envy. With tireless attention to duty, Ellis kept the *Rose* sparkling as brilliantly white above the royal blue hull as on that 1989 day her grandfather passed away and her father assumed ownership.

She dragged a deck chair astern and sank into it, relieved her weekends were free of ferry work and dealings with the general public and that she was free to enjoy her "yard." The harbor's flat sea and lack of activity presented a tranquil, soothing landscape, one she'd come to treasure. Only a quarter of the summer's boats had arrived to date, and they sat dead calm at moorings, even fewer at slips like her *Rose*, and she appreciated the picturesque moment as only a native islander could. Several pleasure craft were put in today; more would arrive tomorrow and in weeks to come, but for now, the serenity and the few gulls swirling above were hers alone.

The silent arrival of Hank Tennon's red trawler rounding Brant Point Light caught her eye, and she wondered if he'd had a successful run. Her father always said old Hank would stay out and starve before coming home "hollow as a hornpipe." She looked harder to see how low the trawler was riding in the water and then nodded at the fisherman's success. *Good for you, Hank.*

There weren't many old-timers left from her grandfather's day, she reflected, and too easily, she fell into memories of years on board with him and her dad. She took great pride in having grown up on the *Rose*, clinging to the "shaky arrangement" with the Atlantic that her granddad and relatives before him claimed to have made. She looked up to the bridge and scanned the wheelhouse, its expansive windshield curved and braced against the brisk onshore breeze. *"Take the wheel, honey. You know the way."*

Today, the *Rose*'s proud bow deck offered plenty of lounging room beneath the watchful bridge, while aft, a fiberglass canopy now extended halfway to the stern, sheltering a head, wet bar, and luxury seating. The open stern deck surrounding her now sat rigged for all preferences of fishing, and she recollected the exciting—terrifying— day, almost twenty years ago, when a great white surfaced on the end of her father's line.

She knew better than to dwell on the past, dredge up heart-wrenching images of their father-daughter team. Though her renovations hardly left a trace of them now, the once utilitarian flat-topped deck with its winches and crane boom, the cavernous holds below filled with pallets of crates and produce, they remained vivid in her mind and always would. She often had to remind herself of the living and maintenance quarters currently below deck, and that she'd done nearly all that work herself. Then, as now, driven by her family's oceangoing heritage, she vowed never to forget how she'd reached this point in life. She was well aware that, in reincarnating the *Nantucket Rose*, she'd honored her past by providing for her present and enabling her future.

The puttering sound of a dinghy's motor interrupted her musing and she was grateful, unwilling to sink into darker thoughts. The little craft drew across her bow and stopped, and the sandy-haired boater pressed a steadying palm to the *Rose*'s hull.

"Hey, Ellis! Have you planned supper yet?" The woman waved a mesh bag full of Nantucket's famed scallops.

Ellis thought twice about the offer. Jan Medeiros ran a successful "middleman" operation, selling fresh catches to many island eateries, and frequently tossed some freebies her way, but they came with a catch of their own. Single and not caring who knew it, Jan was nothing if not persistent.

"Got plans, yes, but thanks."

"Suit yourself. See you at the RC later?"

"Maybe," she answered automatically, having no intention of joining the partying set at the Rose & Crown on this night. "We'll see how the night goes."

"Ah." Jan frowned and pushed off from the hull. "Well, good luck with that."

"Thanks, Jan." Ellis watched her putter away, thinking that accepting one of Jan's offers really wouldn't kill her, that it wouldn't shatter her damn, hard-won independence if she spent the evening—or the night—with such a lively, devil-may-care woman. With *any* woman.

She promptly went below and doused herself in a hot, two-minute shower, pulled on jeans and sweatshirt, and set about finding something in her stores for supper.

"Get off your ass and go shopping, idiot." Pushing cans around in her cabinets, she found little appeal in baked beans, hash, Spam, or any of the other "emergency" staples she maintained on board. Vegetables, meat, and fish were gone from the food cooler, too, not to mention the paltry offerings of the drinks cooler. Only a single can of beer remained among a dozen bottles of water, and the lone bottle of zinfandel promised to nail her head to the pillow come morning. Again, she considered adding a real refrigerator to the galley—and stocking it.

"What a sorry state this is." She straightened with effort and returned topside. "What a sorry state *I'm* in." Begrudgingly, she headed off the dock for the thrilling adventure that was supermarket shopping.

❖

Maggie set the iron aside and trudged back up the stepstool to hang the fourteenth set of curtains. The arches of her feet complained about the narrow metal steps, her back ached from ironing, and her shoulders insisted on keeping track of how long she'd been at this. "Oh, how ambitious I was at seven thirty." It was almost noon, and she had one more to go before she could tackle the fifteen naked windows on the second floor. She'd spent all of yesterday hanging rods in preparation for this.

Retta raced into the common room from the kitchen, knowing, as dogs do, that Bud was arriving, and stood not so patiently to receive attention from her new friend. Her tail whacked rhythmically against a coffee table while Bud ruffled both her ears.

"You're getting there," he said to Maggie, looking around at the warehouse-like assembly of furniture. "Can't decide what goes where, huh?"

"The least of my problems," she said, climbing down and checking the fall of the fabric along the window frame. "One more of these and I'm done down here." She puffed a stray wave of hair off her forehead and headed back to the ironing board. "How's the painting coming?"

"Just touch-up by tomorrow. That's all."

She stopped, curtains in hand, and turned to face him. "*Done* done?"

"We need just a few more hours, yup. Took a week longer than I figured, what with the rain the last two days, but I think we can call it quits tomorrow."

"Wow. The ship's set to sail."

He grinned. "You could say. If you have anything else to add to your fix-it list, now's the time. Tomorrow, we'll be leaving you to all your fun 'n games here."

"Oh, thanks a lot. I only have two dozen recipes to try out, six beds left to assemble, a ton of towels to wash, ten bath—"

"You're still dead set on not hiring help?"

"I'm doing things bits at a time," she said, grinning back at him. "My system of priorities is based on which one of my body parts will wear out first."

"Uh-huh."

"I can't imagine it'll be this insane on a regular basis. I mean, once I have things in place, I can establish a routine."

"And you're cooking, too?"

"Just light stuff, cookies, muffins, things I can offer buffet style, along with coffees and teas."

"Well, don't throw out that woman's name I gave you. You didn't, did you?"

"No. It's pinned to the bulletin board in the office."

"Good, 'cause she's a wiz at this stuff. She worked the Coffin House for years, till her mom took sick and she had to quit to take her in. And she can cook."

"Yes, Bud. I remember what you said." She turned at the sound of her cell phone ringing on her desk. "Excuse me," she said, hurrying off. "Duty calls."

"Okay. Was just checking in. I'll be back later."

Retta watched through the screen door as he left, and then headed for her bed in Maggie's office.

"Well, we're delighted to have you both. I'll email you all the particulars right now." Maggie typed the address onto her laptop screen. "That would be fine, yes. Hopefully, we'll see you that Friday afternoon. Feel free to call any time."

She hung up and spun in her chair to Retta. "Number six, little girl. Maybe we'll hit one hundred percent for the holiday after all." She gave Retta's head a quick kiss. "Gotta get back to work."

"Ms. Jordan? Hello?"

The foreign voice from the common room set Retta back into motion, barking her way to the visitor.

"Good afternoon," Maggie said, pushing rebellious hair off her face. A slim, freckle-faced young woman fondled the strap of her shoulder bag nervously as Retta quieted before her.

"Hi there, sweetie." She offered her palm for Retta to sniff. "Such a good watchdog you are."

"Hello," Maggie tried again and commanded Retta to sit, which she did. "I'm Maggie Jordan. Can I help you?"

A long Irish-red ponytail swung off the young woman's shoulder when she reached forward. "My name is Laura Kelliher," she offered as they shook hands. "I'm pleased to meet you. I believe you know my mother, Irene, at the post office?"

"Oh, yes! Lovely lady, always so helpful."

"I'm sorry to just pop in. You're obviously very busy and I won't take but a moment of your time, but Mom more or less pointed me in your direction, suggested I inquire about any summer work you may have. I'm home now until Labor Day, when I have to go back to Michigan for school. I'm a sophomore."

Maggie waved her in. "I have to be honest. I hadn't planned on hiring for a while, if I could save the money. Just starting out, you know." She pulled two wicker wingback chairs together. "You're welcome to have a seat. Sorry, the place is so disorganized still."

"Oh, believe me, I understand about saving." Laura unbuttoned her jacket and straightened her skirt as she sat, then swung her bag onto her lap. She glanced around at the many disarrayed pieces of furniture and bit back a grin. "Pardon me for saying so, but it looks like you could use a hand."

Maggie laughed. "It shows, huh? Well, you're right. We open in two weeks. Not a full house yet, but getting there, and I'm chugging along. I should have the place ready in time." Laura's disappointment showed in her large green eyes, so Maggie pressed on. She liked this young lady and wished Tuck'r Inn could afford her.

"What's your major? University of Michigan?"

"Yup. Political science—right now, anyway. My parents aren't too thrilled that I've been thinking about switching to theater arts."

"Well." Maggie sat back and studied her closer. "Now *that's* a big change. Do you have a passion for the theater?"

"Oh, I do!" Her eyes flashed. "I've done community theater ever since I was a little girl in Connecticut, and then here with the Theatre Workshop, once we moved."

"No theater opportunities at Michigan?"

"I could only get a lighting assistant job for the production of *Nixon* last winter. Being a freshman, I didn't stand a chance of landing a part, but I still loved being around it all. I should have gone that route from the start." She shrugged. "My dad went to Michigan, too, so…He wanted more for me than what Emerson offered."

"Emerson's a terrific school and considerably closer. Boston versus Ann Arbor?"

"Exactly what I told him." Laura inched to the edge of her seat. Her enthusiasm was heartwarming. "But Dad was a state representative when we lived in Connecticut, and he has high hopes for me. Plus, they're paying my way."

"Sometimes paying off a bank loan is easier than paying back your parents."

"Don't you know it. Are you from around here?"

"Philly, but Albany, originally."

"I bet this is a dream come true for you."

Laura gazed at her, looking a bit awestruck, and Maggie figured plenty of dreams were living in that eager young mind. She found herself doing rapid calculations, crunching budget numbers, wondering if she could, indeed, afford to take on an employee.

"I know you need to move quickly on your job search—actually, it's kind of late to be looking—but I'm afraid I can't swing hiring anyone just yet. I would like to keep you in mind, though."

"I've got three summers of housekeeping experience. Did I say that already? And I've got good people skills, plus I'm in good shape. I swim every day."

"I'm just not at the hiring stage yet, Laura. I'm sorry. As business picks up, though, things could change."

A week later, five days before her inaugural weekend, Maggie awoke at the keyboard with Retta's muzzle on her thigh, questioning eyes asking for breakfast and a bathroom run.

Maggie blinked at the screen, which awakened far brighter than she had. She stared at the spreadsheet, and the anxiety that had plagued her into the wee hours returned. Orders had yet to come in for too many problem items: the largest suite's nightstand (arrived broken); front staircase carpet runners (too big); fridge icemaker tray (arrived broken); freezer bottom shelf (missing); the list went on.

Minor things, like the nonstick mini muffin tins, the four lampshades, and a color-coordinated throw for one of the small rooms, she knew she could hunt down at island shops when she had time, but those others, well, she had to get back on the phone, pronto. And then get to Straight Wharf and Bud's woodcarver for the little plaques she'd ordered to adorn each guestroom door. Hopefully, the painting of the celestial names she'd chosen had been done and she could hang them right away. Meanwhile, the dozens of plants delivered four days ago still needed to go in the ground and into window boxes. Her fading daffodils reminded her that *someone else* would be responsible for entering Tuck'r in the annual festival next spring.

She drifted through her bedroom and across the kitchen. "You go check the yard for invading squirrels, Retta, and I'll get us breakfast." She opened the mudroom door to the chilly, overcast morning. "No digging!" she commanded as Retta ran out, and she sagged against the door frame. "Another night like last night, and I'll probably wake up out here."

Eager for a hot shower, she preheated the oven for her experimental recipes, started coffee, and was scooping dog food into Retta's bowl when her cell sounded from her nightstand. She dashed off, weighing the merits of buying a wireless headset. *How many days left till Friday?* On the spot, she surrendered to the urge to call Laura Kelliher.

CHAPTER FOUR

Ellis waved the last truck off the *Eagle* and stood alongside as the driver crept into the line leaving Steamship Wharf. A temperamental northeast wind blustered against her jacket and threatened her cap as the driver spoke through his partially opened window. She really wasn't in the mood for his idle conversation, but her role supervising debarking traffic held her captive.

"The three-day weekend is supposed to be decent," he said. "I don't know about you, Ellis, but I have my doubts." He inched the truck forward in line, and Ellis stepped along with it to be polite.

"Weather's picked up since the morning run." She scanned the harbor and changed her footing to counter a gust of wind. "The heavy chop out there says something's brewing." *And I'd rather ride it out at home.*

He nodded as he stared through his windshield. "Sometimes I wonder what the TV weather guys look at, y'know? I'm glad this is my last run of the day. You doing the eight o'clock trip tonight, too, because of the holiday?"

Ellis nodded, not particularly thrilled her workday now extended to eleven at night with the holiday and summer schedules. "Yeah, the eight o'clock runs start tonight."

"Hope the weather holds for you. Hell, wouldn't have had to make this trip if I didn't have a few rush deliveries. Most of this load could've waited till next week."

"Customers matter to us all."

"Well, I've got this newbie on my route who's a piece o' work, let me tell you. Called our showroom like three times already." He inched forward again. "Some corporate hotshot's moving in and *had* to have every freaking stick of furniture by today."

"Some timing, huh?"

The man snorted and shook his head. "Got that right. Nothing like picking Memorial Day weekend." He crept forward again, next in line to leave. "It's all about big money, y'know? They're redoing the old Pratt House."

Ellis looked up sharply. The name sent a woeful trickle along her spine.

"The Captain Pratt House?"

"Yeah. I heard the old couple living there finally threw in the towel and took off for Phoenix, sold it to some corporate type. I've delivered there a couple times already this month, and I gotta say, it's good to see the place spruced up again." Ellis wondered how badly the elderly owners had let it deteriorate. "Okay, Ellis. I'm off. Take care out there."

Numbed by his news, she waved the next vehicle up in line and stepped farther aside, not willing to get caught up in chitchat again.

It had been years since she'd seen the house. She'd made a point of avoiding Davis Street altogether. Passed down from her mother's great-great-great-grandfather, Percival Ellis, whose father-in-law had been Captain Pratt himself, the home had remained in the family forever, bearing the Pratt name in tribute to one of Nantucket's greatest whalers. Until…

A fellow seaman called to her from the open belly of the *Eagle* and pointed to the line of waiting cars. He raised his palms, asking why she wasn't directing outbound traffic aboard.

Striding forward, she waved the vehicles on, but her thoughts remained on the landmark house she once called home.

Those thoughts rode with her as uneasily as the sea challenged the *Eagle*, back to Hyannis Harbor, and out again, crossing the Sound on her last run to the island. These trips at night deprived visitors of the best view of the Gray Lady's welcome, the picturesque little harbor with docks offering sanctuary to traveling craft, and for Ellis, it felt like intimacy lost. Brant Point Light provided reassurance, however, and she treasured her ship's curl around it as if pulling into one's neighborhood after a prolonged absence. The specks of mellow light from houses, shops, and church steeples bolstered her spirit, reminded her that islanders—her ancestors included—had soldiered on here for centuries, always with an eye to the sea.

As chief mate, Ellis thankfully had no choice but to tend to her many duties. She assisted the vessel's master with everything: loading and securing freight, safety checks, passenger boarding and control, docking, communications, even navigation. None of them easy tasks when the ocean was cranky and one's mind adrift. Tonight she was glad to be so busy. As the annual holiday rush began hitting its thirty-six-hour peak, the big ship bustled, sold out and cargo deck full. This final run on the Thursday before Memorial Day always drew a maximum load, as would all the trips tomorrow and Saturday morning, and Ellis longed to be flat on her back on her bed, allowing the *Rose* to rock her to sleep.

Headwinds and heavy swells had the *Eagle* ten minutes off schedule by the time it rounded Brant Point, but nobody seemed to care. Anticipation had voices raised and passengers in motion as the jockeying for quick exit began. Ellis squeezed her way through the crowd and descended to the vehicles on the cargo deck in preparation for docking and traffic control.

"Two more days of this," she muttered, watching families pour out of the stairwells and head for their cars, "and Sunday and Monday are mine."

A further treat was the upside of the hour: lack of traffic in town at ten thirty had the *Eagle*'s vehicles flowing like water off the ship and out of the lot. Passengers couldn't debark fast enough, either, scurrying down the zigzagging gangway as fast as seamen would let them, wheeled luggage in tow.

In short order, with backpack over her shoulder and jacket zipped to her chin, Ellis made her way beneath the occasional streetlamps of Easy Street, past the wharves, and through gusts that insisted on blowing her farther inland. *Twenty-knot winds at forty-eight degrees and it's freaking Memorial Day.* She pulled her cap down tighter, crossed the wind off Old South Wharf, and finally reached her neighborhood.

She turned onto sleepy Commercial Wharf, head down into the whipping salt air, and increased her pace to the slip her family had used for generations. A soft yellow light glowed off the tall piling that marked her address, and a dimmer one shone on the *Rose*, both welcome sights. The weathered plank walkway rolled beneath her feet, a bit more unsettled than usual, and she considered how much like the sea she had become, how they resembled each other too often nowadays. With a respectful glance at the restless black liquid around her, she climbed aboard, eager to let the ship's roll and lapping waves calm her overactive mind.

It had been a busy day, but the physical weariness was nothing compared to the thoughts that returned unabated. *Some corporate hotshot? Strangers making themselves at home, oblivious to the banister I rode, the whispers from the chimney, the tales those old walls told...*

She tossed her backpack onto the couch and pulled a bottle of Sam Adams from the melted ice water in the cooler. *Hit up the Boatworks and see about ordering a damn fridge.* The concept made her snicker. "Bet there's a shiny new fridge in that damn house now."

She shed her clothes on the deck and slid under a comforter, propped up to drink and think.

Whose fault is it that I'm not sitting by that fireplace anymore, or sweating off broken pipes or fighting that pain-in-the-ass plaster? She raised her bottle. "Here's to you, Ellis Pratt Chilton, first-class fool." She chugged half the beer without stopping. "Good thing there's only one left." She knew this was one of those rare occasions where, in the past, she would blow through an entire six-pack, dwelling on life's defeats.

She hadn't been able to prevent fate from stealing her father before her very eyes, but she should have been able to save the family business—and should *never* have let the family's legacy slip away. God knew, her four years of sleepless nights and back-breaking effort had been noble enough, just not business savvy or enterprising enough to stay afloat through stiffening economic times. But to have gambled for success, to have put the house on the line for that cash infusion had been...

"The mistake of a lifetime," she grumbled, knowing she'd take that failure to her grave. She sipped her beer again and rubbed her eyes. *Such a know-it-all back then. What the hell does anyone know at twenty-two?* She sighed heavily, mourning all that effort and good intention, and reminded herself that no rationalization would ever mitigate the blame she shouldered for losing it all—father, business, home. And now, to that anguish she added the bitterness of having some off-island bigwig settle into her family's private, long-esteemed residence. *Too bad I didn't hit the lottery. The right name would be back on that deed now.*

Nearly dozing with her head on the back of the couch, Ellis peered at her surroundings as if searching for a friend. The *Nantucket Rose*, paid for years ago, remained her sole possession, her pride and joy, and the day she surrendered the Pratt House to foreclosure, she vowed to never subject the *Rose* to seahorse labor again, to protect *this* home at all costs. She yawned hard and finished her beer, deciding to finish these recollections as well. Ultimately, they would drag her down, flood her spirit, and she'd spent too many years battling the current that sought her soul. Surrendering to sleep, she saluted the Captain Joshua Pratt House and her past.

❖

The stack of correspondence fell over, fanned across the table like playing cards, and covered the billing statement to which Ellis had just signed her father's name. Rocking seven-foot seas made the tedious paperwork chore a challenge as the *Rose* churned across the sound, headed home through thickening fog, but it was her job to tend to business whenever her father manned the helm. She cursed the mess, cleared a space, and continued working until he summoned her up to the wheelhouse.

He gestured for her to take the helm and headed for the cargo deck. "That stern line didn't want to hold earlier. I don't trust it."

She took a step with him. "You stay. I'll go out and check."

"Nope. My turn," he said.

"Well, watch your step. It's bad out there." She called after him, "Don't get cocky, sailor!" She shook her head at his confidence.

He left the bridge and practically disappeared into the fog. Ellis hated dividing her attention this way, keeping one eye on their heading and the other on him. She never felt as "ready" to handle a situation that might arise on either front. But it was their routine, their trusted system as a "two-man" crew, and their livelihood as a family depended on their seamanship as much as that damn paperwork.

She leaned away from the wheel, finally spotted him aft, ghostly nondescript in the gray air. He staggered left as the *Rose* listed on the rough sea, and then right, and Ellis sighed, relieved, when he steadied himself with a hand on the black crane boom and made his way to its far end.

"Damn cowboy."

She turned back to the helm and cleared her forward view with a click of the windshield wipers. She estimated visibility now at hardly an eighth of a mile, and with fifteen miles to go, she hoped previous reports were accurate and this mess would lift in a few minutes. Never soon enough, she thought as she directed the *Rose* through the crest of a wave and surfed down into its trough.

With a hand on the wheel, she looked back again and could barely make out the shadow of her father astern. She picked up the shipboard microphone and broadcast her voice out over the cargo deck.

"Shake a leg, sailor. Get your ass back up here."

The shadow suddenly moved sideways and Ellis focused hard, desperate to see what caused his erratic movement. A wave slammed the *Rose*'s port side and almost dropped him to his knees. The jerky impact snapped the boom's stern line, which, in turn, overstressed the safety cables. They popped like gunshots. Ellis stopped breathing as the boom swung free and its thousand pounds of steel clipped her father's head. Surreal, as if in slow motion, his body hurtled into the fog and the sea.

Ellis screamed, spun, and slammed the engines to full stop with one hand and blared the horn's distress signal with the other. She fumbled with the radio, shouted "Mayday" and "Man overboard" calls, blurted their coordinates, and then ran like hell.

Hands on the rails, she raised both feet and slid down the stairway, then raced across the deck. She ran breathless yet screaming toward the stern she could hardly see a million miles ahead. Fog swirled around her, fought to contain her. The sounds of her pounding steps and thudding heart grew deafening. Salty air stung her teary eyes, filled her nostrils, coated her windpipe, and made yelling seem so useless. The vision of his limp form vanishing into gray mist assaulted her and she ran desperately, ran to it, ran through it, ran until the gunwale slamming across her gut caught her.

Gasping, Ellis jerked upright and wide-eyed on the couch. Her beer bottle clattered to the floor and rolled away, and she stared after it, wondering how it belonged in the trauma she'd just experienced.

Coated in sweat and short of breath, she held out her palms and watched them shake.

"Jesus." She dropped her face into her hands and waited for reality to return as it always did.

CHAPTER FIVE

M aggie emerged from the kitchen with a fresh pot of green tea, just in time to see Laura catch a ceramic lamp en route to its demise. The rambunctious little boy who'd sent that side table rocking raced up the stairs. Maggie mouthed "thank you" to Laura from across the room.

"These are simply divine," his grandmother said, more interested in Maggie's miniature muffins than her grandson's destructive behavior. "Do you get these locally?"

"We just took them out of the oven," Laura said, stepping up to the woman's opposite side. "Ms. Jordan makes them herself."

"Is that so? Tell me, is there a chance I might have several dozen shipped home? There's nothing like them in Alexandria."

"That's sweet of you, Mrs. Cross. Thank you," Maggie said and set the tea caddy amidst an attractive coffee-and-tea station on the corner buffet. "Of course we can send some off for you. So glad you're enjoying them. Apricot and Nantucket's own cranberries added to my grandmother's recipe."

"I thought I detected some of that grandmother-y goodness." Her eyes twinkled behind her glasses.

"I'm hoping they'll become a Tuck'r Inn specialty. Thank you again. And you just let us know when to send them and how many."

"I'll do that," she said and dabbed the corner of her mouth with a napkin. "I must go for a stroll, however, to tear myself away or these will spoil my appetite. My daughter and grandson should be down momentarily. He's excited to see the Whaling Museum. Personally, I'm looking forward to an up-close look at the making of your lightship baskets."

"Both are worth the trip," Maggie assured her, "although I'd double-check the hours." She pulled a brochure from a display by the door. "Yes, the museum will be closing in an hour, but the basket shop is open later."

"Good to know. We might be able to hold Harlen off until tomorrow, then. We're hoping to arrange a sightseeing cruise at some point. That will definitely keep him contained."

"Well, I'd be glad to make some referrals, if you'd like. There's lots of information like this in your room." She waved the brochure. "So, how are your accommodations? Is everything satisfactory?"

"Oh, quite pleasant. Even Harlen slept later than usual this morning—for which his mother and I are quite grateful."

Maggie laughed with her. "Well, I'm tickled to hear it. Enjoy your stay and don't hesitate to ask if either of us can be of any help."

By eight thirty that evening, having sent Laura home by four, Maggie eased into a cushy wingback chair in the empty common room. She'd cleaned up after guests' late-afternoon comings and goings, washed and restocked supplies at the coffee-and-tea station, refreshed the fruit and nut bowls, then baked brownies and oatmeal cookies for anyone passing through or lounging after their evening plans, and finally, prepped ingredients for making breakfast breads in the morning. With a satisfied sigh, she shook her hair free of its clip and took a moment to relax and survey the place.

"Not bad," she said to Retta, who curled up on the little braided rug at her feet. "If this is what busy feels like, we can handle it for a while. Right?"

It would have meant an increased workload, but she would have preferred a full house for this opening weekend instead of starting off at 65 percent occupancy. Considering the bigger picture, the sooner Tuck'r Inn succeeded and she had substantive business records to show a prospective buyer, the sooner she could take on another project.

She gazed around the cozy room and snuggled deeper into the chair. "But this *does* amount to a very respectable start. I can't be impatient, can I, girl?" Retta raised her head as if about to respond. "I'll lose my mind if I don't stay realistic. This is actually pretty damn good for newcomers like us."

She sat up, suddenly re-energized. Retta popped up too.

"I think Mama deserves some of that Italian merlot, don't you think? Let's go for a walk."

Retta bounced in place, then ran off to find a stuffed toy to take on their adventure. Searching for a jacket in her office, Maggie yelled to her, "I can hear you running around out there, Retta. God. I thought *I* was impatient." Retta managed a muffled bark from behind her toy duck as Maggie hurried into the bedroom to find the jacket. "All right already. I'm coming."

Leash in place, Retta tugged Maggie out the door and through the gate in seconds. Maggie reined her in a bit as they picked up speed downhill toward Main Street.

"Will you slow down, please?" Retta obeyed. "Thank you. Sometimes I don't know if you're a bloodhound or a husky."

What should have been a twenty-minute jaunt to and from the liquor store evolved into a more practical stroll around several blocks, and that expanded into a sixty-minute social event, as Retta commiserated with the occasional passing dog, inhaled and snorted at every tree, and then bolted free to chase a rabbit behind the bank. Almost. Maggie actually didn't get a good look at the critter, but Retta had, and Maggie barely managed to stomp on the loose leash before they ended up behind the building in the dark.

"Christ, Retta." She led her onto the sidewalk and resumed their stroll down Main Street. "Enough socializing for you tonight."

At the store, Maggie tied the leash to the nearby bench. "Sit, please. Thank you." Retta stared past her to the lighted doorway as Maggie kissed the top of her head. "Mama's just going to be a minute. Be a good girl now. Stay."

❖

Headed home with her backpack over her shoulder, Ellis couldn't help feeling a bit lighthearted. The next two days were hers, free and clear, and the promise of springlike weather had her contemplating just how she'd spend that time. She caught herself whistling down the dark street like an Old Spice commercial, headed for the liquor store to stock up while she was in the vicinity rather than interrupt her precious free time in the days ahead.

She had just ten minutes till closing as she walked up Main, and she grinned at the dog who sat waiting patiently by the door. Such devotion, she thought, and remembered wanting a dog when she was young. A Lab would have been perfect, and she recalled lobbying hard as a teenager, but her father had been adamantly opposed. Eventually, she came to see his point about their time constraints at sea versus a pet's need for exercise.

She crossed the street, and the dog barked at her approach.

"Hey. Calm down, fella." She noted the animated expression, then the familiar leash. "Hi there." She stopped several feet away and removed her cap. "Remember me? Are you...Retta?"

The dog's dangling ears twitched. She rose on all fours, excited now, and barked again.

"You *are* Retta, aren't you? Well, good to see you, girl." She glanced at the store and remembered the hour. "Look, I've got to go, but maybe I'll see you around, okay? Be good."

Ellis had an image in mind as she stepped inside, several weeks old, but nonetheless vivid from when she'd been tackled aboard the *Eagle*. Retta's owner was that lithe, auburn-haired beauty, with the energetic brown eyes and cute, turned-up nose, the broad, easy smile. They'd come face-to-face more than once.

Retta's owner stood at the register with a wine bottle in one hand, the other raised haplessly at Jason, the young cashier. Ellis avoided eye contact with either of them and went promptly to the coolers at the rear of the store. From such a distance, she couldn't catch their conversation but definitely understood the tone. And it wasn't particularly pleasant.

A six-pack in each hand, Ellis debated whether she should approach the disagreement at the register. The arrival of a third wheel would probably embarrass all of them, so she returned to the coolers for orange juice and took her time selecting a sparkling wine. *Mimosas in the morning.*

A blonde carrying a fifth of Fireball Whiskey hurried to the register, and Ellis figured she'd stalled long enough. *Something's got to give now.*

"Seriously, I'll be here when you open tomorrow morning," Retta's owner pleaded.

"And I can't do it. I told you, my boss would kill me."

The blonde with the whiskey stepped closer and Retta's owner blushed. "I'm sorry," she told her. "I was just explaining to the cashier here that I ran out of the house, not thinking—"

The cashier scowled and turned to service the blonde. "I'll ring that up for you. We're about to close."

Ellis looked away, not wanting to be caught watching and making things worse, but peripherally, she saw Retta's owner put the bottle down.

"Sorry if I delayed your closing." She spun on a heel and walked out.

Ellis set her beer, juice, and spumante on the counter as the blonde left, and picked up the abandoned bottle of merlot. She called to the blonde, who was almost out the door.

"Excuse me. That woman outside. The one with the dog. Tell her to wait, would you?" She turned back to the cashier. "Add this to my stuff, Jason."

"Sure, if you want." He shrugged. "Sorry, Ellis, but I couldn't risk my job just 'cause she forgot her wallet." He took her cash and handed back the change.

"She's a good customer?"

"Well, yeah. She's in here now and then, but still."

"You're in a tough spot, I get it, but things happen, y'know?" She picked up one six-pack, tucked the other under her arm, and gathered up her bag of juice and wine. "Thanks, Jason."

Outside, she found both dog and owner waiting for her to emerge, looking just as attentive as Retta had looked at the bench. *Lighting may suck, but the lady is just as striking as ever.*

Retta barked and lurched up onto all fours, tail swinging low and steady, as if awaiting permission to greet her.

"Hi—oh. Hello," her owner said, and Ellis caught recognition in her eyes. "Did you—I may have misunderstood, but...did you ask me to wait? Is there something you wanted?"

"Yeah. About that in there." Ellis stacked the six-packs at her feet and pulled the previously abandoned wine from her bag. "I think you forgot this."

Now she had the woman's full attention.

"Oh, no. You didn't!"

"Hey, it can happen to anybody. And if you're here at this hour, it must be important."

"I don't believe it. I'm really embar—"

"Don't be."

"You're kidding, right? No. I'm sorry, but I can't accept it. I mean, you're incredibly generous to do this, but—"

"Yeah, yeah. Here," she said and extended the bottle closer to her. "Don't let my money go to waste. I'm not going to drink this."

"Why not? It's very good. Honestly, I really can't let you do this. I *do* appreciate the gesture, though." Retta picked up her toy duck, dropped it on Ellis's foot, and barked.

Ellis lowered the bottle, ready to walk away. It was late, she was tired, and she didn't even know this woman. *So much for good deeds.*

But words continued to come out of her mouth. "Retta says take it and be done with it."

"You know, we've sort of met several times now, and all I've said is 'I'm embarrassed' or 'thank you.'"

"Like I said, there's no need to be embarrassed."

"Well, when your dog knocks a ship's officer onto her butt, I'd say it's justified."

Ellis shrugged. "Seems to me I *do* remember. The rainbow leash."

"Rainbow, yes." She offered her hand. "Could we start over? I'm Maggie Jordan."

"Accept the wine and I'll shake your hand, Maggie Jordan."

"Not fair." Her smile widened as she reached for the bottle. "Thank you very much."

"Y'welcome." Ellis slid her fingers around Maggie's, so much smaller, more feminine than hers. "Ellis Chilton."

Retta barked at their contact, snatched up the duck, and poked it into Ellis's thigh.

"Retta! Be polite," Maggie said. "I'm sorry she's a nuisance."

"Hi, pretty girl." Ellis rubbed Retta's ear. "You're not a nuisance, are you?" Retta let the duck fall from her mouth to lick Ellis's hand.

Maggie drew Retta back. "Boy, you'd think you're a long-lost relative."

"Let her loose. She won't go far."

"Ohhh no." Maggie shook her head vehemently. "This one takes off like a rocket, as you well know."

Ellis stroked Retta's back with long firm motions. "You won't stray, will you, Retta?" Ellis reached for the leash at Retta's collar and noted the matching rainbow pattern of both. *Is there a special woman in your life, Ms. Jordan? If she's an islander, I probably know the lucky woman.* She looked up. "Can I release her, just for a minute? All of downtown's deserted. It's safe."

Maggie almost shook her head. Admittedly a bit captivated by this woman she'd finally met, she fought to remain focused on Retta. "Against my better judgment." When Ellis unclipped the leash, Retta's hopeful gaze turned excited and Maggie sighed at her. "She's such a flirt." She saw Ellis grin at the comment and appreciated the way she diligently supervised Retta's romp along the sidewalk. "Do you have a dog?"

"No. We had a couple cats when I was kid, but never a dog."

"That's a shame. It's pretty obvious you're a dog person. I'd be lost without her."

"My experience with Labs is only through friends, but I do know they're 'people dogs' and very smart."

"Too smart for their own good, sometimes," Maggie added, enjoying Ellis's attention to Retta. It said Ellis was compassionate and kind, the generous sort, and not only toward strangers who shopped for wine with no money. "So you live on Nantucket?"

"Down the waterfront a ways." She turned at last. "And you? Every time I've seen you, you've been towing luggage."

Maggie suddenly felt a bit like Retta, warmed by the attention, flattered that Ellis remembered their previous encounters. She remembered them, too, down to details like the strength in Ellis's hand during that rough ride, the long, lean body sprawled out on the deck, the ocean-fresh scent of her in the doorway at Dell's. And it certainly was a pleasure to have more than a passing moment to share, finally.

Caught assessing her thoughts, she scrambled to respond.

"Oh, I'm working here. My B&B is just beyond the center of town." She spotted Retta wandering toward the far corner of the block and clapped urgently, beckoning her to no avail.

Ellis put two fingers to her front teeth and released an ear-piercing whistle that made Maggie cringe. "Retta! C'mere, pretty girl!"

Maggie shook her head as Retta raced to Ellis, who crouched and patted Retta's hindquarters while being flogged by the whipping tail. "Atta girl, Retta. Great dog you have here, Maggie. How old is she?" Ellis scratched Retta's back and the dog wiggled with pleasure.

"She's three and can be a handful."

"Aw, she's just super smart. She really is beautiful, very fit, great coat—" Retta popped up just enough to lick her chin, then retrieved her toy duck and nudged it against Ellis's hand.

"She likes you a lot." *Understandable, I think.*

Ellis surprised Retta by grabbing the duck and throwing it down the street. Retta bolted after it.

"Bet she's great company, though."

Maggie couldn't help but notice the hint of longing. She studied the distant look as Ellis watched Retta scoop up the duck like a ballplayer fielding a grounder.

"You know, she'd gladly keep you at this for hours," Maggie said, "but we probably should head home."

Ellis swung her backpack to her feet and began loading her bottles of wine and juice into it. "Time for this sailor to hit the sack." Retta arrived and dropped the duck to investigate the backpack. "Gotta go, pretty girl."

Maggie forced herself to stop assessing Ellis's hands, the wide shoulders, and broad back. She tried to recall seeing her without the jacket aboard the *Eagle*, and the Retta incident came to mind, complete with the image of Ellis sprawled out in chinos and snug uniform polo shirt. How long that image had stayed in her head…

Ellis stroked Retta's ear with an easy touch, and Maggie knew Ellis had to be enjoying that warm, luxurious velvet feel. Ellis stood and faced her. "At least we've finally said more than a few words to each other."

"Oh, I agree." She hoped she didn't sound like she'd fallen out of some dream.

"Well, ah…" Ellis settled the pack onto her back. "Maybe we'll bump into each other more often, since you're working on-island now."

Maggie tugged Retta closer. They had to start walking before those dreamy thoughts returned.

"I'm sure we will." She caught herself watching Ellis run those long, weathered fingers through her hair and adjust her cap before crouching again to pick up her beer. She liked that Ellis offered Retta an affectionate head butt to say good-bye before standing and taking a step back.

"Hope you both enjoy your weekend." The throaty tenor reminded Maggie of their few exchanges to date, simple words always delivered in a resonant, earthy tone.

"You, too," Maggie said, "and thank you again for the wine." Ellis waved as she turned away and Maggie couldn't help herself. "Y'know, would you…ah…Well, would you like to meet for a drink sometime?"

CHAPTER SIX

Maggie drank the remnants of her second cup of coffee and took a moment from the warm kitchen to clear her head on the back steps. She delighted Retta with a game of fetch as the sun emerged and her thoughts aligned. How lucky was she that a young woman like Laura could so ably step in and do practically everything right? That Bud was sending her favorite plumber over at eight thirty to solve this morning's crisis with the clothes dryer? Or that, for a change, she had an option to relax a while with someone, do something that had absolutely nothing to do with business? She whipped the ball into the yard again. *Without Retta, how conversational will you be, Ellis Chilton?* Being the sole focus of Ellis's concentration rattled her. *So, since when did a date break my stride?*

Maggie tossed the ball again, completely distracted by the idea of a date. Since her breakup last year, she'd had no interest in dating. Friends had dragged her through a couple of setups, but she'd put a stop to that. Business, honestly, *had* to come first, especially now. *So hip-deep into my latest project, I flirt with some sailor? No, I wasn't flirting, I was being friendly, cordial. There's no harm in having a drink...with a nice, quiet, very good-looking friend.* She sighed. *This is all temporary, anyway.*

A familiar white van crunched onto the driveway, and Cora Perez's smiling face beamed at her from the open window. "Lady needs a plumber?"

"Thank God!" Maggie enjoyed the talented tradeswoman's spirited personality as much as her outstanding work, and took comfort in having her expertise back at Tuck'r again. Plus, that eager smile against that dark complexion was certainly no hardship to see. "It's been what? A whole two weeks or so?"

In jeans, work boots, and her company's yellow T-shirt, Cora looked fit, bright, and extremely capable. She chuckled as she swaggered her small frame to the bottom porch step and looked up, hands on her hips. "So I hear you're not as full of hot air as you want to be?"

"Very funny. I have a ton of wet linens waiting and you're out here making jokes. Come on in. Coffee?"

Cora patted Retta as they followed Maggie inside. "I'd love some," she said and went to the laundry room in the opposite corner. "I want to check the gas, though. You're sure you haven't smelled anything?"

"I'm sure. No one's touched any valves or anything, and Laura and I both sniffed around till our sinuses hurt."

Cora returned and leaned against the counter. "Everything looks good. I don't think that's your issue, but I'll get my meter and make sure."

Less than two feet away, Maggie could sense her confidence, even her concern, and the spicy scent of her skin had Maggie wanting to step closer. *Jesus Christ. Suddenly I'm losing control? Get a grip, girl, and stay on course, for God's sake.* She handed her the cup, avoiding Cora's suggestive ebony eyes.

"Everything else is going well," she said and gestured to the kitchen in general, hoping to fill the awkward silence. "Knock on wood." She knocked on the countertop.

"Excellent. Upstairs bathrooms, no leaks, slow drains, enough hot water?" Cora set down her cup.

"All good, thanks to you."

"Perfect." Cora nodded and turned to the mudroom door. "I'll be right back with the meter."

Maggie watched her stride out to the porch and shook her head. "Nothing like a woman at work."

"And she's really good at it, too."

Maggie spun around to find Laura smirking. *Caught in the act.* She felt her cheeks flush. "Yeah, there is that."

"Cora's in demand all over the island, I hear," Laura went on, and Maggie tried not to grin. *I bet.* "She's come a long way, building her own business. It's so good that Bud hired her to do Tuck'r Inn for you."

"I'll second that. How are things going out front?"

"Smooth as silk. Your banana bread is a smash. The couple from Plymouth, Diane and Brian, have asked for more."

Maggie tugged a sheet of parchment paper from the dispenser and took another loaf off her bakery shelf. She sliced it as Cora disappeared into the laundry room.

"This is your most popular bread, Maggie," Laura said, watching closely. "They'll probably ask to buy some, so maybe you should make more."

"Once the dryer nightmare is over."

Retta ran up, offering her little stuffed duck. "Ew, Retta." Laura laughed at Maggie's grimace. "That's a shabby mess. It's going in the trash soon, young lady, before there's stuffing all over the house." Retta stomped, waiting for her to throw it. "It's what you get for taking your toys on walks. Too many throws onto the bricks."

"You two playing catch on the sidewalk?" Laura asked and wagged a finger side to side.

"Not me. Our new friend Ellis." She tipped her head to Retta. "I think you two would've gone all night if I'd let you."

"Ellis?"

Cora emerged from the laundry room. "Ellis Chilton?"

Maggie looked at each of them. "Yes, you two know her?"

"Of course," Cora said, clipping her meter to the tool belt that now hung off her hips. "A native islander, grew up right here, and was always hanging around the docks. When I was little, she was one of the big kids."

"Once, years ago," Laura added, "we were family sailing a few miles out of the harbor, and Ellis and her father came by and rescued us. I can still see Ellis, jumping onto our boat to fix the jib." She smiled dreamily. "I think I was about seven years old, and boy, was I star-struck. To me, she was a lady pirate."

"That's Ellis," Cora snorted. "Nothing ever fazes her, least of all the ocean."

Maggie couldn't imagine growing up on Nantucket, being "on the water" from childhood. *So that's where the independent, solitary vibe comes from. Could I have managed it?*

"Well, a love of the ocean is probably why she works on the ferry now," she thought aloud.

"She ran freight with her father for years," Cora said, "but after he died, the business just got away from her." Maggie knew such losses had to have been deeply damaging.

"Yeah," Laura said, about to leave for the common room, "her mother died when Ellis was little, and after he passed away, she had a rough time."

The dryer chimed and Cora spun back to the laundry room. "You're good to go," she said and returned with a broad, satisfied smile that swept thoughts of Ellis from Maggie's head. "A simple adjustment. You can run that monster as long as you want now."

"Good. I'm so glad it was something small. Thank you, Cora."

"No problem, no charge. Thank *you* for the coffee." She downed the last mouthful and headed for the back door. "Feel free to call anytime. For anything." She winked over her shoulder before leaving.

Maggie busied herself wiping her hands on a towel, glad when Laura left for the common room with the bread platter. But she'd barely dismissed the flirtation when Laura returned.

"Quite the charmer, isn't she?"

Maggie tossed her a glance on route to the laundry room. "Quite." She filled the dryer with the first load of wet sheets and ignored Laura leaning in the doorway, inspecting her manicure.

"So…Last night? Ellis Chilton?"

"She and Retta seem destined to be pals. Our paths have crossed a few times, including last night at the liquor store. She…well…" Maggie sighed as she closed the dryer and pressed the start button. "Somehow I'd forgotten my wallet and she ended up paying for my wine. It was all extremely embarrassing." She returned to the kitchen to begin another round of bread.

"She *is* very nice," Laura continued, loading the dishwasher. "You know, my mom told me Ellis was the first of the island's mariners to be out, and everyone just took it in stride because they'd known her forever. Apparently, people didn't take to her partner Nicki, though, because she was from Detroit."

Maggie stopped abruptly. "I invited Ellis for a drink sometime."

"Yeah? That's great, especially after she bought your—"

"No, I mean, it didn't even occur to me that she might be involved."

Laura shook her head. "Oh, she and Nicki broke up a long time ago. I don't think Nicki ever hit it off with anyone around town. Sometimes, outsiders just don't get accepted here. I felt bad for Ellis because she was going through hard times." She rapped a tray against Maggie's arm playfully. "So enjoy your drink. I think it's cool." She left for the common room as Maggie began mentally filing all the information.

What does that say, she's evidently been single for a while? At least the island's open-minded—except when it comes to outsiders.

❖

"Shit!" Maggie kicked her trash bin and Retta rushed out of the room in a fright. "Sorry, sweetie. It's okay. Come back."

She stroked Retta's neck absently while glaring at the red cross-through she'd just put on the calendar, a guest cancellation that dropped her total to six for the July Fourth weekend. It was supposed to be one of the summer's biggest, and even though right now Tuck'r had more bookings than any other week or weekend, it had a long way to go to being profitable. "Nine out of eleven rooms every week would be nice," she grumbled. "At least five every week would keep us afloat. This measly 'three here and four there' just won't cut it. And just six on the Fourth is unacceptable."

She ran her fingers through her mussed hair and growled down at her desk. A reprioritization of her operating budget, scaling it back to a minimum at the middle of June, had been smart. Not only did it ease her cash flow enough to guarantee a full summer's operation, it freed some capital for additional promotion. But so far, the returns hadn't shown up on her bookings calendar, and with June about to close, she worried.

Laura arrived with a cup of coffee.

"I'm heading home. You okay?"

Maggie leaned back in her chair and covered a yawn with her palm. "Excuse me. Yes, just tired, I guess. Thanks for another great job today." She knew Laura spent a good portion of the day cleaning the pantry and sorting books on the common room's many shelves, busywork, because four bookings hadn't required much from either of them. "I hope you weren't bored stiff."

"Don't think about it like that, Maggie. It's early yet. There's plenty of summer ahead, and the fall is fairly touristy, too. You've done a lot to get the Tuck'r Inn name out there, and folks will catch on. This is new, don't forget."

Maggie let Laura's genuine sweetness wash over her. She needed a pep talk, a few of them, and although Laura was young and even newer to the business than she was, Maggie welcomed her sentiment with opened arms. *Can't do much more unless I cut my only employee.*

She forced a smile and sipped her coffee.

"Thank you. I don't know where Tuck'r Inn would be without you, Ms. Kelliher."

"Just some honest thoughts, that's all. The ideas you've been coming up with lately are awesome, by the way. Offering guests those package deals with other businesses is brilliant."

"I haven't had many takers yet, but I'm hoping to let the concept sink in before I visit them again."

"Well, the discounted dinner at the Club Car is a great one for guests here four nights. So are the deals for a historical sites pass and for a whale watch. Guests should eat up bargains like those. My favorite is the Jeep rental with Young's."

"They haven't said yes yet."

"Make sure you tell them that Round Town Tours and elegant restaurants like Crest and Sol de Mer have agreed already. Young's is all about family and enjoying the island. I think they'll go for the idea."

"Keep talking. You're good for my spirit."

"Tell you what else I think would be good for business?"

Maggie cocked an eyebrow. "Sure. Let's hear it."

"Really want to hear?"

"Shouldn't I?"

"Well…Have you called Ellis about that drink yet? I think you need to go on a date."

Maggie blurted a laugh. "Oh, you think?" She set her cup back in its saucer before she spilled coffee on her slacks. She'd practically talked herself out of that drink and prioritized her personal life to "distant future status." She couldn't risk losing focus on the job at hand, and something told her Ellis Chilton had the potential to blur that focus in a big way. "Sounds like we're through talking shop."

"No. Not exactly. When's the last time you just had fun? It's good for the soul. And you've been working for weeks without a break."

"I see. And exactly when should I do this?"

"Any time. You *know* I'm free almost any night to come back and *babysit.*"

Maggie dared try her coffee again. Laura's idea had appeal, without doubt. Just getting out for an evening did sound heavenly, in fact, but not wise.

"Hm. It's very sweet of you to think of me. I appreciate that."

"Just do it, Maggie. Call her. It's just a drink or two. It would do your spirit good and you know it. Sounds like Ellis likes you."

"Ellis Chilton—"

"Is tall, dark, and handsome."

"I think you're still hung up on your little girl pirate fantasy."

"She could be your Captain Sparrow, your Johnny Depp." Laura giggled behind her hand.

"God, Laura. Enough, already."

At the door, Laura glanced around the quiet common room and turned back. "Why don't you take Retta for a stroll along the waterfront and think about it? We're empty here, it's a beautiful evening, and you'd love it."

Maggie debated the suggestion for more than an hour, sitting at her desk, trying not to look at the blank dates on the bookings calendar and trying not to feel frustrated. Shadows of defeat edged around her thoughts, compacted her timetable, threatened to overwhelm her business plan. *I've managed slow start-ups before. They're all stressful. This one is no different.*

"I deserve a break." She shut off the laptop, tied a sweater around her neck, clipped Retta to her leash, and headed for the waterfront.

Along Main Street, Retta inspected every shop door, every tree, and every loose sidewalk brick. At seven thirty on a Sunday evening, tourist traffic had dwindled, but Retta greeted the few she passed on the sidewalk, the locals, and everyone seated at every bench with endless enthusiasm, bright eyes, and a wiggle. Maggie marveled at how quickly a dog made friends and thought studying the canine "happy approach" might have merit after all. The idea of island businesspeople becoming friends brought a smile—and the reminder that such acquaintances would be short-lived, if her plan held and she moved on by summer's end. At the same time, however, she yearned for Tuck'r Inn's acceptance, and feared the opposite would happen should she speak of the transient nature of her work, of the inn as the turnaround project it really was. Sincerity, despite omissions, still mattered, but so did this project.

They turned onto South Water Street and strolled to the end, twice stopping to chat with shopkeepers about the arrival of summer weather, the tourist volume, the lovely window box flowers, and dogs. In all, accomplishing little more than strengthening friendships and passing the time. In short order, Maggie noticed the relaxation in her step, the massage of each breath of ocean air, and the absence of tension.

"I guess I can admit it to you, Retta. A nineteen-year-old can give solid advice after all, even if it is to a forty-four-year-old. This is nice, isn't it, sweetie?" Retta actually looked surprised, as if Maggie had just noticed. "I know it's not news to you. Shouldn't be to me, either." She started them on a loop down to and then past Steamship Wharf, and then headed back along the water on Easy.

"Such adorable little places right on the water. Not much room for a girl like you, though, but still so pretty." Retta tugged her along and turned onto Straight Wharf. "Hey, what's your hurry?" Nose to the ground, Retta led the way along the water's edge. "Lots of boats, huh? You want a boat?" Even Retta raised her head to look from one to the next. "Have to make some money first, girl. That's how it works."

They walked along the dock and Maggie couldn't help but admire the variety of pleasure craft tied to slips. Occasionally, a boat owner said hello. A young boy even climbed over the side of his boat to pat Retta. Maggie wondered about pets on board, how sad, if families left pets behind to sojourn at sea.

"I'd hate leaving you behind, Retta," she said as they walked on, passing Old South Wharf. "But there'd be no place for you to run, not much to sniff. Sure, you could go—" She caught herself before saying the "S" word, but not before Retta heard what usually came next. She stopped in mid-stride and spun to stare up at Maggie with immense anticipation. "No, we're not going there. I was talking about being on a boat, Retta. Just imagine how bored you'd be, sweetie. And where would you do your business?"

Now *that* wasn't an issue Maggie cared to consider. "Maybe boaters leave their pets home because it's just better for the pets. Somebody should open a pet hotel, a fun, safe, comfy place boaters' pets can go while their owners zip around on the ocean."

Retta was back sniffing, following her nose onto Commercial Wharf.

"You don't like fish, Retta. Can't you smell it here?" She looked closely at the old trawlers docked nearby, their rusted hulls and decks loaded with coolers, cages, coiled lines and hoses, and an assortment of equipment that boggled the mind of a landlubber like herself. Elaborate rigs reaching high created a nautical skyline, and she contemplated the travails of fishermen hauling in acres of netting, battling the unforgiving sea as part of their daily job.

"Too few appreciate what they endure," she muttered, leading Retta along to another boat. "This one's from Gloucester. That's one hell of a long way." Retta sat by her side and Maggie scratched the short fur between her ears. "Think they all spend the nights on their boats? Cheaper than hotels. Bet if Tuck'r offered them a special rate, we'd be full every night."

Retta looked up briefly, then led Maggie farther down the dock.

"What? Think it might be a little stinky? All right, so it's not my brightest idea."

Retta stopped and stared at two workers on a red trawler, and Maggie suddenly knew theirs had been the background noise she'd ignored for the past ten minutes. Heads down, working on a steel cage, they yelled to each other at very close range.

Retta sat, apparently captivated, as Maggie surveyed the boat itself. The old tub creaked against its fenders, bobbing in place. The *Tenn-acious* hailed from Nantucket, impressive that it still functioned as a working trawler. Steel plating covered its hull, all the way to the bow and as far below the water line as she could see. Its rigging thrust skyward, tall and gawky, and everything on board seemed older than she was.

Retta jumped to her feet and barked, tail swishing side to side in a frenzy.

"Retta, shush. They're busy. Come on." She gave the leash a little pull, but Retta's paws were glued to the wooden planks. "No barking. Stop. Now, let's go." Retta's selective hearing had been activated. Maggie bent to her ear. "No, Retta." She drew her against her leg and tried to turn. "Come. Now."

Retta jerked away, to the far corner of the stern, and Maggie stumbled after her. Then stumbled again, when Retta ran back to the opposite corner.

Maggie's temper rose. Bumbling around on a narrow dock was risky, not to mention embarrassing, and the sharp command she was about to shout died on her lips when someone else beat her to it.

"Retta!"

Both Retta and Maggie stopped abruptly and looked up to see Ellis move to the trawler's side, set a hand on it for balance, and vault onto the dock. Retta nearly yanked Maggie off her feet again, dashing to greet her.

"Whoa!" Ellis said. "Slow down, pretty girl." She squatted and Retta ran into her arms. "You be careful with your mother. Humans on leashes can be trouble."

Maggie swiped disarrayed hair from her face. "Lord. Just when I think she's decided on a favorite boat, she sees you."

"There're just too many boats to choose from, huh, Retta?"

Maggie watched Ellis dote on Retta, watched Retta eat it up and wiggle gleefully beneath Ellis's hands. *Guess I can't blame her.* "You spoil her something fierce, you know," she said, managing to speak past the vicarious sensation of that touch. "She's taken to not listening to me when you're around."

"She and I are buddies now, I think." Ellis stood, a presentation of hard-worked cargo shorts and battered T-shirt, carved arms and calves that Maggie found particularly striking. Ellis brushed at the rusty grit on her shorts and spoke softly toward Retta. "Sorry to be a bad influence."

"No, you're not," Maggie corrected her almost too eagerly. "You're one of her best friends now."

Retta sat, butt wiggling restlessly as she stared up at Ellis.

"You have to obey your mother," Ellis told her, and rubbed Retta's head. Retta licked her hand several times. "I doubt you're listening to me either, right now." She turned to Maggie. "A night off or just taking a break?"

Maggie felt a bit restless herself. The vivid light in Ellis's expression was as difficult to dismiss as the wild, tousled look of her. She seemed much nearer than the six or so feet that separated them, but Maggie didn't mind at all. She spoke over the unexpected jangling in her stomach.

"We're just out for a stroll. We've never been on Commercial Wharf before."

"Well, this is the neighborhood." Ellis extended an arm.

Scanning the boats, curious about their function and routine, Maggie struggled to concentrate beneath Ellis's penetrating gaze. "I can't imagine making a living at sea. You'd have to be courageous and highly skilled just to come home from work safe and sound each day. That's amazing to me."

"You grow with it. Or else."

"No doubt." *You grew with it, didn't you?*

"In this neighborhood, we help each other as much as we can." She nodded toward the elderly fisherman on the red trawler. "That's Hank Tennon. He's got some problems we're squaring away tonight so he can head out later."

"Those cages need to be fixed now? He'll go out *tonight*?"

"Yes. If he's lucky, it'll just take a few days."

"If the weather's good, I suppose that's not totally unpleasant."

Ellis laughed roundly, and Maggie realized it was the first time she'd seen that rugged face light up. Her weathered look brightened with softness and warmth, and the flash of brilliant smile made Maggie's breath catch.

"It's all about respect for the sea," Ellis said. "It owes you nothing. No one here knows that better or has been doing it longer than Hank."

Maggie watched him drag one of the large steel cages across his deck. "I'm keeping you from helping. I'm sorry."

"It's okay. At the moment, we're between projects." She toyed absently with Retta's tail. Ellis's mischievous grin looked out of character. *Lighthearted is very attractive on you.* "Hank and I have to take breaks every couple of hours because he's so single-minded and doesn't always pay attention. We've been yelling at each other for years."

Maggie grinned back, happy to win a glimpse of Ellis's humor. "Well, I'm sure he appreciates your help." That Ellis spent serious time with this man said there had to a considerable amount of tenderness hidden behind that closed persona.

Ellis looked back at Hank with something Maggie couldn't pinpoint. Probably fondness and respect, she thought, maybe a longing to do what he does, or for times gone by. *I know so little about you.*

"Do you live around here?" Maggie surprised herself by asking. Ellis didn't have time for this, and here she was, being nosy.

Ellis nodded at the dock. "The last slip."

"You live on a boat?" She stole a glance past the dozen or so slips to the large craft at the end.

"Yes."

Maggie fought the urge to unleash a string of questions. *Can this woman be any more fascinating?*

"Well, that's just...remarkable." She wished Ellis would offer more details, or better yet, an invitation. "Is it something you always wanted to do?"

"I've been on boats all my life."

Maggie couldn't tell if that was a "yes" or a "no." She looked out along the dock again, as Ellis continued to minister to Retta.

"It must require a lot of work," she said. She waited an extra beat and realized Ellis wasn't about to respond. *Must you be so cryptic?* "Keeps you busy, I bet."

"I enjoy keeping busy," Ellis said without looking up.

"Too busy for a drink some evening during the week?"

Ellis turned to her then, that stoic, totally unreadable look back on her face. "My evenings are pretty full."

I should have known better. It's for the best, anyway.

Over Ellis's shoulder, she saw Hank approach the side of the boat and lean on both hands, his haggard face twisted with discontent.

She tugged Retta closer and prepared to leave. "Well, I'm sorry to—"

"Chilton! You done socializin' yet?"

Ellis responded without looking back. "Hank, don't be rude."

"You a tourist, young lady? Or are you gonna be around a while, so's that slacker can talk with you later?"

Maggie grinned up at him. "Not a tourist, Mr. Tennon, no. The new B&B just up town, I'm—"

"Eh! Another tourist trap." He tossed his hands at her and shuffled back to his work. "Just what we need around here."

"Don't mind him," Ellis said and slid her hands into her pockets. "My, ah, my weeknights are booked because I'm scheduled for late runs next week."

"Oh. Of course. I forgot about the *Eagle*'s schedule."

"Saturday night okay?"

Maggie hid the unexpected surge of pleasure. "Sure, that would be fine. Is there a local place you recommend? I'm afraid I haven't had much time to explore the island."

"The Brotherhood is great." Ellis pointed beyond Maggie. "The Brotherhood of Thieves. Just a few blocks from here."

"Sounds perfect. Meet you at seven?"

Ellis nodded as she stroked Retta's back. "Seven's good."

"Look, I won't keep you any longer. He needs you."

Ellis set a hand on the edge of the boat, about to climb aboard. "See you Saturday."

"Definitely." Leading Retta away, Maggie could feel Ellis still watching but didn't expect her to speak again.

"Glad you two stopped by."

She looked back briefly and waved. "So are we."

Maggie noted the slight, possibly sad curl of her lips before turning away, and pondered the reasons for it. *Are you content, living the dream, independent and free? Maybe it's not a dream life after all.*

CHAPTER SEVEN

Maggie stared into her third martini Wednesday night and saw the hands of her business plan clock spinning past her deadline. Another idiotic promotion scheme like this, and time would tick away with her career. She'd hoped to send her prospective buyer an upward-running spreadsheet of success by now. *The illustrious Jill McGee and her Cavanaugh Resorts will have to wait a bit longer.*

She labored to pay polite attention to the woman beside her at Nix's bar but instead found herself escaping to the serenity of her backyard lounge chair, the distant foghorn and occasional church bells, the blanket of stars overhead. This, her latest brainstorm, had flat-out backfired, and here she sat with an all-too-eager Jan Medeiros, who had some completely different business in mind. When it came to exchanging discounted accommodations for fresh seafood, neither she nor Jan could maintain interest. In fact, Maggie ranked the proposal of having Jan luxuriating at Tuck'r in return for guests' shrimp cocktails as her worst idea to date.

Jesus, I'm getting desperate.

Her watch said ten o'clock was time to go, time to send Laura home, time to talk her way out of Jan's offer of dinner and dancing at the RC Friday night.

"Sounds like fun, but it's difficult for me to get out, Jan."

"No chance over the weekend? It's the Fourth, you know. We could..."

She rambled on as Maggie's thoughts turned to meeting Ellis on the night of July Fourth. *How easily I forgot it was the holiday. She must have, too.*

Jan inched toward the edge of her seat. "Maybe midweek would be less hectic for you?"

"I'm afraid I never know in advance."

"Come on, Maggie. I'd really like to see you." She lowered her hand to Maggie's knee and squeezed. "I think we kind of click together, don't you? Look, let me get us another round and we'll figure something out, okay?" She rubbed her palm over Maggie's kneecap. "There's got to be *some* time we can…you know…"

Maggie turned on her stool, just enough to slip out from beneath Jan's grip. "I appreciate that, but Tuck'r Inn requires my every waking moment these days. I'm sorry, but I hope you understand."

Nodding into her glass, Jan withdrew her hand and hailed the bartender.

Maggie shook her head at him. "I really should run." She tapped Jan's forearm. "Thank you for this tonight, for meeting with me and hearing me out."

"Hey, my pleasure, but remember what I said, okay?"

"I definitely will." She stood and took her purse off the bar. *Won't forget this awkward scene for quite a while.*

"Wait, let me walk you home."

"Oh, that's not necessary." She nodded toward Jan's fourth cocktail. "Enjoy the rest of your evening and your drink. I don't mind—"

"No way." Jan guzzled more than half her drink as she slid off her stool. "Not letting you go it alone." She walked Maggie to the door, and once outside, took Maggie's arm and hooked it around hers. "How could I ever let a knockout like you walk home unescorted and still hope to improve my chances?" She drew her arm closer and Maggie stifled a frustrated sigh.

Unusually humid and thick with the flavor of low tide, the night air settled heavily on her skin, tempting Maggie to swipe it away, off her cheeks and arms like an unwanted blanket. The arm linked with hers was uncomfortably warm and tacky, and she longed to rid herself of it, too. She longed to be standing at the harbor, beneath that immense display of stars as onshore breezes soothed her mind. Nearing the corner of South Water Street, Maggie briefly closed her eyes to the image, and to her surprise, the shadowy form of Ellis Chilton took shape.

❖

"There won't be a crowd of us, El. I know you don't care for that. Just five of us. Come on. I'm doing my awesome ribs on the smoker,

and I *know* you love them. You can catch the last boat home easily."
Jeannie finally took a breath to sip her coffee.

"Thanks for the invite, but I can't."

"You can't? What's up?"

Both donning sunglasses, they walked out of the Hyannis terminal and into the brilliant morning. The *Eagle* sat ready for its next run, and Ellis was pleased the trip looked to be smooth. She'd much rather think about today's steady warm breeze and calm sea than discuss her personal life.

"So how come you can't?" Jeannie smirked over the rim of her cup. "Tell me it's a hot date."

"Well, yeah. I'm meeting someone."

"Do I know her?"

"Not really." Ellis dropped her empty cup into the trash bin, not surprised that Jeannie took the few steps with her.

"Ellis." She tugged off her sunglasses. "Do I or don't I?"

"Well, you've seen her. Remember the woman with the luggage in the doorway at Dell's?" Jeannie's blank look said she didn't. "The one I held the door for?"

Jeannie narrowed her eyes, only to pop them wide open. "Oh, no way!"

"Yes, way."

"I remember her now. Nice work, El. *Very* attractive lady."

Ellis shrugged. "We just keep bumping into each other and figured sitting down for a drink would be nice. She works at some B&B, a manager, I guess."

"Well, it would be sweet if something came of it, don't you think? You've gotta be open to that. You're long overdue, my friend. And you deserve someone nice in your life—besides me, of course."

"Thanks, but I finally have things just how I like them. I'm in no rush to mess things up."

"What a crock. Listen to you, 'mess things up.' You can't take that attitude into your first date, for Christ's sake. Shake that off. Enough time's passed. Get your ass in gear." She dashed to the trash with her empty cup, continuing her spiel. "Now, look. I know nothing about her, but she somehow got you to come up for air—and that's a freakin' miracle, so there's definitely something special about her."

"Who knows? Maybe. She's got a great dog. I like what that says about her." Ellis headed for the gangway and noted the usual shift among waiting passengers to formalize their line. Another seaman awaited her signal to remove the rope barricade.

"Oh, right, El. It's all about the dog," Jeannie said, still tagging along. "I get it. Sure."

"Just drinks. No marriage proposal."

"To hell with that," Jeannie said and stepped closer to whisper. "You just—"

"You need to keep your one-track mind to yourself. Go, get to work. I'll see you in a few hours."

Ellis nodded to the sailor and they began boarding passengers. She greeted them with smiles and one-liners about the perfect weather while he tore off ticket stubs. She kept count with the clicker in her hand, but the repetitive sound faded as her thoughts wandered to Maggie Jordan and what it was about her, *exactly*, that made their upcoming date so… unnerving?

With the last vehicle in place on the cargo deck and the *Eagle* under way, her first stop on the way to the bridge was the snack bar, for coffee for herself and Benny, the ship's master. A glance at the bustling lounge and its full complement of passengers in booths and chairs had her picturing Maggie again, as she'd only half noticed many times before.

But now she had her clearly in mind, and the image was engaging. *"Enough time has passed."* Jeannie's coaching echoed in her head. Time had indeed passed and days were good now, reliable, comfortable, safe…predictable and boring.

She imagined phone calls between them, dinners, dancing, intimate evenings on the *Rose*, the roiling nervousness of a new relationship. A relationship, period. *Shit, Jeannie. You've got me blowing this all out of proportion. I'm not looking for a relationship. Probably couldn't handle one correctly if it hit me in the face.*

She studied the black liquid in her cup, practically motionless as the *Eagle* glided out of the glassy harbor. Gone were the days her hands shook at the helm, when guilt weighed so heavily upon her she thought she'd never smile again. Time *had* passed and brought relief, restored a bit of the zest for life she used to possess, but she just couldn't be sure she had enough yet to share with anyone special.

Climbing the steps to the bridge, she counted the years since Nicki left and scolded herself for having remained in such an emotional hole. *Eleven years. At least it all brought me here.* She stood at the rail, four decks high, and scanned the ship below, the passengers enjoying the summer sun, the arms of Hyannis Harbor gradually releasing them to the Sound, and admitted she'd come to love the job that had, in effect, saved her from herself.

After all this time, I should have my act together. The half dozen or so dates in past years mean I'm definitely rusty, though. Who knows what real dating is like anymore?

She shook her head at herself and took a drink. "It's okay to be anxious," she muttered into the wind and entered the wheelhouse. *But if her type is somebody with smooth moves, we're definitely not on the same page.*

With a plump face to match his short body, Benny turned from the helm and eyed the cups of coffee in her hands. He spoke too loudly, as always.

"Been waiting for that. You go pick the beans yourself?"

"Morning to you too, grumpy old man." She handed him his cup. "Turn those hearing aids up." She pointed at her ear. "I don't feel like yelling for the next two hours."

He took a long drink before setting the cup down and adjusted his hearing aids. "Pretty morning we have, Ellis. Good weather ahead for the Fourth, too. You taking the *Rose* out for the fireworks?"

"Hadn't figured on it," she said and checked the dashboard gauges over his shoulder. Benny had been mastering ships for so long, he took things for granted. She didn't. Reassured that everything was shipshape, she fell into his conversation. *The Fourth is Saturday. Date night.*

A new wave of anxiety rolled through her when she realized Maggie was her first thought. *She might like that.*

"Well, why the hell not?" Benny continued. "You can't keep that tub of yours tied up all the time, girl. She's built to go, not sit 'n rot. You know better."

"I do. We went out last weekend and I cranked it up for a couple hours. The *Rose* is as solid and fit as ever."

Benny just nodded as he stared ahead. She knew he wrestled with adding a reference to pleasing her father, but she appreciated him not bringing it up.

"Y'take company out lately? You should be proud of all you've done to her. Show her off."

"Thanks. I'm content just looking at it myself."

"Well, that's a load of bull crap." He shook his head as he reached for his cup. "You're alone too damn much. Go show her off. Make your daddy proud."

There it was. She knew he'd bring up the subject sooner or later. Making her father proud could never happen. She'd done too much damage. All the work she'd put in converting the *Rose* simply demonstrated how she'd failed at their business, failed him, and she didn't like being reminded.

"I just might take the *Rose* out Saturday." *That will shut him up.*

"Got yourself a date to take along?"

Or so I thought. "We'll see."

Chapter Eight

"Well, I could have asked for a room this weekend, you know, but I was being the good little sister and not pressing for prime time."

Maggie reclined in her chair, her cell set to speaker on her desk. Rachel always bubbled too much. And no, thank God, she hadn't asked for a free room during the holiday weekend. Tuck'r had five rooms left, and Maggie still held out hope that she'd book them to paying guests in the next few days.

"I appreciate that, Rach. Sometime next week, then?"

"So Wednesday and Thursday are good? I wanted to see you, so I'm tagging along with John, my neighbor downstairs. His partner Ian has family on the island, out in Madaket, and I guess we're all going to see his brother in the Theatre Workshop. Wednesday is opening night for *Oklahoma!*, and you're coming with us."

Leave it to Rachel to sweep in with big plans for everyone. "I have to pass. I have a ton of work to do before Thursday."

"Really. Such as?"

"Rach. Not everyone lives off the grid like you do."

"I'm a starving artiste, big sister."

"And I have a prospectus to update for a buyer."

"That slinky babe in six-inch heels you met last summer?"

"She's a property acquisitions attorney out of Baltimore."

"Uh-huh. The one with the superb tits who works for that resort outfit in Miami?"

Maggie sighed. "You're bad. Yes. Jill McGee."

"Whoa. So the shark is coming."

"To check out Tuck'r, yes. Well, she indicated as much. It's not definite yet. Either way, I have to have paperwork ready."

"So I might get to see her in action?"

"Possibly. And that means I won't have a lot of time to play with you. I'm sorry."

"I'm sorry, too. I miss you, big sister."

"Same here, you pain in the butt. Come over early Wednesday so we'll have some time to catch up."

"You sound lonely. How are you staying sane out there in the middle of nowhere?"

"I'm too busy to be lonely."

"No hunky butches on Nantucket?"

Maggie sat up. "Stop."

Rachel chuckled. "No sweater-and-Docksider types taking you for rides in their Land Rovers?"

Maggie shook her head. "Knock it off. If you must know, I'm meeting a friend for drinks Saturday night. Satisfied?"

"Ah. Well, that's something, at least. Is she a voluptuous sculptress, like moi? I know: she's a Mass General surgeon on vacation."

"Rach."

"A poet. Nantucket's a hotbed of poets and writers."

"She's an officer on the ferry."

"Oooh. Make sure I get to meet her on Wednesday. Does she wear a uniform?"

"You're impossible for a straight girl. Good-bye, little sister."

Somewhere amidst her laughter, Rachel said good-bye, and Maggie shook her head in amusement. *It'll be good to have you here. And you don't need to meet Ellis, couldn't on Wednesday, anyway, unless you cross paths on the steamship. But I think you'd like her.*

She typed Rachel's reservation into the system for two nights next week in the single room. She'd already tagged one of the two front suites for Jill McGee for Thursday and Friday, and the name and all it represented loomed large on the register. The Cavanaugh attorney hadn't confirmed her reservation yet, and Maggie wasn't sure she would, which, in turn, made her wonder how many inquiries, how much advance work the corporation was doing without her knowledge.

"God. I hope not." She looked vacantly at Retta, who dozed peacefully on her bed in the corner. "The rumors that would start could make life miserable for us, cost us progress—and a lot more money before we see any profit."

She leaned back in the chair and assessed her work of the past several weeks. All accounts were in order, nothing in arrears; all appliances and structural elements of the inn performed flawlessly; the guests' up-to-the-minute calendar of island events—which she hated tending and usually dumped on Laura—now appeared on a flashy upgraded Tuck'r website as well as in the common room. The landscaping even dazzled, just as she dreamed, and the columns of early-bloom roses framing the front door had her ridiculously giddy with pride. She knocked on her desk three times for continued good luck.

"All I need is to fill in these damn blanks." Her eyes flitted from one vacancy on the register to the next, and knew anyone, especially Jill with her calculating eye, could readily see that occupancy rates barely averaged 50 percent. "She *has* to appreciate a start-up coming this far so fast. Obviously, you don't become established overnight."

Jill McGee had been a whirlwind of corporate-speak and PowerPoint slides when they'd met in Maryland last summer. No stranger to red tape, Maggie nevertheless staggered a bit beneath Jill's aggressive approach and would have walked out with her proposition if Jill hadn't injected a dinner invitation and turned down the business heat. Ultimately, that evening proved beneficial, and Maggie saw serious interest from Cavanaugh Resorts, despite the awkward personal cat-and-mouse game she and Jill played to a stalemate. Maggie was still damn proud of her performance that night. She smiled at her laptop, remembering how she'd offered a good night handshake at her hotel door, how she'd read the unspoken touché on Jill's lips.

"You know, Retta, they're not just a resort company." Retta lifted her head and blinked at her. "They've just begun branching out, and now they own two B&Bs like this in Key West and two on Myrtle Beach. Your mama does her homework, little girl." She gazed around her office and out into the common room. "Should I stay a step ahead and go for something in Provincetown after this? I could probably pitch it to her."

Retta stood and stretched, then meandered to Maggie and sat. Maggie bent down and rested her cheek atop Retta's head.

"Getting ahead of myself, huh? But I really should firm up the next project. That place on the East End off Commercial Street was adorable, and you'd love Provincetown."

Retta drew away and licked Maggie's cheek.

"Okay, okay. One thing at a time." She straightened and eyed the laptop screen warily. "My package deals *are* good, damn it. We have to fill these gaps. I need to push harder, get more restaurants, more activities on board with us. Offering a sightseeing cruise would be outstanding, don't you think?"

❖

Maggie frowned at the tray of scones and muffins she handed Laura. Her confections were top-notch this morning, but her concentration was far from her work.

"What's got you so preoccupied? These look yummy."

"Hmm? Oh, just wishing one of those charter operations would go in on my deal. I went to one outfit Wednesday afternoon, and three yesterday, but it was like pulling teeth. And now the couple in the rose garden just asked about a cruise—the third inquiry this week alone. We're so close."

"Yeah. Seems like every other day, someone asks. Still not even a call back?"

"No. Well, Roberson's called, but I think he was more interested in taking *me* out than our guests." She poured herself a glass of orange juice and leaned against the counter. "So frustrating. Nobody offers anything like it, a stay that includes a cruise, and we'd be unique."

"I don't think you should give up, Maggie. That deal for three nights with cruise and dinner is a steal, and it's bound to be a moneymaker."

"I agree. We've got the stay and the dinner parts nailed down. Too bad the cruise part is missing."

"Hey." Laura came back across the kitchen. "What do you think Ellis would say?"

"Ellis? She doesn't do public cruises. She's on the ferry all day. Besides, she lives on her boat." Maggie allowed the image of Ellis at sea to cruise through her mind for the third—*or was it the fourth*—time today. *Damn it. What is it about that woman?*

"But doesn't she have weekends off? What if Tuck'r offered that great deal on weekends? Think she'd be interested? It doesn't seem like there'd be much work involved on her part, right? An hour or two here and there would mean easy money."

"There's a lot more to it than just puttering around the island with a few passengers. Liability, for one." She rinsed her glass in the sink and spoke out the window. "And somehow I don't think Ellis is much of a people person."

"Couldn't hurt to ask, could it?" Laura went off with her tray, but Maggie lingered over the notion. She pictured herself, practical and reasonably persistent, squared off with Ellis, reserved and firmly entrenched.

The image was enough to draw her and Retta back to Commercial Wharf that afternoon. Retta had seeing Ellis in mind, no doubt, and led the way with typical, dogged determination, while Maggie simply *had* to see where and what Ellis called home.

"She's not going to be here, sweetie. She's working." Maggie kept Retta's leash short, guarding against being swept off the floating pier, but let her patrol left and right and investigate their path.

Maggie inhaled deeply and let the air refresh her. The congested, tightly packed "neighborhood" of their last visit here differed greatly today, and the absence of many trawlers opened broad portals to the bright sky and harbor breeze. The sun singed her arms and legs, though, and beat on her head, and she wished she'd worn the new Nantucket cap she'd bought several days ago. She also regretted not applying suntan lotion. Retta, sporting her water-resistant fur coat, panted steadily yet remained undaunted in her sniffing.

"Hardworking boats," Maggie told her, and they stopped to study the worn scalloper tied to the dock. "Bet this one has seen its share of bad weather." She empathized with the seamen who faced such work. She'd heard that Nantucket's big scallop season came in February, not a time of year to be *close* to the Atlantic, let alone *on* it.

One broad-beamed boat remained as they moved to the end of the narrow pier.

"This must be it." They took in the formidable stature of Ellis's boat. "Wow. This is impressive. Don't you think?"

Retta glanced up at her, as if asking permission to board.

"No." Maggie shook her head. "She's not here right now. We only came to look." She gave Retta a consoling pat on the head. "Did you think she'd have something this big?"

They stepped closer to the piling. Loops of thick, imposing rope drew taut off the large cleats on the dock and secured the boat firmly. She envisioned Ellis handling them with swift precision, never breaking a sweat. A hefty electrical cord extended up and over the side, connected on the near end to the utilities post at the end of the pier. A neatly coiled hose sat nearby at a water spigot.

With no thought as to why, Maggie set her hand on the side of the glistening blue hull, rust-free in stark contrast to its workhorse neighbors. The steel was warm from the sun, and so solid, so fortified. *No surprise there.* She looked down and imagined the blue bottom to be far cooler below the water line. *Probably a lot like her.*

A lone deck chair and tattered paperback sat near the open rear, away from the hard-top canopy that sheltered half the spacious deck. "You could probably park three of our cars in that space. And, God, this thing is long. You can't even see the front end from here." She stroked Retta's head absently and tried to picture a handful of paying guests seated comfortably, sipping cocktails, ogling the island's coast and its many picturesque homes, absorbing Ellis's narration as she drove.

"How she must love this view. Who wouldn't, huh? Parked here at the end, no neighbors from here out, just the harbor with boats passing by." She sighed. "How relaxing can it get?" *What kind of books do you read up there?*

"That's a decent-size cabin for driving, don't you think, Retta?" She pointed to the bridge as they wandered alongside, but Retta didn't seem interested. "It'd be fun, lounging in the sun up there, right in front." She eyed the graceful sweep of the bow as it curved away into an assertive, wave-piercing stance. "Must be a force on the water. Certainly formidable, so long and wide…and so pristine, so well cared for. It doesn't look as if she takes it out much."

She gazed back along the hull. "She must have quite the place for herself downstairs. Too bad we can't see inside. How nosy are we, Retta?" She wished she could lean far enough over the edge of the dock to peek in the small windows. Retta tried in her own way, flat on her belly, front paws hooked over the edge, nose extended as far as possible. Maggie laughed when a little splash against the hull startled Retta back up into a sitting position. "A fish, sweetie. Probably nosy like us. And don't even *think* about catching it."

Ellis probably does her share of fishing, she mused as they retraced their steps. Probably fished these waters since she was a little girl and has a wealth of tales about fish, sharks, whales…

"Maybe someday she'll tell us what it's like to live on a boat." Back at the rear of the boat, Maggie smiled at the name, the arch of pink script lettering outlined in silver. "*Nantucket Rose* doesn't sound like you, Ellis Chilton. I do love it, though."

Pondering the source of such a sweet name, Maggie recalled what little she'd been told of Ellis, that she'd been around the docks since childhood, that this was the boat on which she'd worked with her father. And that he had died some time ago. *No wonder you live here.*

"Do you think she chose the name *Nantucket Rose*, Retta? Maybe for a special love she had? Or maybe her father named the boat, like, after her mother?"

Do memories haunt you? Do you share your Nantucket Rose *with anyone? Would you?*

"God, Retta. She's a bit of a mystery, isn't she?" They started away along the dock. "Maybe everything's just black and white to you, girl, but she's definitely not."

CHAPTER NINE

Fresh from the shower, Ellis stuffed towels and sheets, along with her day's work clothes, into the laundry sea bag she kept beneath her bed and evaluated her housekeeping as she dressed. Not bad, she thought, and spared a thought for her own appearance. Now in dress jeans and a pale blue short-sleeved shirt, she scanned the galley. Dishes washed and put away, floor swept, and everything clean and in its place. She snatched open her new fridge and reassured herself about the beverage selection she'd purchased that morning. There were plenty of jumbo shrimp for shrimp cocktails, and even two varieties of cheese to have with crackers. Topside, where she assessed equipment and its readiness, things were shipshape. *If* a certain pretty lady agreed to a boat ride later, the *Rose* was prepared.

Am I?

Try as she might, she couldn't remember the last time she'd entertained on board, let alone invited an intriguing woman for an evening cruise. And that's what she'd decided to do. Actually, she didn't think she had much choice, and told herself as much, as she walked down Centre Street to the Brotherhood. It *was* the Fourth of July, after all, so the subject of going "somewhere" to watch the fireworks was bound to come up. Watching them off the beach, especially with the harbor and its quaint setting as backdrop, was a "must" for someone who now called Nantucket home. *Did you catch the little parade downtown this morning? A newcomer like you needs to experience Nantucket tradition.*

"Hopefully, she can use a little break as much as I can."

Entering the dark confines of the Brotherhood, she waved to the bartender and spotted Maggie along the bar, seated in front of a half-empty chocolate martini. Ellis checked the bar clock, glad to see she was exactly on time. *She's early.* She looked back to catch Maggie watching.

In linen skirt and jacket, she certainly stood out among the tourists and regulars, especially when she turned on her stool and swung crossed, shapely legs into view. Her warm gaze deepened, and Ellis couldn't help but enjoy the greeting. *Damn if you aren't the finest-looking lady here, Maggie Jordan.*

"Ellis, hi. Good to see you. So you're the punctual type."

"Hi to you, too. Punctual, yeah." She rubbed her naked wrist awkwardly. "I never forget my watch, but tonight…" She accepted the bottle being offered by the bartender and ordered another martini for Maggie.

"Thank you." Maggie nodded at the beer. "Your usual?"

"Syd remembers every time." She turned the bottle to display the label. "You should give this a try. Cisco is Nantucket's own. We're proud of it."

"Next time I will. Glad to support the local cause." Maggie moved to her feet gracefully as her drink arrived. "Shall we grab a table?"

Ellis followed her to corner seats, enthralled by Maggie's relaxed air, her poise and confidence, and for a moment, saw them sitting down for a business meeting. *Well, she* is *a polished businesswoman.*

"I'm usually pretty punctual myself," Maggie said, "although the hours I've been keeping lately have done a number on that. Now I'm lucky if I remember the right *day* of an appointment, let alone the time." She shook her head at herself, and Ellis wondered just how hard a B&B manager worked. Maggie held up her glass. "Today I was early. I'd thought about treating myself to these all day and couldn't wait. Sorry I started without you."

"Oh, I can relate. No problem." *How many drinks ago did you start?*

"I've been shameful. This is my third—and final one of the night. I'm switching to water."

"Well, you're not driving anywhere, right?"

"Right. But I hate not keeping a level head. God, you must think I have a problem. First, you catch me begging for wine, and now I'm swigging down martinis. But to tell you the truth, I haven't indulged in months, too much hard work."

"I can relate to the hard work. If you don't let it push the wrong buttons, you've done a good job. And there's nothing wrong with honest self-examination at all."

"Then here's to self-examination." Maggie tapped the rim of her glass against Ellis's bottle. "I think this could become one of my favorite places on the island," she said, looking around. "I love the low ceiling, the old wood beams and brick walls."

"Tourists love it, too, unfortunately. I mean, we wish we could keep it to ourselves, but I know, if it weren't for the tourists…"

"Exactly. Tourists matter." Maggie fidgeted with the tiny candle at the center of the table. Ellis watched the soft light flicker across her cheeks and couldn't look away from the subtle touch of powder blue eye shadow, the curl of long lashes. She'd just torn herself from the view when Maggie looked up and spoke. "Retta sends her love."

"Give her a hug for me, please."

"I'll do that," Maggie said. "She was beside herself with joy last weekend when a couple from Hartford checked in with their Westie. Poor Retta sulked so badly when they left, I had to take her swimming for three days."

"Loves the water, huh?"

"You can't say the word 'swim' in any form without her going crazy. She's even learned how it's spelled."

"She's a great dog. I enjoy her very much."

"Thank you. That's sweet. Too bad you never had one. Have you really spent your whole life here, on the ocean?" Ellis nodded. "Has that been by choice? Never a desire to…to see the world, as all good sailors do?"

"I've seen enough, and Nantucket still is my choice. I think islanders here develop a special strength and integrity from living with these waters, the seasons, and I wouldn't change that for anything. I think that's why we're all so protective of this place. It's who we are and we're grateful for the nurturing."

"So I'm learning. Mr. Tennon didn't seem too thrilled to hear I run *another* B&B, even though I'm sure he's aware of what tourism means to the island's economy."

"To him, it's 'despite' the tourism. Hank would turn back the clocks to the nineteen seventies, if he could, when things were simpler all around. There are some topics I just don't bring up with him. It just gets him too worked up for his heart meds."

"But you have to agree, growth is good for everyone, native islanders included."

"Oh, I try to enlighten him when I can, but I agree with him on some things, too. I'm one of those 'native islanders' who is happy we've put in some killer restrictions. It's kept the chains, the McDonald's of the world, from turning Nantucket into Coney Island, thank God. Off-islanders who don't have a clue aren't welcome to come here and fumble around."

Maggie nodded and slid her half-empty glass aside. "Well, I don't think I've heard it stated quite so succinctly before. I hope I can do justice to a Nantucket B&B."

"I didn't mean to offend you. I bet you and your B&B will fit in well. But some outfits just think hit-and-run. They just show up for the big bucks and don't give a damn about impacting the island, that's all."

"Well, I did my homework for this. Establishing Tuck'r Inn as a classic Nantucket destination is a goal I'm proud to work toward. Granted, our first season is a bit of a struggle, but I'm working hard at it."

"Running a business by yourself can be tough, I know." She sipped her beer, knowing she'd rather change the subject than get too far into that one. "Look, this is spur of the moment, I suppose, but... What would you say to a run out into the harbor to catch the fireworks tonight?"

Maggie's eyebrows rose as she sat back. "You mean on your boat?"

"You could probably use a break from the routine as much as I can. And if you want to become an islander of any kind, you *have* to see them from the water."

As they strolled through the humid twilight toward the *Rose*, Maggie contemplated the wisdom of sailing with a virtual stranger, and being so one-on-one with a woman so remarkably intriguing. But those concerns paled in comparison to maintaining the impression of "becoming an islander," as Ellis understandably believed. The urge to level with her rose strong and loud, and actually upset her stomach. She wasn't the deceitful type, hated false impressions.

But what little she knew of Ellis advised Maggie to keep her master business plan under wraps. She couldn't afford to be seen as one of those "unwelcome hit-and-run off-islanders," and, surprisingly, it mattered whether Ellis saw her as one. Right now, Ellis didn't have a clue about the kind of woman Maggie was at all, so it was too soon to come clean. They definitely needed more time, like this evening's boat ride, to get to know each other. Besides, Maggie enjoyed Ellis's easygoing style and her quiet demeanor, was a bit enchanted by the attachment Ellis held for Nantucket, and didn't want to spoil any of it with a misconception.

"Lots of boats going out tonight," she offered, as Ellis returned the wave of a family sailing past. At the *Rose*, Ellis climbed over the side and retrieved a two-step wooden box, which she promptly dropped into place on the pier alongside the boat.

Maggie accepted her offered hand and stepped up, over the side, and onto the spacious white deck. So big, it didn't tip a bit, she thought. Awfully big for one person. Big enough for at least twenty guests to lounge comfortably.

"Welcome aboard." Ellis seemed a bit undone at the moment, hands in her pockets, scanning her surroundings as if she expected to find something out of place. "Ah, would you like to look around before we get under way?"

"I'd love a tour, yes. Thank you." She slipped off her sandals and left them by the side. "The *Rose* is huge."

"Consider this my sun porch," Ellis said, then led her beneath the canopy and opened the saloon door. Maggie took in the benches and small round tables with teak swivel chairs, the little counter and cabinets at the rear, the nautical accents on the walls.

"It's just perfect, Ellis. What more could a woman need?" She was pleased to win the hint of a grin before Ellis turned away.

"Well, we don't need to go there, do we?" At the far wall, Ellis stopped at the top of a narrow flight of stairs and looked back. "Something to drink? Come below and choose your poison."

"Well, I *did* get off to a powerful start tonight, so I probably should behave right now," Maggie said with a laugh, following her down. "Maybe save a real one for later." Ellis had two chilled bottles of Perrier in hand by the time Maggie arrived in the galley.

"I like that idea, too."

Maggie stood in place and turned in a circle. Surprisingly spacious, the table, countertops, and sink looked taken from high-end boating magazines Maggie had seen. The three-burner stove and oven were impressive, as were the polished teak walls and cabinets. The overhead roominess of the kitchen struck her as well, having expected the typical low-ceiling claustrophobia of boat cabins. Ellis even cleared the ceiling with plenty to spare.

"Oh, this is beautiful, Ellis. Spacious, but homey, cozy." She placed a palm on the refrigerator. "All the comforts." She examined the decorative wreath of pink artificial beach roses on a door in the corner. "And this is just gorgeous, so real. Did someone make this for you?"

"For my father, actually. A close family friend who passed away a few years ago."

"Nantucket roses," Maggie said and turned to her. "You've made a lovely home here."

"I...well, thank you. It's taken a while, but I think I've finally run out of projects."

"These are all your renovations?"

Ellis shrugged. "The *Rose* carried freight since the sixties." She gestured toward the bow. "I have a full bedroom forward now, where there used to be just a small bunk-and-galley combination. The rest of all this held cargo. I just sort of pushed things around."

She swung open a rear door and Maggie went to the threshold. The open airiness of the room with its bright, pale gray walls and dual purpose took her aback. Wider than it was deep, the room offered a living room on the near side, with an upholstered couch and chair, wall-mounted flat screen, and lobster trap coffee table; and a library of sorts on the far side, complete with a simple antique writing desk, computer, and shelves of books.

"It's not your typical family room," Ellis explained, "but it suits my needs. Beyond that back wall is aft storage."

"It's like a cute loft apartment. Looks so comfortable." She sent Ellis a sideways look. "You're far too modest. This really is lovely." Ellis obviously knew her way around interior construction, and Maggie suddenly wanted her opinion of the work at Tuck'r. "I'd love to know what you think of the renovations I had done for my B&B. Would you come by sometime?"

"I'm no expert," Ellis said, leading them back up the stairs. "All this was...you know, good enough for me."

"Like I said, you're far too modest. I bet you'd enjoy seeing what's been done to my place and I'd love to hear your thoughts. Please say you'll stop by."

They reached the open deck and Ellis started up to the bridge. "Well, all right. I could do that." She scrambled up the steps and started the engines. Her agreement sounded like a concession. *Damn, she's hard to read.*

"I'll be right with you," Ellis said from above. "Give me a minute to get this..."

Engines rumbling to life beneath her feet startled Maggie, and she quickly took a seat. She watched Ellis slide down the steps with a hand on each rail and cross the deck with purpose.

"Could I be doing something to help you?"

"Nope. You're good. I just need a minute."

Maggie watched, intrigued, as Ellis vaulted over the side and unwound the tie lines and tossed them onto the deck. Just as deftly, she gave the boat a shove and jumped aboard as the *Rose* inched away from the pier.

Ellis moved swiftly toward the stairs but stopped short in front of her. "You're welcome to come up with me, if you'd like."

"Aye aye, Captain." Excited about their little excursion, she followed her up the steps as quickly and carefully as she could and joined her at the helm.

Maggie sipped her fresh martini, crossed her ankles in the lounge chair, and took in the view of Nantucket's humble silhouette as dusk faded to night. Brant Point Lighthouse slashed a beacon through the darkness, and Maggie found herself watching for its indefatigable return, realizing how, in just barely two months, she'd come to take it for granted. So much about life here mustn't be overlooked, she thought, and wished all visitors would pause for moments like this and appreciate the view, the history.

Bobbing silently in place just off the channel, the *Rose* provided the perfect viewing station for the fireworks, now only minutes from starting. Dozens of pleasure craft of all sizes sat scattered within shouting distance, dotting the dark sea with yellow cabin lights and red and green navigational lamps. A steady, warm breeze carried laughter and conversations, even the aroma of grilling steak, and Maggie shook her head at the scene.

"I can't believe I'm out here. It's so beautiful," she said as Ellis drew up a chair beside her.

"We lucked out this year, with a perfect summer night and flat sea."

"Someone told me that they play serious music right there on the beach. It must be magical."

Ellis nodded, her eyes focused on the crowded beach. "The Boston Pops came out here in nineteen ninety-seven." She straightened in her seat. "The music just exploded out over the water. It was a pretty special night and made a ton of money for the Cottage Hospital."

"There's so much about Nantucket that visitors don't know, don't realize. I'm learning, too, just how much of a community this is. I encourage my guests to take in as much of the history and the feel of the island as they can."

"I hope you do well. Nantucket needs residents who 'get it.' "

The first fireworks of the night whooshed up into the darkness and lit up the sky.

"It's a tightly knit little place, that's for sure," Maggie said as they stared upward.

"I believe it has to be. It's a survival sort of thing. Fitting in takes determination and effort, sometimes courage."

"And money."

"True, but mostly old-fashioned New England ingenuity and hard work."

"That's for sure. It's not easy, but I'm no quitter."

"So where are you from, Maggie? How'd you end up here?"

A huge bang echoed across the harbor and made them both jump. They laughed when several boats sounded their horns in appreciation. But Ellis's question lingered like the scent of blasting powder, and Maggie hurriedly composed a truthful response.

"I'm originally from Albany but ended up getting lucky with real estate investments in Philadelphia. When I spotted the listing on Nantucket, I guess my imagination took over."

"Philadelphia. You must have quite an imagination."

"I guess I do. No regrets, though."

She watched the sky's luminescent blue, gold, and red soften to pastels across Ellis's rapt expression and wondered if Ellis had regrets, if she'd chosen to remain on this idyllic but rugged island...or if the island had chosen to keep her. Maggie mused over that as she smiled up at another colorful sky burst. *Can a place do that? Would I ever allow that?*

"The competition must be pretty steep," Ellis finally said. "We have quite a few B&Bs on-island."

"I'm trying to be creative." She elbowed Ellis playfully. "Use some of that ingenuity you mentioned."

Ellis turned, and a breath of onshore breeze mussed her hair over her forehead and darkened her sculpted features. The flash of appreciation on her mouth, the fireworks' silver sparkle in her eyes made Maggie's heart skip.

Another boom echoed across the harbor, fluttering against their clothes. "Whoa," Ellis said with a chuckle. "*That* was big." She swiped away her hair and scanned the colorful sky. "So just how are you being creative?"

"Ah, well. I'm offering combination deals with other attractions, great restaurants, tourist sites, things like that, to increase the draw, but…maybe it's just too soon."

"No takers?"

"A few, but I know I can do better. I *do* have one idea that's yet to take off, however." She sipped her drink and decided to learn Ellis's opinion. "I'd love to offer guests a sightseeing cruise, to package it with, say, a three- or four-night stay."

"Sounds like it would be popular."

She thinks it has potential.

Fireworks now roared rapid-fire into the sky, and night became day. Layer upon layer of brilliant sparks and smoke splayed across the canopy of stars. Explosions overtook easy conversation. Occasionally, stubborn sparks rained into the sea around them, and Ellis guardedly observed their progress.

Maggie left her chair to stand at the side. "This is unbelievable!" She gaped at the display, gestured around her, above and below. "It's as if we're in a kaleidoscope."

The *Rose* floated on a sea of twinkling colors as the celestial show sliced black waves into millions of brilliant, shimmering lights. Spectator boats and their reveling passengers, now fully illuminated, sounded horns in appreciation, while the beach came alive with cheering and applause.

"A great show this year!" Ellis shouted over the din. "Glad you agreed to come out!"

The last, mightiest bang nearly rocked them in place, and everyone united in a final, rousing cheer.

"Wow, what a super show," Maggie said. Unthinking, she gripped Ellis in a quick hug and kissed her cheek. "And thank you so much."

Ellis felt her face heat and she fumbled for her drink. She raised it to Maggie and waited for her to match the toast.

"To becoming an islander," she offered, and Maggie clinked her glass.

"To Nantucket."

They finished their drinks and Ellis tipped her head toward the saloon. "Let me refill these. I made a pitcher earlier. We can do one more while we wait for this traffic to die down."

"Allow me, then," Maggie said and took Ellis's glass just as the *Rose* rocked in the wake of a departing boat. She stumbled sideways and Ellis caught her by the arm. "Lord, thank you. I'm so sorry. I'm not that experienced on boats."

"That will change over time."

Ellis went for the pitcher in the saloon and met Maggie halfway back. She poured where they stood, replaying her last comment in her head. *Was that too suggestive?* "Most islanders are familiar with boating," she added, "but it's not a prerequisite."

Maggie laughed lightly. "Well, that's good because I have enough on my plate right now."

"Ah, yes. Ingenuity." She led them back to their seats, a palm lightly—comfortably—pressed to Maggie's back for steadiness. So many boaters heading home had churned up the sea, and waves now slapped randomly against the *Rose*'s hull.

Maggie sat and turned to face her. "Your honest, educated opinion. Do you think offering sightseeing cruises would be a draw?"

"I know they're popular. We have a few operators who do well." Ellis couldn't tell if Maggie's frown meant she disagreed or was simply confused.

"I guess my *ingenuity* hasn't impressed them. Not so far, at least."

"Well, maybe that's just because you're new here."

"You know, I didn't really think the subject would come up tonight. Hell, I wasn't even sure I wanted it to, but if you don't mind, could I toss something out for your consideration?"

"Of course."

"I'm..." Maggie sighed. "Well, I'm not very good at beating around the bush, so...Would *you* ever consider offering cruises?"

To say Ellis was surprised by the question was an understatement. She knew her face must have gone blank, judging by the way Maggie inched forward on her seat and wrapped both hands around her glass.

"You mean, on my *Rose*?"

Maggie nodded.

"Well. Wow, Maggie...I...Hmm." This was a huge issue to Maggie, and one that Ellis needed to swirl around in her head for a while. *Or do I? It's crazy, right?* Yet she stopped short of blurting a reactionary "no."

"I don't know what to say, where to start."

"Ellis, I know I've got a nerve asking, but I really see it as a win-win situation. There's a lot to it, I realize, and I'd simplify as much of it as I could for you—if you'd consider it at all."

Ellis absently scratched the back of her head. She didn't know what to think, except that opening her *Rose* to the public just hit too close to home. Literally. But that was her gut reaction, and she thought it prudent to keep that to herself. At least for now.

"I'm curious, I'll grant you that."

"The bottom line is that I'm trying desperately hard to boost business. Offering exclusive excursions would certainly help Tuck'r get its feet on the ground, so to speak, get through this first season." She looked out toward the beach. "We've been getting by so far, but… Sightseeing by boat is the most frequent request I get, and no cruise operator is interested."

"And you'd like me to offer my services on the *Rose*."

"I'm asking if you'd consider it, yes."

"The *Nantucket Rose* is my home, Maggie."

Maggie's wide-eyed optimism dimmed slightly but held. "I understand."

No, you don't. You have no idea what you're asking.

"My *home*." She blew out a breath and scanned the pristine deck around them. "Why should I disrupt my life, my home? That's what would happen, you know."

"I'm not talking crowds of people, Ellis. Not groups of like forty or eighty or whatever. Probably no more than a half dozen, I'd guess, and definitely not every day. For instance, weekends. Details could be worked out to our mutual advantage."

"And where would these cruises go?"

"Well, I was imagining all around the island, Tuckernuck, too."

"The shallows off Madaket…" She shook her head. "Not routine passage."

"Oh. I didn't realize that. Obviously, I don't know as much as I should, but…well, that makes a shorter cruise more manageable, don't you think? More doable?"

This isn't how I saw tonight unfolding. Keep your head.

"Operators here offer cruises for whale watches, fishing, dinners, sunsets, and other things, so are you looking at private runs like those in the long term?" Just the thought of all that pushed Ellis to change the subject.

"Well, I have dreamed about the possibilities, but, no, I hadn't considered them seriously—and wouldn't unless we discussed it." Maggie set her glass down and sat back quietly, folding her hands in her lap. Rubbing her crossed thumbs said she was nervous, maybe impatient, and Ellis remained silently curious about what Maggie would say next.

"Would you at least give it some thought? Enhancing Tuck'r Inn's appeal and the extra income in your pocket would benefit both of us."

"You're asking a lot, Maggie. It's my home you're talking about."

"I know." She leaned forward and rested her fingertips on the back of Ellis's hand. The tender touch registered instantly and threatened to unsettle her. "Believe me, I know, but remember, I'm not suggesting a huge commercial operation. More like…" She raised her eyebrows tentatively. "More like having an intimate group of friends visit for a couple of hours or so on the weekend."

Ellis had difficulty picturing that. She wasn't one for entertaining; a hostess, she was not. Quite the opposite. The answer surely seemed like a no-brainer.

"What do you think, Ellis? Consider it, at least?"

The anxious expression in the soft light pulled Ellis's emotions to the surface, right where she didn't want them. They edged her conscience aside and allowed room for something more, and she knew she had to respond rationally before her common sense buckled.

"There's a lot to think about. Look, I'm fine with my life the way it is—and I love my *Rose*—so I have to tell you, right up front, that I'm not keen on this."

Maggie gripped her glass with both hands again. Ellis fought mounting frustration, irked that the evening had somehow morphed into business, and disappointed that Maggie appeared to welcome it. She labored to keep her irritation in check and still find the right words that wouldn't shatter the entire night.

"I don't want to burst your bubble. I mean, obviously you've given this a lot of thought, and I appreciate your situation, but…" Maggie's gaze, previously warm and hopeful, fell away, and anxiety tightened her elegant complexion.

Ellis sat back and sighed, listening to the silence between them, feeling her staunch refusal soften. She shook her head at herself. "Only as a favor to you, I'll consider it, but don't get your hopes up."

CHAPTER TEN

A warm, vigorous tailwind and easy seas beneath a sunny sky made for a perfect crossing and finally, plenty of time to think without the pressures of work, passengers, or exhaustion. Ellis ran through a mental list of issues in need of resolution, and Maggie Jordan figured into all of them, except for that aggravating little leak in the *Rose*'s bilge pump. Today she'd make some decisions. It was why she'd swapped assignments this morning to work the freighter *Sankaty*. She wasn't really a fan of freight runs because they not only stirred up her past, they now involved a freighter as large as her *Eagle*. But the duty demanded less of her time, and she'd jumped at it.

She reached the open bridge deck, awash in rapidly heating sunshine, and narrowed her eyes to scan the horizon. "Figures," she mumbled in resignation. "Just when I was seeing things clearly."

A prevailing wall of fog ahead sat much closer than the usual hint of land she expected to see. It was a sobering phenomenon, especially out here in the sound's busy shipping lane. Fog gripped you right where you stood, removed all your tangible surroundings, and left you with nothing but deep thoughts.

For Ellis, that always meant flashing back to the tragedy of her father's death. At least the passing of time had lessened that pain, and the nightmare rarely recurred now, but she knew she'd soon be plunged into a world of introspection. Considering how heavily Maggie weighed on her mind today, she thought it ironic that the fog should appear on this trip. *Sometimes being unable to see what's right in front of you is a good thing; a different perspective can be so revealing. Talk about forcing my hand.*

Frowning, she stepped into the wheelhouse, and the ship's master looked up from his gauges and acknowledged her concern with a grumble.

"Yeah, I'd thought it would have burned off by now, too," he said.

"Maybe it's thinner than it looks, Frank." She joined him in staring through the windshield. "The *Eagle* said it wasn't pea soup on their run."

"Yeah, well, they also predicted it would be gone by the time we came through. Obviously, it's not."

His heavily wrinkled brow told Ellis that veteran mariner Frank Thomasello shared her disappointment at the interruption of their smooth sail. He had captained ferries for twenty-four years, known her father and grandfather, and knew that Ellis, with decades of experience of her own on this water, valued their mutual respect.

Frank sighed hard as he piloted the *Sankaty* closer to the consuming fog bank. "Okay. Here we go." He sounded the horn, a long, chest-rumbling blast.

He powered the engines down from cruising to meager headway speed, and their steady drone, so monotonous as to normally go unnoticed, dropped to a whisper. Beside him, Ellis logged their coordinates, status, and time, and wondered how long they'd be held captive by this ocean-bound cloud. She had serious personal things to think about and wanted this crossing to return to automatic in a hurry.

But she knew the drill. Being no stranger to the anxiety sea fog created, she always managed to give procedure priority over emotion, although sometimes that was tough. As a little girl, she'd found magic in the otherworldly shroud of fog; in her early teens, she'd known enough to fear the blindness; but as a young woman and her father's right hand, she'd developed the knowledge and skill that every sailor worth her salt needed. *"Emotional reactions should never top practical common sense. Someone could get hurt."* Her father's voice always returned, loud and clear.

Heavy mist condensed around the bow, and the *Sankaty* slipped into the fog as if to its own demise. Wordlessly, Ellis and Frank watched the bow vanish, watched as they surrendered their forward deck. The bridge pressed into the fog, and waves of mist rolled up the structure and billowed against the windshield, spreading left and right, engulfing everything in an opaque mask of gray until only the interior of the wheelhouse remained of the world.

She wiped her moist palms on her thighs.

"Makes you want to take a breath, just to be sure you still can."

"Like being dropped into a vat of whipped cream," he said, "not being able to see a thing, after seeing so much."

Ellis settled into the chair beside his. "Good thing I'm not claustrophobic." She could feel that both wind and sea had gone dead calm, making any evaluation of exterior conditions impossible, and the unsettling stillness carried only the soft hypnotic hum of the creeping engines. Gauges were their only measure available, and she trusted them implicitly, but nothing beat being able to see outside.

"Gonna take a look," she said, unable to sit idle.

"Well, don't take off."

"No chance." Long ago, she'd learned a hard lesson about venturing into the fog. All local mariners shared in that heartbreaking loss of her father and wisely continued to remember. She waited as Frank sounded the horn again before stepping out onto the bridge deck.

Getting instantly misted from head to foot wasn't unexpected, and she tugged her cap down farther over her forehead to peer through the fog, hoping to judge its density. "Jesus." She could barely see her hand at arm's length. No chance of looking down at their load of eighteen-wheelers, delivery trucks, and cars. The deck rail was visible in front of her, but nothing beyond it. Just gray air. Nothing above the wheelhouse door, either, or to her left or right.

So easy to succumb to the nothingness out here, miles of ocean in every direction hiding just feet away. How imposing but, thankfully, not unknown. How immeasurably vast yet intimate. She swiped the mist off her eyelashes and marveled at the union of sea and sky, its ability to touch her. *I know you're out there.*

"Constant contact," she said softly. "Without it, where would I be? *Who* would I be?"

She couldn't fathom the concept of sharing that connection with Maggie's commercial enterprise. Been there, done that. And learned the hard way that it wasn't meant to be. Somehow, Maggie would have to understand.

"This is a big ocean, Maggie, and I survived a hell of a ride to get where I am." She shook her head and gazed into the fog. "Lucky just to have the home I do. No way I'd turn it into a business."

Sorry, Maggie.

She went back inside.

Frank didn't bother to turn around. "Satisfied?"

"Could hardly see my shoes, for God's sake." She wiped her face with a paper towel. "Must be like being in a submarine. The world is completely gone except for our little bubble, right here."

"Couldn't pay me to be *under* water," Frank mumbled.

The intercom from the cargo deck beeped and they both jumped.

"How much longer?" Seaman Wes McCall was impatient—and skittish as usual, Ellis thought. He grunted into the intercom and swore colorfully. "Can't see for shit down here."

"Sit tight, Wes," she said. "Could be ten minutes. Hard to call."

"Ten minutes?"

"Roger that. Just sit tight. Write another letter to your mama."

"Screw you, Chilton."

Frank laughed when she hung up the mic, but his attention never left his gauges. He was holding a true and steady course through the fog and she was thankful to be with him for this.

Ellis climbed back into her seat and tried to compose a considerate, diplomatic response to Maggie's proposition. But Maggie was a complex topic that swamped her brain as thoroughly as this damn fog corralled the *Sankaty*. Yes, Ellis knew she owed her an answer— and that Maggie wouldn't be pleased. Yet Ellis held on to hope that something special between them still might be possible. *There was that prolonged hug when we parted the other night.*

Frank blasted the horn again and sat back. "So, how's life treating you on the *Rose* these days?"

"Good. Relaxing." She laughed at herself. "I was going to say that I'm finally used to having a job I don't stress about." She tossed a hand toward the windshield. "But then this stuff turns up."

"Eh," he said, eyes on the radar, "every job has its moments. Seems every night, the wife expects me to announce my retirement. Girl's put up with too many years of this, so I suppose I owe it to her to think about it." He flashed her a sideways look. "No one looking out for you?"

"Still the independent soul, Frank."

"Your pop was so hooked on the sea. It's in your blood just like it was his, your granddad's, all your people."

She smiled because it was true. Her "people" were whalers and fishermen whose lives were linked to the sea, and whose return voyages drew worried wives and mothers to rooftop widow's walks, yearning for sightings. Staring through the grayed glass, she bit back a chuckle at the impossible notion of Nicki ever standing watch for her. Suddenly, Ellis wondered if Maggie knew what a widow's walk was.

Like a sheet fluttering in the wind, the mask of fog rippled against the windshield and lofted out from the bridge. Gradually, mist fell away, the *Sankaty*'s bow reappeared, and dim light brightened. The curtain of fog parted and the *Sankaty* emerged into brilliant sunshine, with Nantucket Island clearly visible on the horizon.

Fate has one hell of a sense of humor.

❖

"Listen, could I borrow your car for a run out to Madaket? John's brother's theater friends are partying after rehearsal, which should be wrapping up in about a half hour."

Maggie handed her credit card to the waiter and eyed her sister skeptically. "No problem, just don't get buzzed and go four-wheeling on the beach. The last thing I need is to have you get busted in my car."

Rachel pouted across the table. "I'm not seventeen anymore, Mags."

"No, you're thirty-four going on twenty-one. And it would be nice to have you awake and coherent at a decent hour for breakfast so we can catch up more. Jill McGee is due in around one thirty on the Hy-Line, so after that I'm off limits."

"She decided to come after all? Sweet."

"Yes, she did, and no, it's not 'sweet.' It's turned me into a nervous wreck. Tuck'r numbers aren't knockout impressive, nor is my business plan thus far, so keeping her interested means a hard sell on my part."

Rachel's fluffy auburn curls bounced when she leaned across the table. "So you need to chill tonight. Come party with us. It'll be a blast. Let your hair down, girl."

"No can do. I'm meeting Ellis later."

"Oh, well, *that* I understand. What time?"

"She's off duty by eleven."

"Uh-huh. You spending the night?"

"We're going to talk business."

"Sure you are."

The waiter returned with Maggie's card and she signed for their meal. "Let's go," she said, standing. "Drop me off at Tuck'r and take the car, if you want."

"You've got over an hour to get ready for Ellis, you know."

"I have things to do before that," Maggie said as they stepped outside.

"I still think I saw her on the ferry today. She's tall with like, these laser-blue eyes, right? Wonder what she would've done if I'd said, 'Hi, I'm your girlfriend's sister, Rachel.'"

"We're not girlfriends. Please get in the car. We just hung out on the Fourth, that's all."

"Did she kiss you good night?"

"I'm not discussing Ellis with you anymore if you—"

"Is she a good kisser?"

"No! I mean we didn't."

"Oh." Rachel sat back and fastened her seat belt. "Bummer."

Okay, so yeah, it was. But it's time to pull on the damn big-girl panties and not lose focus.

"Look, if I can tell Jill that Tuck'r has this sightseeing package deal, it'll brighten my entire prospectus. I have to concentrate on business."

"Right. And you're sure Ellis is going to agree?"

"Pretty sure. She could have turned me down with a one-liner on the phone instead of suggesting we meet at eleven o'clock."

"I guess…if she was an asshole."

"Well, she's certainly not that. I just didn't hear any negativity in our conversation this morning, so I'm crossing my fingers."

She checked her watch as she entered the Tuck'r Inn, relieved to see she had plenty of time to finish a little work, shower, and still fuss about what to wear. *And I'll fuss because…because I want her to see how much this means to me, that I appreciate what she's agreeing to do. And, yes, because her smile is a killer.*

CHAPTER ELEVEN

Ellis walked the deserted route from Steamship Wharf to downtown, closed shops on both sides of the street guarded by bright-eyed window boxes, alert through the night. Occasionally, faint laughter from the RC and Nix reached her on the breeze, but the pat of her boat shoes against the bricks provided the only other accompaniment. And that was fine with her. The quaint tranquility provided a unique comfort, a familiarity she'd grown to appreciate more with every passing year, and she wouldn't have it any other way. *If only outsiders could experience this, feel it, too. They'd appreciate just how deeply our values are embedded here.*

In the halo of light on the corner of Main and Centre streets, Ellis leaned against the lamppost, hands in the pockets of her chinos, and tried to sort her thoughts. She and Maggie didn't need some social setting to discuss this damn cruise idea. In fact, what she had to say wouldn't take long at all, but she wanted to extend Maggie the courtesy of an explanation. And a simple stroll along a quiet street would suit the purpose.

Suddenly seeing herself as some devious character from a classic Bogart film, she straightened off the post and shoved her uniform cap into her backpack. She finger-combed her mussed hair into place just as the silhouette of woman and dog appeared at the top of Main.

Ellis raised a hand in greeting and Maggie waved back. Retta barked, and when Maggie unhooked the leash, Retta was off. Ears pinned back, she raced downhill, hitting top speed almost instantly, and Ellis tossed her backpack onto a nearby bench and went to one knee to brace herself.

"Whoa, pretty girl!" Retta roared into Ellis's arms, spinning and slamming sideways into her chest. Ellis quickly set a hand on the ground to keep from toppling over. "Get a grip, there, Retta. Easy, girl." Retta bopped on her front paws to lick Ellis's face. "Down. Yes, I'm happy to see you, too."

"I'm the only other person she greets this way," Maggie said.

Roughing Retta's fur with both hands, Ellis looked beyond her to the pink toenails in sandals, and up the slender legs to shorts and fitted sleeveless blouse, and finally, to the amused, delicate lips. *Such a vision. You glow even in this light, do you know that?*

Ellis swallowed hard and managed to stand as Retta bounced around her legs.

"I'm flattered. Dogs know dog people. She's a joy."

"Thank you. That she is. So…How are you?" She clipped Retta's leash back onto her collar.

"I'm well, thanks. I-I thought we'd just take a walk, let her stretch her legs, if you don't mind."

"Oh. Well, no. That's fine."

Ellis slipped an arm through her backpack and led them down the street. "I appreciate you coming out at this hour. Work doesn't leave me much free time during the week, here or in Hyannis."

"The summer schedule must be tough. You can't really be a night *or* day person, can you?"

"Not really, no." Ellis kept her attention on Retta's enthusiastic maneuvering along the sidewalk. Strolling with Maggie made her edgy, despite the soothing quiet and soft breeze, and she couldn't tell if the easy intimacy, Maggie's allure, or the point of this meeting unsettled her most. The venerable trees that occasionally interrupted the sidewalk dappled the lamplight, but their swaying shadows weren't enough to mute the impact of Maggie's attention. Although Retta frequently drew them away, Maggie's eyes hardly left Ellis's face. *I wouldn't have handled this well on the* Rose.

"My schedule at the inn has become quite flexible," Maggie offered, "except for early mornings. But once breakfast is past and housekeeping starts, Tuck'r pretty much runs itself." Ellis only nodded. "I'm thankful, believe me, because the first couple of months have been tough. It's such a big place." They stopped to let Retta investigate a tree root. "I really hope you'll stop by sometime. Being a native, you must love the old homes."

"I do." Retta tugged them along, but Ellis could still hear her abrupt answer lingering pointedly.

"I thought so," Maggie said. "I'd love your opinion of the place in its new incarnation, now that that forlorn, haunted look is gone." She sighed heavily. "I couldn't be more grateful it was built so well, so many years ago. I had my doubts when I first laid eyes on it, all boarded up as it was."

"We treasure our homes here, and it's a wonderful thing you've done, bringing an old one back to life." Ellis dropped her backpack onto a bench on the corner. "Sit a moment?"

"Sure." Maggie reined Retta in closer and sat. Retta waited for Ellis to sit before plopping down at her feet.

"I have so much respect for your work ethic, Maggie, your devotion to your B&B. I don't doubt for a minute that you put everything into it that you can."

Maggie sat back, keenly focused on her. "Failure is not an option. It's not who I am."

Ellis leaned on her knees and stroked the length of Retta's side. *Failure wasn't me, either, until it swallowed me up.*

"Well, I'm glad of that—for your sake. The dissolution of a dream can be heartbreaking. You've earned success, and I hope it comes soon. We all strive for contentment, satisfaction, and try like hell to keep it when we find it."

Maggie bent forward to pat Retta as well, and now considerably closer, she spoke gently without looking at Ellis.

"I hope you know I respect you a great deal, not just for what you've done with your own amazing home, but for your perseverance, too. I never intended to imply otherwise by my proposition. I apologize if you took it that way." Maggie paused, and although Ellis knew Maggie waited to have that assumption corrected, she couldn't bring herself to elaborate.

Maggie cleared her throat and sat back again. "You say quite a bit with few words."

"I suppose I internalize a lot." She met Maggie's eyes as she straightened. "I *have* given it a lot of thought."

A surge of tiny wrinkles appeared at the bridge of Maggie's nose. "You're turning me down, and I'm disappointed." She took a breath and exhaled evenly.

"I'm sorry, honestly, but there's a lot involved, using your home for business—as you well know. And I'm just not much of a…a public person. It wouldn't be a good fit."

"I might not know you very well, but I have to disagree. I *do* know you're kind and considerate, helpful, and God knows, you have the knowledge and skill." Maggie tipped her head slightly, eyed her suspiciously, and Ellis could almost feel Maggie probing her mind. "You wouldn't have to play social director, you know, if that's a concern. I would accompany my guests, provide refreshments. I'd play hostess." A glance told her Maggie wasn't ready to concede defeat. "Ellis, these are things we could work out together. I think it *would* be a good fit."

Ellis fought the onset of a headache. Her pride wanted out of this predicament and had been prepared to make a stand. The rational part of her, however, saw possibilities, and the conflict was physically uncomfortable. *Why am I even seeing potential here?* Feeling so torn just proved that she'd failed—once again—to become the secure, bulletproof, independent woman she'd set out to establish years ago. Actually considering Maggie's scheme said her subconscious sought to fill a void, and she mentally shuddered to think one still existed in her life, that she really hadn't risen all that far from the depths of past failures. She *did* know that feeling torn made her vulnerable and insecure, and that felt a bit scary. *How does she always end up in my head this way?*

"You used to have a shipping operation, not long ago," Maggie said, "with your father, I've heard. If you don't mind me asking, why did you stop?"

I really don't want to go there, Maggie.

"I wasn't the businessman he was."

"I see. My guess is you miss the work, though, miss running your own boat."

Don't.

"Living on it means everything to me."

"I'm sure, especially with all the memories." *You may know more than you're letting on, Maggie, but there's no way you know how I feel.*

"How often to you take the *Rose* out?"

"I shoot for at least once a week. It keeps us both shipshape." *Is that what you wanted to hear, propping me up to see things in a positive light? Please don't make me resent you.*

Retta bobbed up onto all fours when Maggie stood. Tail wagging tirelessly, she looked from Maggie to Ellis and back, and Maggie patted her head appreciatively.

"You're sending me sulking back to my drawing board, Ellis, but I simply can't give up on this. Just so you know."

"I like you, Maggie. A lot, and I wanted to explain."

"I appreciate that. I do understand, but—"

"The *Rose* is far more than a business tool. It's personal."

"And I can appreciate that as well, fully."

"But you won't let the idea go."

She longed to hear Maggie agree to drop the whole scheme, to finally see things from her perspective. If Maggie knew about the *Rose*'s history, and it appeared she at least knew some of it, she should respectfully back off. But Maggie didn't respond immediately. Instead, she seemed content watching Retta sniff the hedges. At last, she looked haplessly at Ellis and shook her head.

"No, I can't seem to let it go."

Ellis jammed her hands into her pockets and exhaled toward her feet. *Damn if she isn't as stubborn as she is beautiful.*

"Business isn't my thing. Hasn't been for more than ten years now."

"I know you're not in the freight business anymore, so maybe I should have realized that a formal business proposition was the last thing you'd want to entertain." She clasped the leash in both hands and tipped her head curiously. "What if we didn't call it business per se, and just connected as friends?"

"Meaning what, exactly?" *How many have you made since moving here in April? Probably not many. But friends do favors for one another. Is that what you want? Or are you suggesting something else entirely?*

"We *are* friends," Maggie said, "so maybe nothing has to be formalized. Maybe we could work out a now-and-then arrangement, or maybe you'd consider a retainer-type option, you know, on an as-needed basis?"

Ellis held up her palms. "Maggie, I—"

"Something to think about at least?"

Ellis let her arms drop with resignation. "Something we could have a drink over, yes."

"That's a great idea."

Ellis returned the little coy smile and had to shake her head at Maggie's persistence. Friendship with a woman this attractive and refreshingly assertive appealed in a big way, almost enough to draw Ellis out of her solitary habit, but *this* was just asking too much.

Why does it feel like this conversation isn't finished? Did I make my point at all?

"We'll talk," Ellis said with finality, and took a step forward to pat Retta.

"I hope so. Even if you didn't have the answer I hoped to hear, I'm glad we saw each other tonight." Maggie bit her lip as she took a breath, and Ellis saw the disappointment she'd created.

It's better this way. Let it go.

"Always enjoy seeing you, Maggie. Good night."

❖

Maggie shut down her printer and stepped into the kitchen in time to see Rachel rummaging through the fridge, an overflowing beach bag at her feet. Wearing shorts and a bikini top, T-shirt slung over her shoulder, the little-sister image of many years past sent a nostalgic whisper of home across the room.

"Heading to the beach now?"

"Yup." Rachel turned, showed her the orange juice, and poured it into her water bottle. "I'm getting out of your hair. Is that what's put the glimmer of sunshine on your face?"

"No, dummy. I just took our biggest reservation of the season so far."

"No way!"

"An all-female bridal party just took every room we had left—for a week, starting Saturday."

"Oh, my God, Mags! That's awesome!"

"How serendipitous, huh? Right when I need to show Jill the books and I had only two parties reserved."

"No kidding. How'd this happen?"

"Well, I guess the hotel they'd booked in Yarmouth just had a fire, so they found us online. Thank God."

"Yeah. And all women? Lucky you, big sister." Rachel stuffed the water bottle into her bag. "Well, now you're *definitely* too preoccupied to hang with, and you're only going to get worse, with Miss Lawyer due in a couple hours, so I'm leaving."

"I'm nervous, that's all. Tuck'r has to make a good impression."

"Oh, I know. So I'm out of here." She settled oversized red-rimmed sunglasses into place and grinned. "Breakfast was yummy, by the way. Eating outside on such a gorgeous morning, with the birds, the flowers…It was just perfect. I'm glad we had the time, just us. Thank you." She stepped closer and put a hand on Maggie's shoulder. "I'm sorry Ellis turned you down."

"Thanks. Me, too. Shame on me for getting my hopes up. Wouldn't you know, the bridal party asked for a boat cruise? I had to think fast, so I looked up one I'd heard decent things about and booked it."

"Too bad it won't be Ellis. But she might come around, you know. She might like the informal arrangement idea."

"It *is* her home, for God's sake." Maggie shook her head. "Jesus, I sounded so pushy that night, and right after we'd had a great time together. I don't want her thinking I'm inconsiderate. Aside from the fact that an informal arrangement probably wouldn't work anyway, and I have *no* idea what I was thinking, it was grossly unfair of me to put her in such a position." She sagged against the counter. "Guess I'm just worried."

"Hey, chin up. Take a good look." Rachel waved a hand around the room. "Try to see all this with new eyes. It's wonderful, what you've done here." She poked Maggie in the stomach. "Personally? I can't imagine parting with all this. Hell, I'd move in and never leave. But, look. Word will get out, I'm sure, and places will start calling to team up with Tuck'r. I just know it."

"Thanks, honey. I just need Jill to believe that."

"Oh, she's bound to, Maggie. She's no fool. Tuck'r is freakin' gorgeous and intimate, convenient to everything, not overpriced." Rachel tugged her into a one-armed hug. "Tuck'r is young and promising. She'll see."

"I love you."

"And I love you, too. And now I'm going to find me a beach and flirt with some hot, ripped guys." She patted her cheek and spun away. "You're going to meet Jill at the boat?"

"Yes. I want to walk her up here, have her enjoy the stroll and take it all in."

"Smart idea. Good luck—and good luck to me!" she yelled as the back door slapped shut.

Retta ran to watch her leave. "Auntie Rachel's on a mission," Maggie said, and Retta whined to go out. "We'll be going out soon."

She refilled Retta's water bowl as laughter filtered in from the common room. The house seemed empty without it, and she thanked her lucky stars that Tuck'r at least would be moderately busy during Jill's stay.

But Rachel was right, everywhere one looked, appliances, furniture, woodwork, decorative schemes, even the landscaping, drew an appreciative eye. Tuck'r *was* a gem and she was damn proud. Now, if only business would grow to sustain it as fast as her hopes had broadened to sell it.

She chuckled as she put the OJ back in the fridge. "If you moved in, little sister, I'd make you finally learn to pick up after yourself." The concept of Tuck'r as "home" made Maggie pull out a chair and sit. Reverently, she ran her palm across the antique tabletop, a fixture she'd always dreamed of owning. "I might have to take you with me when this is over."

She sat back and sighed. "But where would I put you?" The large oak farmer's table certainly wouldn't fit in the galley kitchen of her Philadelphia condo. Moving somewhere to accommodate the table seemed silly. Besides, it had come with the house, actually had been in it for more than a century, and she recalled her excitement at having its surface refinished, the generations of nicks and dents perfectly preserved. "I think you belong here," she whispered and, for the first time, wondered if she did as well.

Chapter Twelve

You're spoiling me, Maggie. This espresso is scrumptious. And your precious little muffins would be a marketing sensation all by themselves." Jill took a deep breath of the fragrant air and shook her head as they lounged on the front porch. "The prospect of leaving all this right now for our boxy little office in congested Boston is just *so* unappealing."

"I'm glad you're pleased. In fact, I'm selfishly thankful we *don't* have a full house right now just so you can appreciate the serenity. It's addictive."

"I agree, totally. You'll have your hands full in just a couple of hours, though. A houseful arriving all at once will break this spell quite pointedly."

"Nothing we can't manage. I'm excited. They'll be praising Tuck'r wherever they go for years to come. Many will return because Nantucket is difficult to resist."

"How I wish I had discovered the island during my college years. The Dickensian allure truly is charming. I loved your tour yesterday, and the five-star dining? All over-the-top, Maggie."

"And don't forget the wine. More will be waiting when you get home."

"It was outstanding. Thank you for that." She squeezed Maggie's hand. "You have me longing to stay and I haven't even left, you know."

"Please come back any time." Maggie slipped her hand away and feigned a pout. "I hate to put a damper on this, but—"

"Oh, you're right! Speaking of leaving."

"Let me walk you to the waterfront," Maggie offered, and they headed inside. Jill rolled her suitcase to the door as Maggie clipped Retta to the leash.

"She's well behaved," Jill said, inching away when Retta nosed her hand.

"She's very popular around town. Folks ask about her as much as they do Tuck'r." She led them down the walkway, but on the sidewalk, she turned to see Jill hadn't followed them through the gate. Instead, she stood looking back, assessing the house again.

"So very pretty," Jill said, finally joining them. "Quaint, immaculate, and very pretty. I'm glad we connected last year, Maggie. Tuck'r has terrific potential and Cavanaugh *definitely* is interested."

Maggie fought the urge to skip down the street.

"Occupancy could be better," Jill went on, "but it is coming along rather well. Your marketing has been first-rate."

"Thank you. That's so good to hear. I know I have high hopes, but they're realistic. I think you'd agree, they're justified. Nantucket tends to sell itself." They crossed Main Street's cobblestones at the intersection with South Water, headed for the Hy-Line ferry on Straight Wharf. Retta stopped them, a tree much more important than their walk, and Maggie seized their pause to emphasize the obvious.

"I don't think this little square has really changed in some three hundred years. It doesn't get more precious than that. Islanders preserved everything they could through the generations, from the cobblestones, to the buildings, the street lamps, this horse trough memorial in the center, even the trees. And they tell me that the Nantucket Stroll in December is a magical trip into a true Dickens Christmas."

Retta tugged them toward the next tree, but Maggie urged her onward. Jill hadn't reacted to the little tour guide narrative, and Maggie hoped she hadn't bored her with details. *It's important she understand the scope of the island's appeal.*

Now in the boarding line on Straight Wharf as the ferry docked, Jill turned from the sleek modern vessel and focused evenly on Maggie.

"Nantucket has won you over."

"I found it charming right from the start, yes."

"Will we still have business to conduct when I return on Labor Day?"

"I'm looking forward to it. Thank you for giving Tuck'r the summer to prove itself."

"I'll bring the necessary paperwork with me then."

❖

A boisterous cluster of young women settled along the *Eagle's* promenade deck rail beside Ellis, laughing and gesturing with cocktails in hand at the majesty of Brant Point Light. She knew more of their group remained sunning themselves on the open deck above and was thankful the entire bunch hadn't chosen to disturb her favorite moment of every arrival.

"What's the tradition about throwing pennies?" a tall redhead asked, drawing the attention of her friends.

"When you round Brant Point as you leave, you make a wish for a quick return," Ellis answered, and smirked when two women pitched quarters toward the lighthouse.

"We're just so excited to finally get here," the redhead continued. "It's Jenny and Leigh's honeymoon and we are ready to parrr-tay!" The eight women cheered her statement. "So, hi," she added, sidling closer along the rail and extending her hand. "I'm Ali, maid of honor."

"Ellis Chilton," she said and shook her hand.

"Well, it's very nice to meet you, Ellis Chilton. Do you live on Nantucket?"

A petite blonde leaned in between them. "Don't answer that, Ellis Chilton. You could be in danger." She rapped Ali's shoulder playfully and muttered, "Down, tiger," before rejoining the others.

"Ah, yes. The wedding party," Ellis said. "I saw you all come aboard. You're in luck because the week's forecast calls for great beach weather."

"We're going cruising, too, I think, all around the island on a boat rented just for us."

Ellis hoped that operator was prepared for this lively crew. "Sounds like a fun time."

"We really lucked out, considering we had to change hotels last-minute. Leigh found a place called Tuck'r Inn and landed this great package deal."

Ellis was all ears now and hoped Ali would hurry up with more details. In a few minutes she had to be on the cargo deck for docking.

"The deal included the boat ride?"

"Sure did. Three hours' worth." Ali leaned against her shoulder. "Insanely expensive, I guess, but the inn is eating almost the entire thing. Drinks and lunches, included."

Ellis found herself calculating the expense of a three-hour cruise and wondered who the operator was and if Maggie was being charged by the hour or the person. There were about twenty of them, she recalled. *Why do I even care?*

"Well, I'm sure you'll have a terrific time." She wished them well as she left the rail and hustled down the stairs to her post, completely distracted.

Seaman McCall joined her as the *Eagle* inched into place at the wharf, its now-opened bow gingerly meeting the asphalt of the parking lot ramp. Together, they worked speedily with Steamship Authority dockworkers ashore to secure the ship.

"Quite the bunch, that wedding group," he said as they surveyed the load of vehicles ready to be waved off. "You know any of them?"

"No, Wes." Ellis sighed at his snicker and began waving drivers ashore. "I'm just glad none of them is driving. They'd already had a few when they boarded, and it ought to be entertaining just watching them make it down the gangway."

He laughed as he pointed directions to drivers. "You meet the bride? Er...the blond one, that is. She's a looker, huh?"

"They all were cute."

"Hell, Chilton. For someone who ain't picky, how is it you don't have a woman of your own?"

Here we go again.

"Told you before. The Steamship won't give me time off."

He roared as he usually did when she delivered her standard response. Somehow, though, it didn't make *her* laugh as much anymore. In fact, it made her think too much, and that usually wasn't a good thing.

There hadn't been a woman in her life for years, not since Nicki, but remembering her father's pleasure at her happiness back then made her smile where she stood. An elderly woman in a Mustang inched onto Nantucket soil and winked, thinking the smile was for her.

Damn. Most of those seven years were exciting, romantic, so full of promise. And then her father passed. Her heart still clenched whenever she recalled his memorial service and Nicki's whispered "You're free from all this now." But she refused to abandon her legacy, and life became a doomed, all-consuming struggle to carry on in his name. Their relationship lasted just four stormy months more.

"So I *am* free," she sighed aloud, watching the last vehicle leave the *Eagle*. She reset her cap and focused on the line of parked cars waiting to board. "Off and on. Back and forth." A family in a Ford

Explorer crept aboard, three children waving as they passed. Ellis waved in return. "I wanted carefree and that's what I got."

I like the job, love the home, but, Jesus, really? Can I spend any more time wallowing?

Raucous laughter drew her attention to the gangway, and she watched the wedding party bumble its way to ground level. Wheeled luggage toppled, one brunette did also, and created a massive, comedic logjam. Wes and two other seamen sorted out the mess and ushered the women along.

Ali spotted her alongside the crawling line of traffic, and the entire party chorused Ellis's full name, laughing its way across the wharf, ready to invade downtown.

"Have fun, ladies," she said, mostly to herself, and wondered how long it would take them all to reach Maggie's B&B. *They've probably booked every room. Look out, Maggie, wherever you are.*

"Those were the days," a woman said as she edged her Lexus past Ellis. "Oh, to be a pretty girl in my twenties again, so carefree."

Ellis offered a chuckle but realized she couldn't automatically agree.

And her spirit slid into the trough of introspection she'd been in since parting ways with Maggie. Since she'd convinced herself that nothing mattered more than her privacy, that never again would she permit outside influence in her world, the life she'd salvaged from scrap.

Back on the bridge as the *Eagle* glided away from the dock, she scanned the bustling open deck below and the passengers preparing to toss pennies toward the lighthouse. How many passengers would return, she had no idea, but figured most would someday. For now, though, they were off to God knew where, homes, jobs, loved ones eagerly awaiting their arrival, and she remembered such anticipation with a flash of melancholy.

Back when their runs had them away from home for a day or two, in good weather or bad, day or night, no greeters ever awaited the *Rose's* arrival. But she did remember times as a child when, with tiny hand secure within her mother's, they watched her father and grandfather cruise into view. Though slightly less vivid now, the memories provided a lifeline to home that Ellis cherished above all else. She'd clung to that lifeline over the years, not only to survive the profound losses in her life, but to construct—and keep—what she had left. She'd spent the past several days examining that rationale, wondering if she was still clinging, if she was defending her life or avoiding it.

How carefree am I, really, when I'm spending more and more time analyzing it? When's the last time I had purpose, for me or anyone else? God forbid, some woman takes a liking to this façade. When did single-minded turn into pathetic and lazy? Who am I fooling, carefree at middle age?

CHAPTER THIRTEEN

If Ellis had been able to fall asleep promptly, the beautiful day that beckoned beyond her porthole would have had her up hours ago. Sunday was her free day and a list of chores awaited. But tossing and turning, thinking, questioning herself for most of the night had her tired and grumpy. She stared at the teak ceiling, wondering what Maggie was doing, if that wild wedding crowd had driven her crazy yet.

She threw off the sheet. "Got my own business to take care of."

By midmorning, Ellis had managed to clean the head and shower, wash dishes and sweep the galley, swab the entire exterior deck, and do the week's laundry at the Laundromat—all without stopping, so thoughts of Maggie wouldn't leave her staring vacantly off into space. Finally, she arrived at the bilge pump repair on her list, and knowing it posed no immediate crisis, she allowed herself a relaxing moment in the sun. She hadn't meant to doze off.

"Ellis! Hey, wake up!" Ken Whitley pounded on the *Rose*'s hull and jolted Ellis from her deck chair. "Tug" rarely raised his voice except when passengers needed to hear him over the sound of his engines, so Ellis woke up instantly on edge.

"Hell, Tug. Something on fire?" She hopped over the gunwale to the dock, watching him fuss with his black and white captain's cap. He ran a hand over his bald head and put the cap back on.

"That'll probably be next, the way the morning's going. Listen, I've got a problem and need your help. Like now."

Ellis rubbed her face hard to wake up. *I should have gone to work.* "What is it?"

Tug pointed at her hull. "I've got a fuel leak. Don't know how long it's been, but—"

"Jesus, Tug." She was awake now. A fuel leak ranked as *the* most dangerous situation a boater could have, next to sinking at sea, and with his seventy-foot *Roustabout* at Straight Wharf, surrounded by tourists, pleasure craft, and artisan shops, he had a genuine nightmare on his hands. "Let me get my tools." She vaulted back aboard the *Rose*. "Does Sam know?" She stopped for his answer before going inside.

Tug glanced out at the harbor and up at the cloudless sky. "Well, I thought I'd try—"

There was no excuse for circumventing safety protocol, especially not for a veteran mariner like Tug. Hands on her hips, Ellis glared at him. "Call him now, Tug. Shit. You know all the crap the harbormaster has to go through."

"I know, but those damn regulations will cost me a fortune."

Ellis stormed back to the rail. "Your leak isn't contained?"

Tug scowled up at her, defensive, embarrassed to admit the magnitude of his problem. "You fucking sound just like your old man. I came asking for help, not to be judged. Now, you coming or what?"

Ellis swore under her breath all the way down for her toolbox and back up and onto the dock. She couldn't imagine what she'd find below the *Roustabout*'s deck. And she knew she didn't have replacement hoses or gaskets for the quick fix Tug probably expected.

"If it's anything but a drip, Tug, it's got to be called in. And you know what Sam's going to do." Tug mumbled an obscenity as they hurried along the waterfront. "He has no choice, Tug. You can't blame him. Coast Guard's got to be notified."

"Look, I'm crossing my fingers it'll be something small, like when you fixed Whitehall's last summer."

"That wasn't small," she corrected him, and they hustled up the *Roustabout* gangway. "He was going to replace the fuel pump anyway and had the new one right there. He just didn't know the process." Tug lifted the hatch and they climbed down to the engine.

"Well, I've got a tour scheduled for two o'clock. I really need this buttoned up in a hurry."

"Jesus, Tug. Smells like a refinery down here." She set her tools down gently and looked around. "There's diesel on the deck over here and could be…" She lifted a hose, and her hand came away covered in fuel. "God damn. You better start making calls."

"Maybe it's just a clamp," he said, hovering at her shoulder. "Was a time I could get down in there and do stuff like this, but the ol' body won't cooperate anymore."

Ellis didn't want to hear him minimize this situation, didn't want to hear the usual litany of ailments. Somehow, Tug Whitley managed a very lucrative touring operation that could well afford a skilled mechanic, but he never parted with a cent. The man hadn't changed a bit since her father helped his childhood friend start the business, but how—why—her father put up with Tug's whining had always been a puzzle.

"It's almost twelve thirty, so you better reschedule that tour, at least for today."

"Can't. Don't have an opening any other day. I've got a ton of money riding on this. Some wedding group staying at the Tuck'r."

Maggie, no. Damn sightseeing cruise. On the Roustabout? *Not the height of luxury, granted, but ordinarily a reliable option—until now.* The idea of Maggie and her happy-go-lucky guests cruising around the island for hours over a hemorrhaging fuel pump didn't sit well at all.

"I'll do what I can, Tug, but I can't promise."

He sighed heavily and shuffled around as he watched Ellis troubleshoot the leak. She was tempted to call Maggie with a heads-up. *It's really not my place, but she'd best find another boat.*

And that thought led to the obvious.

Too proud? Too selfish? Too pigheaded to have said yes when she asked? Now look. It's not her fault she's stuck with Tug and his mess. If it's anyone's fault, it's mine.

She sat back on her heels and wiped her brow with her forearm.

Diesel fuel dripped steadily into the bilge, and she knew a colorful sheen had to be growing in the water along the hull. She yelled at Tug to shut off his pumps. She cleaned her hands on a rag from her toolbox and wrote a list of replacement parts he needed, noting he'd returned to messing with his cap.

"Changing out this old pump is long overdue, Tug. You've pushed it too far."

He shook the slip of paper she'd given him. "They're at lunch at the Boatworks now. *If* they even have one, I won't get it for another hour. How long will it take to change it out?"

Ellis bristled at his assumption she'd do the job. "Not all afternoon, but face facts, Tug. You've got to clean this mess up. And cancel that damn tour." She couldn't help but feel disappointed for Maggie. She closed her toolbox and went topside. Tug practically climbed up her heels.

"There really *is* a quick fix here, Ellis. You know that, right? I mean I can just blow this shit out, once I clear the harbor."

She sent him a hard look and peered over the side. "Notify Sam, will you?"

"Look," he said, sounding more desperate by the minute, and pointed down at the shimmering rainbow of fuel on the water. "It's not *that* bad. And it won't grow any bigger with the bilge pumps off."

"Why didn't you shut them off when you first noticed it? And if *you* noticed it, others probably have already. You *have* to tell Sam."

The longer she stayed, repeating herself, the madder she became. He had trouble on his hands, and she really was done thinking about it. What kept returning to mind, however, was Maggie's dilemma, the one she didn't even know she had yet…and what would solve the problem.

Moments later, standing on the *Rose*'s stern deck, Ellis wondered if the hot sun or lack of sleep or both had contributed to her lapse in common sense. The phone ringing in her ear just might be warning her, allowing an extra second or two to reconsider. But her head didn't seem to be a player in this, making an offer she'd decided against some time ago. She'd done all the thinking she could pack into the six-minute walk back to Commercial Wharf, but the decision boiled down to *feeling* she was doing the right thing.

"Ellis? Hi."

The soft, welcoming familiarity of Maggie's voice sent a finger of warmth tripping down her chest. And realizing that Maggie had programmed her name into the phone, Ellis had to turn away briefly to clear her throat, take a breath. *Concentrate.*

"Hi. Hope I'm not bothering you."

"No bother at all. This is a nice surprise. How are you?"

"Oh. I'm well, thanks. Look, there's this…ah…See, it so happens it's a good thing today's my day off." *Jesus, get to the point. That sounded like you're about to ask her out.*

"Well, you picked a beautiful day. Are you going fishing? I thought the fish didn't bite on hot days like this."

"Fishing? No. I think I'm going sightseeing—with you."

"What? Actually, I *am* hosting a cruise this afternoon. You heard? I'd love to have you join us, of course. I'm sure Ken won't mind."

"Forgive me for being cryptic, but *you* will be joining *me*." She pictured Maggie's confusion, the crinkling of her nose, the way she bit her bottom lip. "I'm calling for several reasons, Maggie, and considering the hour, the most important ones are that Tug Whitley's boat is out of commission as of right now, and I'm offering the *Rose* to help you out of this jam."

"You're not serious. Are you serious?"

Damn, she's cute when she's flustered.

"Completely serious. I'll fill you in on the tedious details of Tug's situation if you want, but if I'm going to be cruising around Nantucket this afternoon, you probably should fill me in on your details."

"I-I'm speechless. Yes, I want details...but later, sure. Um. Wow. I'm due at Straight Wharf in twenty minutes. I was about to load the car with drinks and food. My guests know they're expected to board by two, so they'll be along—to the *Rose* instead? Really?"

"I'll be at Straight Wharf, once I gas up. You'll just have to keep an eye out for your people."

"Ellis, I don't know what to say. You're a lifesaver. I hope you know that."

"Hey, I can't say I'm willing to do it for a living, mind you, but...I couldn't drop the ball here, if you know what I mean."

"I think I understand."

"Give me a half hour?"

"Anything you want."

❖

Laura knocked and called from outside Maggie's bedroom door.

"Everything's in the car. Just brought out the shrimp cocktail, but the ice is already melting. You have ten minutes to get there."

"Thanks. Hey. Come in and tell me what you think."

Laura peeked in and Maggie held a white tank top above plaid navy blue shorts. "Too twenty-something for forty-something me?"

Laura laughed. "Not at all. Boy, one phone call and you're a disaster. She has an interesting effect on you."

"She's just thrown my whole day—the biggest booking of our summer—into turmoil. I can barely think straight."

"Uh-huh. Think she's willing to do this more often?"

Maggie dug a pair of white Nikes from the bottom of the closet. "I doubt it. Something apparently happened to Ken's boat, that's all."

"Well, maybe this is just the push she needed."

Maggie took the door from Laura, implying Laura should leave. "I'm not getting my hopes up again."

"Well, I think it's promising." Laura backed out, shutting the door.

Maggie dressed, explained to Retta that she couldn't come, and drove her carload of food and drink bins through the maze of tourists, shoppers, and boaters on Straight Wharf before giving much thought to the significance of it all.

Whatever made you agree to this, Ellis, must have been big. I can't imagine you've had some epiphany, that somebody turned your head around. Damn. Maybe today's adventure will persuade you to reconsider the bigger picture after all.

She parked at the end of Straight Wharf and piled her bins onto the small utility cart she'd remembered to bring at the last minute. At the beginning of the long sliver of pier beyond the wharf, she stopped and pulled the brim of her Nantucket cap down farther to look out to the very end. As promised, the *Rose* sat waiting, sparkling against the harbor's darker water. She took serious note of her amazing good fortune. Ellis appeared on the back deck, jumped onto the dock, and began jogging her way.

You're one difficult woman to figure out, Ellis Chilton, but so help me, I really like what little I know.

Ellis slowed as they met on the boardwalk and ran a hand back through her hair. Maggie appreciated the windblown look, the vital, energized air about her that made every task seem routine, including this one. Ellis wore light gray cargo shorts—several sagging pockets said she needed to—and did sweet justice to her corded shoulders and biceps by wearing a Red Sox tank. In Docksiders and Ray-Bans, she was the epitome of an adventurous New England boater.

"Hi, again. No Retta?"

"I just couldn't. I have enough on my mind today."

"I suppose, but she's welcome any time." She reached for the cart. "I'll take this aboard." Her hand slid over the handle and Maggie's fingers.

They looked down at their hands and turned to each other.

Maggie searched in vain through Ellis's black lenses. *You certainly sent me reeling the other night, seriously bummed me out and cost me a few nights' sleep, but damn if you haven't come to my rescue today.*

Frustrated by her own reflection, Maggie let the handle drop and removed Ellis's glasses. "Before we go one step farther..." She slid her palm along Ellis's smooth cheek, drew her down to within a breath. "Thank you." She kissed her lightly and returned the sunglasses.

Ellis raised an eyebrow. "You don't thank everyone this way, I hope."

"Only handsome, kindhearted women who live on the ocean."

"Jesus." Ellis glanced at her feet. "I suppose the only thing to say is 'you're welcome.'"

Maggie picked up the cart handle. "Now, where were we?"

"Right here." Ellis took it from her. "Did you park?"

"No. I have to go back for that, but I should wait on the wharf to round up my troops."

"I'll meet you aboard, then."

"Aye, Captain."

Nodding, Ellis smirked as she slid on her glasses and turned away with the cart. Maggie returned to her car, wondering where kisses like that could lead.

The daydream of making love on an isolated piece of Madaket Beach had all the elements of an afternoon's preoccupation, and Maggie had no idea how long she'd been in another world, with Ellis, both of them naked, when the bridal party's commotion doused her with reality. The group assembled around her as Maggie gathered her composure.

"We found you," Ali said. "Only ten minutes late."

"That's fine," Maggie said and led them along the extended pier.

"We're going all the way out to the end?" Ali asked.

"No, twerp," a friend quipped. "We're throwing you off in the middle of the harbor."

Jen, one of the brides, moved up to walk beside Maggie. "Ooh! So that's it? The *Nantucket Rose*?" Maggie nodded with an unexpected flutter of pride as Jen babbled on. "I just love the name. It's appropriate for a Tuck'r Inn outing, don't you think? With all your gorgeous roses around the door?"

Maggie definitely agreed. She'd found the irony in it some time ago. *Such a nice coincidence.*

Introductions came easily, once Ellis helped Maggie aboard and they guided the others onto the open deck. For her part, Ellis appeared suited to the role, rattling off safety instructions and demonstrating use of the mountain of life jackets she'd added to her usual supply for the day. She didn't initiate much casual conversation but didn't shy away from it, and laughed and smiled often, which Maggie relished immensely.

Several woman apparently deemed Ellis their main attraction of the afternoon, and Maggie soon realized she had to monitor Ellis's personal as well as professional space. Adding to her hostess chores, she kept an eye up to where Ellis drove and narrated through the speaker below. Rarely was she alone up there, and Maggie noted that one leggy blonde had climbed the steps three times in the first half hour. *Yes, ladies, she's dashing and rugged, arousing...*

Maggie ventured up with a plate of her confections, wanting a moment with Ellis for herself, not just her opinion of the tasty creations. At the top step, she found the blonde lowering her arm from Ellis's shoulder.

"We probably should let our captain do her job," Maggie said, feeling like a chaperone. The blonde's complexion reddened and she promptly returned to the open deck. "I'll keep better tabs on them, Ellis. I apologize." She set the plate on the dashboard.

"You've got enough to do. I can take care of things up here."

"I don't want you feeling put upon, or..."

Ellis picked up the plate. "Did you make these?"

"I did. My brownies are amazing, if I do say so."

Ellis bit into one and squeezed her eyes shut in ecstasy. "Please save me some from the gaggling girls."

Maggie laughed. "You can have as many as you want."

"The brownies, not the girls."

"Oh, *so* glad you cleared that up." She adored Ellis's lighthearted side. "They're right out of college."

"Pretty but young."

"A few of them like older women, I heard. One has a partner who's older than I am."

"Older than thirty?"

Maggie grinned and poked Ellis in the stomach. "Flirt." She went to the steps, wishing she could press her whole hand, both hands, to those hard abs. *Losing it. God, the pheromones are too strong on this boat.* "Going back on hostess duty. Can I bring you anything? Pepsi? Water? I brought plenty of alcohol and the girls are doing mojitos and vodka shots, if you're interested. Want me to sneak you a beer from your fridge?"

"No drinking and driving, but a Pepsi would be nice. Thank you."

"Just so you know, I told everyone that the saloon stairs are off-limits. No one goes down to your quarters. There's plenty of room and a bathroom on the main deck, and they're all good with that."

Ellis's prolonged, searching look held Maggie on the top step for an extra beat, and Maggie wondered what Ellis saw, what she hoped to see, and if she found it. Maggie hoped it was the honesty and gratitude she felt, and the affection, too. The last thing she wanted was Ellis regretting this decision to open her home, her life, to strangers.

Maggie walked back to her and set a hand on her arm. "Is there something I can do? Is everything okay?"

Ellis's faint smile sent a wave of uncertainty through Maggie's chest.

"Everything's just right, Maggie."

Don't kiss her again. You'll drive her away.

"I'll be right back with your soda."

Left at the helm with her thoughts, Ellis admitted that this tour guide gig really wasn't so bad, telling tales as they cruised just offshore, answering questions the women posed from below. That Maggie initiated the most astute discussion pleased her. *An islander* should *care about things like erosion, wind farms, fishing, Native American history, and such.*

Ellis frowned when one of the partiers—and not Maggie—joined her on the bridge during a photo stop off Sankaty Head Light.

"Hi. It's Ellis, right? I'm Taylor. Love this boat of yours. You do this for a living?" She gazed off at the flashing beacon atop the cliffs.

"This is a favor to Maggie. I work on the Steamship, brought all of you here, as a matter of fact."

"Guess I missed meeting you on the ride. It can get crazy when we're all in one place." She leaned over the rail, cocktail in hand, and gestured toward Maggie, far astern. "She's something else, you know. There's nothing she won't do, always one step ahead with information, drinks, anything we need. She's making our stay perfect."

Ellis watched her, too, the infectious smile, the easy laugh, the purposeful stride and tireless drive, the way she buzzed from one guest to the next, always helpful and unassuming. Headed back to the saloon with an empty tray, Maggie stopped before disappearing directly below them and looked up. She sent Ellis a thumbs-up and moved on.

"Damn." Taylor elbowed Ellis and winked. "Gotta say, your girlfriend's beautiful."

Pulled from dwelling on Maggie's image, Ellis turned back to the boat's controls. "Beautiful, yes. Girlfriend, no. We're friends." Her conscience flared like a kick in the shin.

"Friends? You two seem pretty connected. How long have you known her?"

"Since the spring." But she vividly recalled earlier occasions when Maggie had been the captivating stranger on the *Eagle*, the stunning businesswoman constantly buried in paperwork.

Ellis reached the edge of her comfort zone, no longer good with the topic. Emotion had begun to creep into her head, and drifting off on romantic fantasy was not allowed. She had a sizeable oceangoing vessel in her hands with twenty-one passengers counting on her expertise. *Never had to slap myself before.*

Taylor nudged her like an old pal before heading to the steps. "Good talking with you, Ellis, and thanks for taking us out today."

An hour later, having maneuvered into the thin, tricky waters off Nantucket's remote western side, Ellis dropped anchor and most passengers dove into the ocean.

"You've chosen the perfect spot," Maggie said when Ellis arrived beside her along the gunwale. "At least everyone's eaten well, so they're not totally smashed." Maggie finished her bottle of water and pulled two deck chairs closer. "There's still some fried chicken left, so be sure to try it. You *did* eat, I hope."

"I had one of the Italian sandwiches," she said, taken by Maggie's concern. "Just the bread itself was outstanding."

"It's a favorite of mine, too, and a big hit at the inn. I can't bake it fast enough."

Contentment seemed written all over Maggie's face. Today's big plan, the participants, the weather, all cooperated, and Ellis felt her share of appreciation and relief, but Maggie simply beamed. *There's so much to be said for enjoying what you do.* She pushed aside recollections of happy times working her own business. The laughter and splashing nearby had *her* smiling now, too. This *was* fun. *Snooty tourists or unruly kids probably wouldn't be, but how often—*

Heavy contemplation stopped when Maggie leaped toward the gunwale and spiked a soaring beach ball down to the water. There was no ignoring Maggie's lithe build, the shapely backside and toned thighs, or the way her snug white top detailed her torso when she was only three steps away. Ellis exhaled subtly and stood.

"Ten minutes, ladies!" Maggie called over the screeching and splashing, and turned right into her. "Ooops!" Palms on Ellis's chest for balance, Maggie blushed. "Sorry. I didn't know you were—"

Ellis shook her head. "It's okay." Realizing she held Maggie by the waist, she squeezed a little before letting go. "Really. I-I was just heading up." She backed away a step. "Everyone seems to be having a great time. That's good."

"A terrific time, yes. They're crazy but happy." Maggie followed her into the saloon. "Thanks to you."

"I'm glad it's worked out so well." Ellis pulled two waters from the cooler and handed her one, surprised when Maggie gripped her hand with it and stepped closer.

"Come to Tuck'r and have dinner with me, won't you?"

Gut check time. Her brain spun, unable to conjure the standard, no-strings response, the one that usually provided escape whenever "attachment" threatened. *Probably because...I like her. She's different. This is different—and has nothing to do with business. Besides, my unhealthy habits need to change, right? And...I like her.*

"No pressure, Ellis. Whenever it's convenient." With a hand stuffed into her back pocket, and discerning eyes rich with warmth, Maggie's ready pose hinted at mischief. "I promise not to poison you."

"If you prepare a meal the way you prepared this outing, it would be great."

She drew Maggie aside when partiers began returning to the deck. The volume of laughter and jostling chairs rose several decibels.

Maggie leaned closer. "Well, Captain? Was that a 'yes'?"

"Yes." Ellis straightened the brim of Maggie's cap, surprising herself with the affectionate gesture. The touch had just been so automatic. "I'd love to have dinner with you." *Another automatic response.*

Maggie curled her fingers around Ellis's upper arm. "Let's make it soon?"

"Hey, Ellis!" Taylor arrived next to her, toweling her arms and dripping around their feet. "Are we heading back now?"

"Yes, but we're in no hurry."

"Gotcha. Thanks."

She returned to her friends and Ellis lowered her head to Maggie. "Soon sounds good." Without a second thought, she leaned in and kissed her lightly. "Thank you."

Chapter Fourteen

"She told me she couldn't wait to come back, spend more time," Laura said from the laundry room. "And not just to see the island, by the way."

The comment took Maggie by surprise and stole her concentration as she slid her latest batch of cookies from the oven. Laura had no idea that Jill McGee would return to buy Tuck'r, and Maggie had to keep it that way. It helped that Laura believed Jill had other motives in mind.

"So, you're insinuating she's interested in me?"

Laura sent her an impish look over an armload of folded sheets. "She couldn't praise you enough. I wouldn't be surprised."

"Hmm." Maggie looked down and patted Retta, who now sat at her feet, eyeing the cookies. "Was I *that* oblivious? I just thought it was good business to show her around because she has some serious connections."

"Good business?" Laura repeated. "Well, I'll say. She really enjoyed the guided tour you gave, loved your baking, and she *raved* about Tuck'r. Bet she comes back before the summer's over."

"Funny you should say that. She emailed me already with a change in plans. She's coming in August instead of Labor Day weekend."

Laura smirked as she passed. "I see that hopeful little smile on your face, Ms. Jordan. You can't fool me."

I hate having to fool anyone. This is ridiculous. Reviving a whaling captain's home into a B&B should be seen as a boon to the economy, regardless of whether I'm the owner. If only islanders weren't so parochial about change... She sighed as she reached for the spatula. *And if they weren't so parochial, Nantucket wouldn't be so...appealing.*

Maggie reconsidered leveling with Laura as she layered cookies on a platter for the common room. So hardworking and devoted to Tuck'r,

Laura nevertheless was a long-term islander who undoubtedly would resent Maggie's plan to flip the business, be crushed to see Maggie as another of those conniving, disingenuous hit-and-run money grabbers that Nantucket staunchly rebuffed.

It won't matter that I care about the island or that I'll probably leave a piece of my heart here when I sell. She pushed into the common room, and two couples on the couches and an older woman at the brochure rack all greeted Maggie at once, delighted by the arrival of cookies. *No, this would never get old.*

"This is the most charming house, Maggie," the older woman said, "and you are such a lovely hostess." She bit into an oatmeal cookie. "Oh—still warm." She set a palm on Maggie's arm. "I meant to ask you at breakfast yesterday but was too excited about taking that little boat ride you arranged earlier. It was quite informative, by the way. Mr. Whitley was a bit gruff around the edges but so knowledgeable. So, before I get distracted again, I would like to book ten days with you next July. For myself and my daughter and son-in-law. Could you pencil us in now, or should I contact you around the first of the year?"

"Tuck'r would love to have you, Mrs. Lowell. Come with me and we'll get you on the register right now." She led her into the office as the other guests headed for the cookies. "We already have several bookings for next July," she said proudly, "so I'm glad you didn't wait." She brought up her calendar on the computer and logged the dates.

Tuck'r twelve months from now wasn't hard to picture, but Maggie acknowledged—with a twinge of regret—that *she* wouldn't be bustling about this kitchen or trimming the roses out front or introducing excited travelers to the wonders of this island. She'd be somewhere else by then, maybe hip-deep into that Provincetown project. *That wouldn't be so bad at all. Legalities, construction, decorating, marketing, they should keep Tuck'r out of my head. Plus, who knows what could happen in the LGBTQ capital of America?*

Provincetown's multitude of shops, artisans, and boaters came to mind next, along with an image of Ellis on a wharf. Maggie blinked and caught herself staring out her office window, disappointed by the unlikelihood of that reality. The *Rose* could make the journey easily and Ellis could visit, but why would she, when there'd been little more between them than quick thank-you kisses?

Maggie grabbed her phone and dialed. *Inviting Ellis to dinner Saturday night will help us both see if this is worth pursuing.* The call went to voice mail, and Maggie kicked herself, forgetting Ellis was on duty. But the low, soothing recorded voice captured her attention and stirred butterflies in her chest as she scrambled to leave a message. Afterward, slumped back in her chair, she doubted she'd done the smart thing. *If I'm gone at the end of the summer.*

❖

Ellis checked her watch and frowned at being ten minutes late. Jan Medeiros had spotted her leaving the docks and didn't get the hint that Ellis had somewhere to be. Now entering the liquor store, Ellis could hardly remember a word of that gossip about the new bartender at Dell's, and she grumbled at still being unable to name Maggie's favorite merlot, the one she'd purchased for her a few weeks ago. Finally, after a hurried search of the aisle, she found it, paid Jason, and dashed out the door and up Main Street. On the corner of Centre, however, she drifted to a stop.

"Shit. I don't believe this."

It had never occurred to her to ask the specific address. Of course, she knew the area like the back of her hand. After all, her old homestead wasn't far away, and that threatened to unnerve her. But Maggie and Retta always headed home this way, up Main Street, so Tuck'r Inn was in this direction. But so were several other B&Bs on several other streets. Was it on or off Main?

A bit embarrassed, she dialed Maggie.

"Hello, Captain."

Ellis shook her head, glad Maggie couldn't see her grinning like a fool. "Hello, Ms. Jordan." She paced from one curb to the other and back. "I-I'm just a bit late, I know, but I have a really stupid question."

"Oh? Well, as long as you're not backing out of our dinner engagement, I'm game. Shoot."

"No, I'm not backing out. Not at all. Actually, I'm probably just a couple minutes away, but, well, I don't know what street you're on."

Maggie laughed. "How did that never come up before? Tuck'r is on Davis. I'll be in the kitchen, so come around back. It's the old Captain Pratt House."

Ellis froze in mid-stride and almost fell off the curb. *No. No. No.* Her spirit sank like an anchor and she instinctively looked up Main toward the intersection with Davis. *I can't—I haven't in…* She shivered in the warm, early evening air.

"Ellis? Are you still there?"

She stared vacantly at the cobblestones, turning in place as several tourists stepped around her and crossed the street. *You have no idea of its history, do you? No idea what or how long it's taken to recover from losing so much, from losing the foundation of my family.* Running a hand through her hair, she wandered to the building nearby and leaned against the bricks, her knees suddenly unsteady. *Yes, I'm a failure all around, Maggie. If I'd warned you, would this invite still stand?*

"Ellis? Hello?"

She swallowed hard against the panic in her heart and closed her eyes. *She knows I'm on my way. Jesus.*

"Yes, I'm here. Davis. I-I got it."

CHAPTER FIFTEEN

The last of her guests out for the evening, Maggie returned to the kitchen and almost tripped over Retta, who was rushing to the back door.

"God, Retta. Slow down." She set the perfectly cooked rib roast on the stovetop to rest. "I never should have told you she was coming." Retta bounced and barked and seemingly lost her mind in the mudroom, those sharp, amber eyes no doubt focused on a friend.

Maggie took a final assessment of her spotless kitchen, the stoneware settings on the table, the large candle flickering in the middle, the way the late-afternoon sun warmed the dark woodwork into a homey setting. Relaxed and informal. *She'll like this.* She took a breath to steady her nerves and noticed Retta had gone silent.

Maggie stepped up behind her and looked through the screen door to find Ellis gazing at the house, around at the manicured, flowering yard. *A black polo never looked so sexy.* Bagged wine in one hand, Ellis ran the other through her hair and brushed at nothing on her jeans. *She's nervous.* Ellis surveyed the property with an intense curiosity, her bearing steadfast and strong, *ever the sailor searching the horizon*, but Maggie thought it clashed with an air of uncertainty.

Retta shifted impatiently and whined.

"Sailor lost at sea? Or should I bring wineglasses outside?"

"It's beautiful, the yard." Ellis started up the steps. "Guess I got a little swept away."

"Well, prepare yourself," Maggie said, pointing down at Retta, "because as soon as I open this door, you'll be swept down the stairs." She gripped Retta's collar, pushed the door open, and Retta reared and wiggled. Ellis entered and ducked through the mudroom to the kitchen.

"Ready?" Maggie asked and waited for Ellis to put the bag on the counter before releasing Retta.

Ellis knelt and received the charge, but only had time to rub both floppy ears before Retta zoomed off.

"That was quick."

"Oh, she's coming back. Look out."

A stuffed toy duck in her mouth, Retta returned at full speed and spun her backside into Ellis's knees. She writhed and snorted repeatedly as Ellis scratched her back and butt.

"Hey, Retta. How's my pretty girl? Nice duck." She snatched it away and tossed it toward the laundry room. Retta dashed off.

"And you'll be stuck playing with it now."

"That's fine with me." Ellis reached into the wine bag and pulled out a smaller one and set it aside. "First, this is for you." She passed the bottle to Maggie.

"Oh, Ellis. Thank you. Let's get right to it." Retta hurried back with her duck and looked up at Ellis. "Don't say I didn't warn you."

Ellis took the smaller bag off the counter and crouched in front of Retta. "All pretty girls deserve presents." Retta promptly sat and let her duck drop to the floor, her attention now on the bag. Ellis took out a stuffed seagull, and Retta leaned forward to sniff. "For you, Retta." The wide amber eyes flashed up in disbelief. Ellis wiggled the toy and Retta pounced. She spun away, seagull in her soft grip, and settled under the table with her new prize.

"You spoil her, you know. That's very sweet of you," Maggie said, working a corkscrew into the wine. "And you spoil me. Thank you so much for this."

"You're welcome. My pleasure."

"You remembered. I'm touched." *Don't make her blush. She seems shy enough as it is.* "So did you do something fun on this gorgeous day? Go fishing?"

Ellis's attention remained on Retta and her toy. "I replaced the bilge pump. Finally, no more slow leak." Retta brought the seagull back, and Ellis tossed it across the room.

"Oh. I hear the bilge is a real vacation hot spot. You put on sunscreen, I'm sure."

Ellis snickered, still looking only toward Retta. "I'd been planning to fix it, but a certain *unexpected wad of cash* made me decide to replace it. Thank you again for that. You didn't need—"

"Don't." Maggie shook her head as she handed her a glass of wine. "We settled this argument already."

"But it was far more than the cost of fuel. The cruise was a fav—"

"End of discussion. Now come. Let me give you the nickel tour." She caught Ellis eyeing the stove. "Unless you're starving. I hope you're okay with a rib roast."

Ellis approached the commercial-grade stove, looking rather awestruck. "Rib roast? God, yes." She examined the stove, its burners, griddle, double ovens. "This is spectacular."

"Our supper or the stove?"

"Oh, the roast looks as good as it smells, Maggie. You've gone to too much trouble here." Retta sat at her feet, toy abandoned and nose aimed at the feast on the stovetop. Ellis scratched between her ears.

"No trouble at all. Puttering at the stove is a passion of mine. Granted, I may have gone a bit overboard, treating myself with this monster when I only really *cook* for myself. If Tuck'r were an official inn, this stove would get a workout, but we're basically a B&B, so I just bake lots of goodies—which is fun, too, of course." She patted the corner of the stove. "But it's a long-term investment. I splurged on a few of them, hoping they'll serve well through the years."

"So modern." Ellis looked around the room again. "But it works in here." She jutted her chin toward the far empty corner. "What do you plan to put there?"

"A potbellied wood stove. Well, that's the goal, anyway, if Tuck'r earns its keep."

Ellis wandered to the spot. "It...ah...I bet there used to be one here."

"As a matter of fact, you're right. I want to keep as much of the old charm as I can afford. The sink is a reproduction in its original spot." She set her glass down on the counter and pulled bread from the oven. "I see I'm not getting you out of this kitchen, so let's eat while everything's hot." She put the loaf on a small breadboard and brought it to the table. "Have a seat."

"Can I can help you?"

"You could tackle the roast, if you'd like." With Retta as escort, she brought it over on a platter and set a carving knife beside it.

"Be honored to," Ellis said and grazed a palm along the edge of the oak-plank table.

"An amazing table, isn't it?" Maggie asked, at her side with bowls of vegetables. "I marvel at it every day. I've had it refinished, but I'm thrilled to have an original farmer's table. Nineteen-oh-something, I was told. It came with the house and I often sit here, imagining who sat around it all those years ago, what foods they prepared on it." She chuckled. "God knows what they did on it."

"God knows. It's...special. There's no doubt."

All through dinner, Ellis seemed to hang on Maggie's every word, thoughtful and attentive as Maggie recounted her design process. Maggie reveled in their newfound mutual interest, especially moved when Ellis inquired about further changes to the house and fell silent to listen and gaze around the room. Maggie couldn't have been happier, seeing her so enraptured by all that had been done to the place.

Caught up in the conversation, she hardly noticed dinner, except to note the meal turned out well and Ellis, remarkably gracious, didn't hesitate to confirm it. Maggie wondered how long it had been since Ellis enjoyed a home-cooked meal, spent any quality time in a *house*. The urge to be *the* woman in *this* place whenever Ellis sought such comfort or rejuvenation came as a curiously appealing surprise.

With dusk approaching, Maggie resisted the temptation to turn on the overhead light. The candlelight mellowed the atmosphere, lessened the space between them across the vast table, and she conceded that being closer to Ellis was really what this evening was all about.

Retta crawled from beneath the table and put her chin on Ellis's thigh.

"Too bad you're a dog, pretty girl. This is people food." She patted her head. "An outstanding meal," she told Maggie. "Thank you. I truly appreciate it."

Maggie raised her glass at the compliment. *I do love your sincerity.* "You know, it did take me a while to get you here. You could have had several by now."

"I think you've made up for that in just this one meal. Do your friends and family know what a fantastic cook you are?"

"Well, back home a bunch of us enjoy experimenting in the kitchen. My family, not so much."

"They haven't been here yet to experience all this? Do they live locally?"

Maggie immediately credited the intimacy of the shared meal for Ellis's first-ever inquiry of her background.

"Manhattan. No, they haven't visited yet. They've promised to come for the Christmas Stroll, but...We'll see." She refilled their glasses. "They had to cancel their Labor Day visit because Mom's so busy, especially now. She's planning a fund-raiser for one of her *many* causes, and her co-chair is *abandoning her* to have surgery."

"And your father?"

"He's a financial consultant for Citicorp. For some reason, I followed him into the field, originally."

"So you were in finance before this?"

"Originally, yes. Dad still holds out that I'll join him," she added with a chuckle. Ellis nodded toward her glass, suddenly distant.

Bad move, bringing up memories of working with one's father.

Despite a craving to know details, Maggie kept her questions to herself. Ellis had finally eased into a conversational mode, and Maggie had no desire to see her withdraw.

"Let me just clean up a bit and we'll take the tour."

They put leftovers away and loaded the dishwasher while Maggie offered amusing tales about the complicated appliance. At least Ellis *seemed* amused. She remained rather quiet throughout the chore, and Maggie wondered if too much domesticity had brought on the reserved mood.

Maggie narrated as they left the kitchen and passed the large pantry and storage room with its commercial freezer, and when she pushed open the common room door, she saw Ellis's jaw flex as if to hold back words.

Every detail of the room appeared to fascinate her, the built-in bookcases and cabinets, the sitting areas, the velvet sheen of the old floorboards. She wandered to the staircase and stroked the banister, ran her hand around the newel post. Retta nudging her with the seagull couldn't break her concentration.

"So beautiful. Such a credit to you, Maggie. It's…it's hard to take it all in." She turned completely around and finally noticed the room's most dynamic feature. "God. The stove."

Maggie couldn't hide her enthusiastic pride. "My favorite piece in the entire house. We just put the finishing touches on it, in fact. It's big, I know, and not exactly your typical wood stove, but the minute I laid eyes on it, I wanted it out front here."

"Wow." Ellis placed her splayed palm on the cast iron surface.

"A wood- and coal-burning cookstove," Maggie said. "Apparently, it had been in that kitchen forever, and I just couldn't keep it hidden. I suppose someday it could return to the kitchen and I could open this fireplace, but having it here adds so much nostalgic charm. Plus, it'll help heat the house, and, God forbid, I can even cook with it, if need be."

"It's beautiful." Ellis studied the claw feet, the brilliant nickel-plated trim, and the buffed black satin finish, all the way around to the back, where the stove pipe fed into the fireplace. "Amazing. May I open it?"

Maggie warmed at Ellis's interest. "Be my guest. I've been assured it's in tip-top condition now, no cracks, no missing pieces, and is ready to go."

Ellis opened the oven, the firebox beside it, then lifted one of the round cook plates on top, shaking her head as she went. "This workmanship is unreal. It takes a lot to restore one of these."

"Oh, you can say that again. Me and my bright ideas."

Her expression stoic, Ellis ran a hand along the stove trim reverently before stepping back. Maggie was touched by the sentimentality.

"My office is right over here," she injected, "and this grisly-looking string bean is the one who built the place." She pointed to the sepia tintype hanging at her office doorway. "Captain Pratt himself." Ellis moved closer. "You think it's any surprise he had to chase the whales?" Maggie asked, biting her lower lip. "I'd run from him, too, he's just *so* handsome."

Ellis reviewed the faded image at length. "It's appropriate, though, having his picture here."

"I thought so, too." She waved Ellis to follow and noticed she seemed reluctant to leave the picture. *Islanders and their history.* "This is my *huge* office, and it opens here to my suite." She gestured to the bedroom around her, and Retta strolled in and flopped down on her own bed. "There's a full bath back in that corner," Maggie continued, pointing. "The house extends so deeply off the street, we were able to put this little suite between the common room up front and the kitchen in the rear." She led Ellis, and now Retta, into the adjacent room. "This is my living room, which leads," she opened yet another door, "back to the kitchen."

Ellis appeared to have taken it all in, the clutter in the office, the Mediterranean-styled bedroom with its king-sized bed, the chrome-and-glass motif of the little living room, and had said virtually nothing. Maggie watched surreptitiously as Ellis steadied herself on a chair back and sipped her wine. *It's a lot, I suppose. Maybe I came on too strong, shoved my success down her throat. Your own home is just as remarkable, you know. And probably equally historic to you.*

"I'd show you the upstairs, but it's just beds and baths, and many are occupied, so to speak. Tomorrow afternoon I'll only have three parties and this place is going to feel empty."

"It's a lot of house, Maggie, and you've done an incredible job. Seriously."

"Thank you. Sometimes *I* find it hard to believe it's real."

"I'm sure all your guests love staying in a place with deep island roots."

"Oh, Ellis. What's not to love, right? I mean it has so much heart, so much history." She knew Ellis had to remember the place during its heyday, or at least the past forty or so years. "Hey, I have an idea." She took Ellis by the hand and led her back into the office. From beneath a stack of folders, she pulled a shirt box and set it on her desk, then drew up an extra chair for Ellis. "Check this out with me," she said, patting the seat, and opened the paper-filled box as Ellis sat. "I haven't looked at this stuff yet—I set it aside for a rainy day project—but you might get a kick out of all the title research my attorney did on the house."

"I'll get us more wine." Ellis retreated to the kitchen.

The bottle clinked against the glass rims as she poured, as her hand shook with the pounding of her heart at the prospect of what was about to be revealed. *Guess it was just a matter of time, anyway. Too bad I didn't have the guts to speak up sooner. Too busy wallowing.*

"Boy, there's a lot here," Maggie said. "No wonder I put off reading all this."

Ellis returned to her seat and watched Maggie sort through the pile. The heap of property title research came as no surprise to Ellis. She'd had her turn at it when her father died and the estate landed in her lap—and again when the bank foreclosed on her. Now it was Maggie's turn, and all she could do was observe and wait for the moment Maggie spotted the familiar name.

I could spare her the shock.

"If you'd rather do this another time, Maggie, that's okay."

"Oh, I'm looking for the summation, the guide that takes you through the paperwork."

"It's a pretty imposing collection of stuff."

"It is, isn't it? God knows how far back she went."

"I'd guess very far." Her heart rate slowed to a crawl when Maggie found what she wanted. Sipping her wine, she waited for the inevitable and tried to appear interested.

Maggie was mesmerized by the photocopies of historic documents. Like scrimshaw on parchment, archaic script flowed into barely decipherable words, and Maggie eagerly scrutinized the scrawl of black lettering.

Ellis knew that Captain Pratt built the home in 1851, probably with his own hands and ship components, and that the mighty arched roof braces, or "ship's knees," were still as solid today as then. She wondered if Maggie had marveled at them in the attic as she once had.

"This works as a legend," Maggie explained and showed Ellis how the attorney's list of details corresponded with the stack of photocopies. "It says here Captain Pratt's only child Abigail didn't inherit the house when he died in eighteen seventy-seven. It went to her husband, Percival Ellis, instead. Popular name." Maggie sent her a grin. "God, what women put up with in those days."

Maggie ran a slender finger down the itemized notes and picked out another document.

"The house became a fisherman's home around the turn of the century."

Ellis nodded somberly. "Kerosene and then electricity had replaced whale oil anyway, so what was left of the whaling industry moved to New Bedford. Our mariners turned to fishing."

"And the son, Thomas, and then his son, George, carried on as fishermen."

"The island had begun looking to vacationers before that, believe it or not."

Maggie moved farther down the list, scanning documents a bit faster as typewritten text replaced the antiquated handwriting. Ellis braced herself for what Maggie was about to discover.

"This page says George left the house and business to his sole heir, Victoria, and her husb—" Maggie flashed Ellis a wide-eyed look, "her husband, John *Chilton*." She dropped back in her chair. "*Chilton?*"

Ellis watched Maggie refocus on the list, then flicker down to the most current documents.

"Do these say what I think they say?" Maggie didn't look up. "I...I don't believe it." She reread a previous document and jumped ahead. "John Chilton transitioned the family business from fishing to freight." She lowered the page and stared at Ellis. "It says his estate assets included the *Nantucket Rose*."

Ellis nodded. "My grandfather."

"Un-freaking-believable." She exhaled heavily toward the ceiling. "I don't believe this," she repeated and reached for the last sheet of paper. "Your father Philip inherited it all in eighty-nine, and then when he passed in ninety-nine…?"

Ellis didn't know what to say. "Yes. I was twenty-two."

"And then the bank…"

Ellis nodded. "In two thousand five. The last time I was here."

Maggie shook the document and glared with disappointment and irritation. "You knew I'd find this." She shot out of her chair and stalked to the doorway before turning back. "I just can't believe—Why didn't you ever say anything?"

"I didn't know Tuck'r was my house until a couple of hours ago, Maggie. I found out on the phone, remember?"

"Oh, my God. That's right." Maggie dropped back into her chair. "I'm so sorry." She took Ellis's hand and entwined their fingers. "One hell of a shock, I'm sure. It was no way to find out."

"You've nothing to be sorry for, Maggie. A lot went down in a short span of time back then, and hell, I almost went down, too, but that was eleven years ago. It's…it's okay."

"Eleven years is a long time to be hard on yourself, Ellis." Maggie squeezed her hand.

"Once in a while, the memories flash back, but I deal with it far better now than I used to."

"And you let me take you through the house, brag about all the changes I've made to what you used to own?" She tossed the paper onto the desk. "Jesus, Ellis. How much fun can a girl have in one night, huh?"

Thank you for understanding.

"Honestly." Ellis found herself wanting to be *very* honest. "I was surprised to be more fascinated than sad. Yeah, on the surface, things look different, but they *fit*. I-I never expected to feel…well, relieved. You haven't destroyed the feel of the place. You've captured it, breathed new life into it, and that's what matters."

"Well, it matters to me what you think, especially now." She stood and tugged Ellis into the kitchen. "We're taking this wine onto the front porch."

"I see."

Maggie stepped outside and motioned to the glider. "When's the last time you sat with a lady on your front porch?"

"Now you're asking me to dig up the past?"

"I guess I am," she said as they sat side by side. Retta nosed through the screen door and curled up at Ellis's feet. "She adores you."

Ellis stroked Retta's ear. "And I love having her around." *Pretty fond of being around you, too, Ms. Jordan, even if the locale makes my head spin.*

Maggie pushed off and set the glider swinging. "Forgive me, but I just can't conceive of someone so strong and independent, so self-sufficient ending up on the short end of things. At the risk of overstepping here, would you tell me what happened?"

"Things just got messy. I'm not the businessman my father was." She nodded toward the house. "I paid the price." Not the most telling response, she thought, but accurate and all that she cared to convey at the moment. Talking with Maggie came easily, but recounting life's devastating failures amounted to shameful exposure. And now, the gloominess of those times threatened to overtake her, spoil what had been a warm, stimulating evening.

"Ellis. I'm sorry—for your sake—that things turned out so poorly. I can only imagine how hard you fought to make it work."

"Ironic, isn't it? Things turning out like this."

Maggie sighed as she shook her head. "Holy crap, you can say that again. Quite a surprise." She swirled her wine. "But I'll admit, I kind of like our connection. Knowing you makes this house feel more like a home, and I'm glad you're here."

To a degree, Ellis agreed, but the overwhelming nostalgia really felt more like a blanket pulled up over her head. She steadied her breathing and tried to relax in the warmth of Maggie's welcome and her surroundings, but she wrestled against a threat of suffocation.

"I think it's time for me to head out," she said, standing, and Maggie rose beside her.

"I'm sorry to hear that, but I understand. Please don't let the past weigh you down, stop you from enjoying the present—and that includes this place. I don't want you to be a stranger, okay? Certainly not here."

Ellis wished they were anywhere but here right now. The *Rose* would have provided a perfect setting, because she so wanted to thank her for the meal, the hospitality, the understanding. Thank her in a big way. Like sweep-her-off-her-feet big. *It's been how long?* Maggie's allure surpassed the long legs, statuesque figure, and sultry eyes; her sincerity and engaging personality were irresistible, as magnetic as the home she had established. *She deserves this house—and good fortune to go with it.*

"Got a lot on my mind right now, and I think the walk will do me good."

Retta hurried to her with the seagull. Ellis threw it into the yard and watched after her.

"She'll go crazy when you leave," Maggie said softly. "She'll sit at the window for hours."

Ellis grinned inwardly. *Do they make widow's walks for dogs?*

Retta returned promptly and Ellis tugged her closer by the toy in her mouth and kissed the top of her head.

"If you let her out, she'll follow me."

"I'm sure she remembers where you live."

Ellis threw the gull again and Maggie touched her arm.

"Anytime you need to chill, have a drink, I'd love it if you came by. You're more than welcome."

A corner of Ellis's mouth inched upward. "I appreciate that, Maggie. Thanks for...everything. Tonight was very special, to say the least."

"I can't tell if that's melancholy or mischief on those lips, but I'd like to see more of your smile." Retta romped back from her successful forage in the shrubs and dropped her toy at Ellis's feet. "Now, how can you turn down her invitation?" Ellis chuckled and Maggie persisted. "Please know I want you to feel comfortable here. Lord knows, you're entitled."

Her chest tightening, Ellis fought the sudden urge to flee. Standing on this porch, the roof she played on as a child now overhead, she felt the house closing in. Her jaw flexed, a nervous habit, and for a moment, she saw herself paralyzed by anxiety. *Those days are long gone. Collect yourself.*

"Maybe I've become a bit of an isolationist these past years, Maggie, or maybe I'm just out of practice, but please don't take it as a reflection on your hospitality. I apologize if I've made you uncomfortable." Unable to resist the urge to touch, she curled a strand of Maggie's hair behind her ear. "You just give me pause, make me think."

"About good things, I hope."

"Things I haven't given a lot of thought to in a long time."

"I'm not sure if that's good or bad, but I certainly don't mean to pressure you."

"You've applied no pressure, Maggie." *I've applied plenty.* She cupped Maggie's cheek and lowered her head, spoke against her lips. "I enjoy the smile on your lips, too."

Chapter Sixteen

Ellis had just isolated her sixth constellation when she detected reggae music off the water. *Another steamy night, another party at sea. Have you booked any more cruises with Tug, Maggie?* Reclined in her lounge chair on the stern deck, she refocused on the stars, but just as she'd found throughout another workday, thoughts of Maggie refused to abate.

That exquisitely soft kiss, lips freely offered, created a yearning Ellis hadn't felt in years. *And I initiated it without a second thought.* There had been no reservations, no inhibitions, just that need to experience more of her, to taste her, be as close to her as she could.

Just where is this going? Why? What exactly do I want from her? Companionship? Sex? Sanctuary? She didn't like what sanctuary implied. It forced her to look inward, and she hadn't been particularly proud of what she saw for a long time. But she'd never been one to dump her troubles on anyone, and she certainly would never hide from them, use another's strength to avoid them. She conceded the companionship and sex, although she did think Maggie took things a lot more seriously than that.

What is she looking for? A friend—or business partner with benefits?

There was the possibility that Maggie produced dinner and the tour of her achievements simply to demonstrate that a business connection between them would be just as professionally executed. *Improbable. It couldn't all have been to persuade me into a business handshake.*

Barefoot in boxers and T-shirt, Ellis walked the narrow starboard rail and sat on the bow deck. "No," she told the flat, black harbor water. "She wouldn't be underhanded." *She's interested in something that*

I'm...I'm what? Not ready for? Not interested in? Who am I kidding? "It has nothing to do with *her,*" she argued with the night. "I almost pulled it off, too, putting up the cordial front while everything came rushing back."

Every room had tested her resolve, and she lay back on the deck, beneath the starry, moonless sky, and saw every detail. Memories and impulses had collided so vigorously that keeping her cool under Maggie's observation had been an incredibly emotional struggle. *Past has become present...for me, too.*

The staircase, the kitchen table, the old faithful cookstove, the uneven wood floors with their gouges and scuffs—the direct touches of family. The picture of Captain Pratt. *Where did she find that?*

"Face it. Not very smooth under fire. You were about to lose it."

Memories Maggie had unknowingly revived now tapped on her heart with as much insistence as they had in the house. *Better to face them, remember them one by one, than dwell on them as a whole. Maybe then the whole won't be as hard to take. To think, a knee-jerk business plan turned it all into collateral. Collateral, for God's sake.*

Seeing her family's century-old cookstove missing from the kitchen corner had almost broken her, but then discovering it, rejuvenated and full of life, had taken her breath away. Now, feeling tears rise, she sighed out into the darkness. "Thank God." She snickered at her emotional attachment to a simple stove. The venerable Glenwood seemed invigorated in the common room, intent on offering visitors an immediate, tangible connection to the home's history, and she was, admittedly, damn proud of it. Visions came to mind of stoking its firebox after a hard day's work, of huddling around it with Granddad and her parents during winter storms, of her mother standing close, stirring a pot of oatmeal. "It *should* be in a place of honor," she muttered and wiped away a tear.

Too bad I wasn't smart enough years ago. Everything about the place deserved respect I failed to give. Maybe someday I'll explain it all and Maggie won't think as little of me as I do. In so many ways, it's all about finding the courage.

Ellis stood, hands on her hips as she battled her guilt to another stalemate. "Jesus, Maggie. The closer we get…"

Some things are just a given. I earned that tour through the past like Ebenezer Scrooge, and this torment will last as long as Maggie and that house are in my life. Or until...what?

She dove off the bow to cool the hell in her head.

❖

"So all you can offer your starving artist sister are glorified hamburgers?" Rachel shut the refrigerator door and followed Maggie out to the grill. "What's wrong with this picture?"

"This is Kobe beef, I'll have you know. Chill." Maggie started the grill and pointed a spatula at her. "You're lucky I could whip this up, considering you *just dropped in unannounced.*"

"Well, hell," Rachel said, settling into a lawn chair with a bowl of chips and a glass of wine. "It's a wonder you're not giving it to Retta. Did you at least make the hamburger buns?"

Maggie turned from the grill and looked around the yard. "Is Mom here?"

"God. Don't accuse me of sounding like her." Rachel leaned forward with another thought. "She'd be on your case about your date with Captain Moby Ellis Dick. Notice I haven't started nagging you."

"You only arrived an hour ago."

"By the way, my room is just as beautiful as the last one I had. Absolutely love the bedspread. Remember that at Christmas. And thanks for letting me escape for a few days."

"As if you gave me a choice." Maggie pretended to talk on a phone and pranced around Rachel's chair, mimicking her. "Please, please, pleeeease can I stay with you while they paint downstairs? You *know* I'll end up hospitalized from those fumes. You *know* Mom and Dad will rush up here and blame you if you don't."

Rachel ignored her and fed Retta a chip. "You miss me. Admit it. Your social life is as wimpy as your spaghetti, so you need me."

"I beg your pardon. There's nothing wrong with my social life *or* my spaghetti. You just don't like spaghetti, period."

"Never mind that. Have you and your Nantucket whaler bumped uglies yet, huh? Right. Like *no.* Have you seen her since that night?"

"Ellis has been busy. And please use her real name."

"Hmm. Well, I think it's pretty weird that she finds out you own her house and now she won't even face you. Hasn't even called, I bet."

"Not yet. I was going to call her tonight."

"Don't you dare!" Startled, Retta jumped to her feet, ready for action. "It's been almost two weeks. Whatever her problem is, she needs to get over it." Seeing no one going anywhere, Retta sat and accepted another chip from Rachel. "Do *not* get hung up on this woman, Mags."

"Stop worrying, *Mom*. I'm not hung up." *Am I?* "I'd just like to see more of her, and…I guess, I'd like her to want the same."

"Be careful, big sister. Remember that you're leaving by the end of the summer, so…"

Not the first time it's crossed my mind.

"I'm just taking one day at a time, Rach. That's all."

"Know what I think? I think you're having second thoughts about leaving. It's getting tougher, isn't it? Does she have something special that would keep you here?"

"Everything is special here. And Ellis has a way about her. I don't know. She's honest, kindhearted, and there's a vulnerability about her that…She's refreshing and I enjoy being around her."

"Uh-oh. Remember what Mom thinks about islanders."

"That's just because your ex never left the house, let alone his island."

"It was off the coast of Maine. Why bother?"

Maggie snorted. "And *that* left a distinct impression on our cosmopolitan mother."

"As if either of us has pleased Mom in the past twenty years."

"Well, Ellis probably wouldn't either. She's a pretty private person, sometimes even aloof."

"Hard to get to know?"

"Yes."

"So she's related to this house. What else do you know about her?" She patted Retta and gave her another chip.

"Rach. None of those for her, please."

"Okay, Mom. So? Shit, Mags, this is like pulling teeth."

"Ellis grew up working freight runs inter-island and to the mainland with her father and grandfather. She's been sort of a wharf rat all her life."

"Interesting. She have family here still?"

"I don't think so, no."

"Where'd she go to school?"

"She's never said. I haven't asked."

"Oh. How old is she?"

Maggie shrugged. "My age, I guess."

"Would she like my work?"

"I don't know if she's into modern art."

"Hobbies?"

Maggie put the finished burgers on a plate and shut off the grill. "Come on before these get cold. I don't know if she has any hobbies."

"Christ." Rachel unfolded herself from the chair, grabbed the spatula, and followed Maggie and Retta into the house. "So do you know anything else?"

"She lives on Commercial Wharf."

Rachel laughed as she coated her burger with hot sauce. "Most wharf rats live on a wharf." She glanced up and caught Maggie's frown. "Wait. Your girlfriend lives on a boat? No shit?" She sat back, an eyebrow raised suggestively. "Ohhhh, *now* you're talking. Very nice."

"You can't call her my girlfriend. And the boat is gorgeous, actually. Not modern but classic, as boats go, I'm told."

"So it's not an old freighter, I take it."

"Well, it's the family freighter, yes, but she's made so many modifications, you'd never know what it used to be, except it's big."

"So Ms. Hunky Whaler lives on a boat. I love it."

"Ellis isn't 'hunky,' Rachel. She's lean and strong."

Rachel smirked as Maggie delivered their salad. "Uh-huh."

"Dig in, would you?"

"She should have contacted you by now. You realize that, right?"

"She said she'd stop by."

"What the hell does that mean? She likes you, doesn't she? You cooked a dynamite meal for her, didn't you? Is being in this place too hard for poor Captain Ellis?" Rachel stabbed her salad with a fork. "Shit. What's the name of her boat? I'll hunt it down and paint it pink."

"The *Nantucket Rose*," Maggie said with a laugh. "Pink is good for roses, but I doubt it's her color."

"Listen, you better hear from her before I leave or I'll be pissed."

CHAPTER SEVENTEEN

Maggie ended her phone call with Tug Whitley and stared vacantly toward the kitchen. Sporadic clanging yanked her thoughts from arranging another ridiculously expensive boat cruise. Probably looking to escape, Retta moseyed in and curled up on her bed.

"Rachel, are you waging war in my kitchen?"

"I'm making our supper. Mind your business."

"Since when do you cook?"

"Get back to work. I'm busy in here."

"Will I recognize my kitchen when you're done?"

Hands covered with flour and wild hair barely contained by a red bandana, Rachel leaned against Maggie's office doorway and puffed a curl off her forehead. "You'll recognize coquilles St. Jacques pretty quick, I bet, won't you?"

"Is that what you're making? I thought my pots and pan were rebelling."

"Listen, ungrateful sister. It's going to be awesome and you're going to kiss my butt that I'm staying here until this disgusting rain stops."

Maggie *was* grateful, regardless of the disaster she'd have to clean up. A delicious meal with Rachel promised to bolster her failing mood. If she didn't stop paying Whitley's inflated prices for his lackluster cruises, Tuck'r would be broke by the end of August. Room reservations for the next month hovered at a 60 percent occupancy rate and seemed to be going nowhere.

No more. I won't let you nickel-and-dime Tuck'r into the poorhouse, Captain Whitley. You know damn well that my package deal would've kicked us both up a notch for the rest of the season, if you hadn't been so damn greedy. At least Ellis thought a mutual arrangement could work.

She shut off the computer. *Two weeks tomorrow, Ellis. You're avoiding me, and I deserve to know why.*

She leaned back and sighed. "You're a sweetie for making supper, Rachel. Thank you. I'm sure it'll be a treat, and I could use one."

"More bad news?" Rachel waved her to follow back to the kitchen. Retta obeyed, too.

"That party of six coming in tomorrow afternoon asked about a cruise for Sunday, but Tug won't come down on his price."

"Tug? That's cute."

"Ken Whitley is anything but cute. This is the fourth time I've hired him, so you'd think he'd give me a break. He's the only private operator available on such short notice, and he knows it."

"That's like extortion or something, isn't it?"

"Kinda." She gathered all the ingredients for brownies and set to work beside Rachel. "So, I'm done. No more cruises after this, and that kills me because they're so popular. We just can't afford his prices."

"Hate to hear you sound defeated, Mags."

"I guess you win some, you lose some, and I need to accept that. Jill McGee expects to see an upward trend when she comes back in a month, but she might be in for a surprise." She set a bowl of batter on the mixer. "I might be, too, if she says Tuck'r doesn't show enough promise."

"Maybe you can persuade the sexy Ms. McGee with your wily ways. She's hot for you."

"Rachel."

"She is. She hardly took her eyes off you when she was here. Okay, so I wasn't around the whole time, but I know what I saw."

"Don't kid yourself. She inspected every nook and cranny of this house, didn't miss a trick."

"Or the halter top you wore when you took her on that little tour. Her eyes were—"

"Enough. Jill's all business. Even her flirtations are about business. And...and so were mine."

"So you're really not interested? She's high-roller glamorous, Mags, and could probably turn your life around."

I'm not looking to turn my life around. I just want it to go forward.

"It's all about Tuck'r making a good impression. If I could only have shown an upswing on the books, I'd feel more confident that I'm on the right track."

"The track to sell and leave all this behind."

Rachel's gentle voice rang as loudly in Maggie's head as the clanging pots had earlier. She actually blinked at the impact and tried to focus on getting the brownies in the second oven. Working at this stove had become her salvation since arriving on Nantucket, and she knew she'd miss it. In fact, she'd miss everything about the house, the island, even Ellis, confounding as she'd been lately.

Rachel didn't look up from her work when she mumbled, "It's a shame Ellis turned you down."

"In retrospect, it was inconsiderate to ask her to open her home to my guests. I really can't blame her, but it might have been the best arrangement of all."

"It sounds like it, because I can't think of a better promotion, having a direct descendant of Captain Pratt take houseguests on a sightseeing cruise."

"Tell me about it."

"You should try again."

"No, it's too much to ask."

"Just one more shot. What've you got to lose?" Rachel snickered. "Is she going to start avoiding you? Will she stop calling?"

Maggie couldn't argue. But she'd much rather ask Ellis about her two weeks of silence before she brought up business. Both were foreboding issues.

"Let's just concentrate on this and enjoy dinner."

"And dessert. Brownies with vanilla ice cream. I saw some in the freezer."

"Yes, there's ice cream."

"And you still won't join us later? Laura said we'd love the RC's band tonight. I hate to think of you here, brooding. You could use a night—"

"Thanks, but no, especially on such a miserable night."

"The rain might stop later, so that's no excuse."

"I'm not up for tromping through a deluge. Retta and I will be just fine, snug and dry here at home."

❖

Wind-driven rain pelted the *Eagle* as it docked for the night, and like her coworkers, Ellis repeatedly apologized to debarking passengers for the awful conditions. She didn't like it any more than they did. Having to finish her workday slogging through the dark as rain drenched her cap, soaked her chinos, and seeped through her windbreaker just topped off a rough day. Only the promise of the *Rose*'s cozy confines made the trek bearable, and she couldn't wait to settle in, relaxed enough to plan tomorrow's call to Maggie. *Unforgiveable, wallowing in a funk and dropping off the face of the earth. Don't be surprised when she refuses to see you. Shame on me—again.*

The irregular wind carried faint music from the RC, interrupting the sounds of splattering water, and she let it entertain her as she strode on, head down, shoulders hunched. Then a frantic call made her stop. It came from the Main Street intersection, and she advanced to the corner and peered toward the historic horse trough that sat in the center. Barely lit by the streetlamps, a woman without rain gear or umbrella stood in the middle of the intersection, cobblestones routing glistening rivulets around her feet as she raised her hands to her mouth and yelled again.

"Retta!"

Ellis broke into a run. "Maggie!"

The dark form spun around and her features materialized as Ellis drew near.

"Ellis! She's been gone well over an hour!" Hair hanging in bedraggled strands around her face, Maggie swiped at her cheeks and issued another call down Main Street. Drenched from head to toe, she turned slightly and shouted in another direction.

Ellis looked about, oblivious to the rain. She called in the opposite direction.

"I didn't think she'd want to be out long," Maggie said and sniffed deeply. She rubbed her eyes with the heels of her palms. "Just ten minutes, and when I called her to come in, she wasn't in the yard." She yelled down the street again.

"Has she ever taken off before?"

"No. I-I can't believe it. I searched our neighborhood for half an hour. Then down Centre and back on Federal. I was about to start..." She wiped her cheeks again before gesturing toward South Water.

"By now, she'd go somewhere familiar."

Maggie turned quickly, hope displacing panic in her eyes. "You think I should check back at the house?"

"Yeah. Up that way. Got your phone with you?" Maggie nodded as she scanned the streets around them. "Go back, then." Ellis touched her cheek. "I'll search down here."

Maggie backed away, her fearful eyes as dark as her wind-whipped hair. "Thank you."

"She'll turn up, Maggie. Go." She waved her on. "Keep in touch."

Ellis decided to chance checking the docks, knowing how much Retta loved the water. Between her own calls into the night, she heard Maggie's grow distant as they separated. *Come on, Retta. You're smarter than this. Did you have to pick such a wretched night?*

She yelled out across Straight Wharf and squinted into the darkness, desperate to spot movement along the row of slips or in the tiny, neatly manicured yards of homes that extended into the water. She hustled on, now wondering if Retta remembered Commercial Wharf and where the *Rose* was docked.

On the unsteady walkway, a savage gust of wind forced her to turn away, and her call dissipated instantly. She ran her wet sleeve across her face and peered ahead, along the row of trawlers and down each wooden finger pier that separated them, but saw nothing. Finally, she reached the *Rose* and lifted her hands to call out.

A scrabbling noise at her bow made her turn. She peeled off her backpack as she ran to the end of the narrow pier and pulled her flashlight from a side pocket.

Some twenty yards off the *Rose*'s bow, Retta dog-paddled in place, angry waves splashing her face and negating her progress.

"Retta! Jesus Christ!" Ellis dropped to her knees and let Retta see her reaching over the edge. "Retta! Come on, pretty girl! You can do it!" She had no idea how long Retta had been treading water, battling and struggling to keep her muzzle above the rough surface, but judging by the blank look in her eyes, she'd bet *too* long.

Then Retta sank. Ellis ripped off her deck shoes. She flashed the light back onto the water just as Retta bobbed back to the surface. Ellis punched in Maggie's number on her cell and began emptying her pockets into her shoes. She tossed down her windbreaker, and then her cap, just as Maggie answered.

"Ellis?"

"Come to the *Rose*."

"No, really?"

"She's in the water, but I'll get her." She hung up and shoved her phone into a shoe. Again, she checked with the flashlight. The only headway Retta was making was down. Another wave pushed her under too easily, evidence of her dwindling strength.

"Retta! This way! Come!" She stood on the edge and checked Retta's position once again, then set the flashlight down, took a deep breath, and dove as far out into the blackness as she could.

Struck by the cold and now virtually blind, she fought off a full-body shiver and propelled herself upward and outward. Breaking the surface, she caught a glimpse of Retta's head before it disappeared again.

Ellis gulped air and shot back beneath the waves, reaching, stretching each stroke, praying she'd make contact and not swim past.

She slammed into Retta's torso and locked one arm around it, pumped upward with the other until both their heads popped up into the rainy night. Retta thrashed, clawing desperately, narrowly missing Ellis's face. Back paws dug into Ellis's hips, and Ellis had all she could do to outmuscle her and hang on. There'd be gashes in the chinos, in her skin, too, she was certain.

Several feet from the end of the pier, she saw Maggie running toward them and spat out a "thank you" of salt water. Now they faced the chore of getting one terrified, frenzied dog ashore.

"Ellis! Oh, God!"

Maggie threw herself into a prone position at the edge and offered both arms.

"My windbreaker," Ellis yelled from just below her reach. "Throw it."

Maggie didn't think. She balled up the jacket and dropped it into Ellis's hand. She watched, breathlessly, as Ellis maneuvered in the inky water and Retta continued to twist and splash. *I'll never let this dog out of my sight again. And, Ellis Chilton, were you meant to save me from myself?*

Ellis's hand shot out of the water clutching a sizeable knot of fabric. "Grab this!"

Extended over the water almost to her waist, Maggie pushed up the sleeves of her sweatshirt and reached as far as she could until she fisted the knot in both hands.

"Got it!"

"Now lift!"

Oh, please, let me be able to do this.

Maggie hauled upward with all her strength, hoisting Retta in the sling Ellis made, and just when she didn't think she could lift high enough, she felt Ellis pushing up from below. Right hand gripping the walkway for leverage and left arm looped beneath Retta's hindquarters, Ellis boosted Retta up, over the edge, and Maggie pulled her onto the pier.

As Retta scrambled to her feet, Maggie grabbed Ellis's shirt and helped her up.

Ellis just sat where she landed, catching her breath. "Thank you. It's okay now." She turned her face up into the rain and closed her eyes.

Maggie wasn't so sure, and she hauled Retta to her chest and kissed the salty fur atop her head. Panting hard, Retta sat as soon as Maggie untied the windbreaker. Ellis still hadn't moved. A million emotions pushed Maggie to tears. Even for Ellis, she thought, this excitement must be extreme.

Retta eventually stood and shook, much longer than usual, then quickly lay down.

"Rest, sweetie. My best girl." Maggie gently rubbed her side and kissed her ear before turning to Ellis.

"I-I don't know where to begin, what to say. Nothing measures up to what I'm feeling right now."

"Wet and tired?"

Ellis leaned wearily on one outstretched arm, hair disheveled, clothes outlining her lanky frame like a second skin. She looked like a creature the ocean had tossed back, when, in fact, she'd snatched a treasure from its clutches. Maybe the discerning glint in her eyes said she was aware. All Maggie knew for sure was the merciless wind and rain did nothing but enhance her appeal.

She crawled the few feet to Ellis and sat back on her heels.

"Wet and tired, yes," she said, sliding hair off Ellis's forehead, "but they're somewhere down the list." She took Ellis's hand and squeezed. "Grateful actually is at the top." She looked down and gasped. "You're bleeding." She lifted Ellis's arm and inspected the gash that extended from mid-forearm to the back of her hand. A watery trail of blood trickled to between her fingers.

"She got me," Ellis said, also looking, "but it's not as bad as it seems. The rain—"

"God, Ellis. You might need stitches." She rose to her knees, still holding Ellis's hand. "Maybe a run to the ER—"

"It's all right, Maggie. The salt water is good for it. Please don't worry."

"But—"

"Shh. I'm fine." Ellis nodded toward Retta. "She will be, too." She rose to one knee and the tear and dark stain on her chinos appeared.

"She got you there, too. Your thigh."

Ellis looked down, apparently just realizing it. "Like I said, just scratches. Don't worry."

"I will," Maggie insisted as they stood, "and I'll replace the pants. I'm so sorry about this." Her voice cracked and tears blended into the raindrops on her cheeks.

"It's not your fault, Maggie. And you're not replacing my pants."

"Of-of course, I will. This is all…God."

"The Steamship will replace the pants. Okay? No problem. Honest. And all this is *not* your fault. Retta's fine and safe, and that's what's important."

"Because of you."

Ellis gripped Maggie's shoulder and crouched slightly to look up at her, but Maggie didn't dare look back. She knew she'd fall apart. Even weary and soaked to the bone, Ellis projected strength and surety Maggie urgently needed at this moment, support that lifted her heart, and the reassuring hand on her shoulder had her craving more.

She sniffed and shook her head at herself. *Take a breath and get it together.*

"Did you drive down here, by any chance?" Ellis asked, moving to Retta. Immediately missing the contact, Maggie watched her run a tender hand over Retta's shoulder and cherished the soothing timbre of her voice. "How's my pretty girl doing?" Ellis stroked Retta's head and side repeatedly. "Worn out, huh? You rest right here for now."

"I don't have my car, no," Maggie said, joining Ellis in administering to Retta. "When you called, I just ran like hell."

"Right now, she's too beat to walk back."

"I'll run home and get it."

"I can get my truck, if you don't mind having her across your lap."

"Oh, not at all, but we're all too wet, so sitting in the back would be fine. Thank you. Could you help me carry her off the docks?"

"I'll carry her. Two of us could be disastrous." She surprised Maggie with a smirk. "No more swimming tonight."

"Good point." She touched the back of Ellis's hand where it rested on Retta's hip. "We should look at your wound before we do anything else." The bleeding hadn't stopped, and diluted by rain, it now covered her wrist and hand.

Ellis wiped most of it away with her shirttail, but a fresh stream started down her arm.

"I have a first aid kit on board. I'll be right back." She headed for the *Rose* and Retta righted herself to watch her every move. Maggie stroked her head.

"She's something, isn't she?" Still panting rapidly, Retta blinked against the rain but didn't look away. "I know you didn't mean it, honey, but you hurt her. What were you thinking in the first place? Did you fall in?" Retta flopped back on her side, still watching Ellis. Suddenly, she lifted her head.

Maggie followed her line of vision and saw Ellis walk halfway back to them and stop.

"We probably should let her recover a bit more, so...Let's go aboard."

Chapter Eighteen

Ellis vaulted onto the *Rose* and back off a second later with the two-step wooden box. She was glad to see Retta show enough energy to sit up, but knew there couldn't be much left in her.

"Come on," she said, cupping Retta's head. "We'll take it slow."

They walked tentatively back to the steps and Ellis squatted and lifted Retta, who barely managed to object. Ellis climbed both steps and was over the gunwale and onto the deck promptly, thankful she'd managed it without a wobble or a grunt for Maggie's sake. *She already feels guilty enough.* She set Retta onto her feet and reached for Maggie.

"After a while, you don't even bother with steps," she said, "but they do come in handy sometimes."

"Well, I certainly appreciate them." With a firm grip on Ellis's hand, Maggie gingerly stepped up and over, and Ellis automatically put a hand on her waist to guide her down to the deck. Maggie's soggy sweatshirt was cold, and Ellis hoped pressing it against that sweet curve of hip didn't make things worse.

"Look. Somebody's already snoozing," she said.

Retta had found shelter from the rain beneath the hard-top canopy and was back on her side, eyes closed. She'd stopped panting, but her chest still heaved at a steady clip. She never moved as they tiptoed past and Ellis opened the saloon door.

"We'll let her rest. She's going to be okay." She shut the door behind them, and the absence of rain and wind intensified the quiet. "The first aid kit is below," she said, moving to the stairs.

But just two steps from the top, Ellis looked up at Maggie, past the exhausted slouch in her posture, the soaked clothes, and the wet, disheveled hair, and saw the spark in her eyes. She saw companionship and consideration, ambition battered but not defeated, and an appreciation *for her* that she didn't think she'd received from anyone before. Moreover, realizing she wanted Maggie to see the same in her almost staggered her. *And I still owe her one hell of an apology. Shit. What a complete ass.*

"Please come down and have something to soothe the nerves."

"A really good idea."

The galley below provided the warmth of close quarters and the whisper of rain, an inescapable intimacy Ellis hoped Maggie appreciated as much as she did.

"What's your pleasure?" she asked, opening the liquor cabinet. "I just stocked up last weekend."

Maggie stepped closer to peruse the shelves. "Whoa. Did you stock up for the year?" Bending over to read the labels, she gathered dangling strands of wet hair in one hand. "Look at all this. How's a girl supposed to choose?" She held up bottles of vodka and amaretto. "I can make us Godmothers, if you like. I think you're officially Retta's dogmother now."

Ellis chuckled. "I suppose I am, aren't I?"

Maggie set the bottles on the table. "Glasses, please—and that first aid kit."

"No." Ellis spun to another cabinet and handed Maggie two glasses. "First, I'm checking on my goddog." She bolted up the steps, hearing Maggie laugh behind her.

First aid. Dry clothes. Dog aboard. Woman below deck. Maybe I've redeemed myself.

She stopped in the saloon and took a breath. "Jesus. I *do* need a drink."

She opened the door cautiously, not knowing where Retta would be, but was relieved to see her right herself and wag her tail.

"Hey there, pretty girl." She crouched before her and cupped her head. "Still don't feel like standing? A flight of stairs might be tough, huh?" She stood and patted her thigh. Pain shot through her leg and she remembered her other wound. "Come."

Retta rose with effort and followed. Ellis took three steps down, turned, and beckoned, but Retta looked from the steps to her and sat, decidedly opposed.

"That's fine, too. I get it." Ellis went back up and pressed her cheek to Retta's head. "Trust me. Just like earlier, okay?" She wrapped her arms around her and Retta squirmed fearfully. "Steady as she goes, pretty girl. Steady." She lifted and worked her way down and found Maggie waiting at the bottom.

She had no wiggle room of her own, couldn't make way when Maggie leaned in very close to kiss the top of Retta's head. Loose hair swung across Ellis's face, Maggie's ear brushed the tip of her nose, and Ellis closed her eyes at the sensations.

The plush, velvety warmth of Maggie's lips pressed against her mouth, just long enough for Ellis to instantly register shock, pleasure, and arousal, and to initiate a response, before the connection broke.

In the shadow of the tight stairway, all three of them stood close, although Retta tossed her head as a reminder of where she was, and Maggie's eyes went to Ellis's lips.

"Retta got one and I-I thought you should, too."

Her body still humming, Ellis gently set Retta down, and they watched her ruffle her fur with a thorough shake and curl up beneath the table.

Ellis couldn't find words. *Maybe there aren't any. Maybe I don't need any. Talk about an emotional night.*

"Um…" Obviously uneasy, Maggie went for their drinks on the table and held them aloft. "Godmother for the new dogmother."

She's moved on. Just an emotional night, that's all.

Maggie hoped Ellis would take the glass before it started to shake. Her nerves thrummed so hard, she thought her heart would flutter. *Could she have looked any more surprised?*

Finally, Ellis accepted her drink and peered into the glass with trepidation.

"Smells powerful."

Maggie shrugged sheepishly. "It is, but tastes a whole lot better than scotch." She relaxed a bit when Ellis brought their glasses together.

"Then here's to dogmothers everywhere." A suggestive curl formed at the side of her mouth. "Thank you, Maggie. I'm honored."

They sipped, and when Ellis blinked and blew out a breath, Maggie laughed. Ellis pursed her lips thoughtfully and took another sip.

"Damn, that's good." She offered a chair, but Maggie shook her head as she swallowed.

"Not sitting in these wet clothes. I don't mind standing if you don't. Besides, we probably should call it a night after this." She really didn't care about wet clothes or standing or the late hour. What she cared about was the persistent temptation to kiss her. "First aid now."

"Ah." Ellis produced a brown plastic tackle box, its voluminous interior and three trays filled with assorted bandages, gauze, tape rolls, ointments, and surgical implements. Maggie shook her head at how well prepared Ellis seemed to be for everything.

Ellis washed her forearm in the sink and scrubbed away dried blood all the way down to her fingernails. "It's not as bad as it looks, you know." She dried the wound with paper towels as Maggie dug a bottle of hydrogen peroxide from the box.

"I don't care what they say, this is going to hurt." Maggie handed her the bottle and studied the concerted look on Ellis's face. The picture of determination. *Guts never looked so good on a woman.*

Ellis took a hearty mouthful of her drink, sent her a glance, and poured the peroxide. Maggie winced for her as the bloody four-inch slice filled with white foam. Ellis threw back another swallow before disappearing into the next room. In an instant, she was back with towels. "I should have offered you one of these right away. Standing around soaking wet isn't good."

Maggie wiped her face and the back of her neck before running the towel across her hair. It had become a lost cause long ago, but the soft warmth was a comfort. *Now these wet clothes are an issue. I really should go.*

Ellis dried her own hair, a quick one-handed job that fluffed her short style into a jumbled mess. Maggie delighted in the carefree attitude that left it untamed as Ellis poured more peroxide into her wound.

"Let me," Maggie said, rushing to wipe spilled liquid off the table. "You're obviously not left-handed. Would you please sit?" Ellis obeyed. "You can't get this stuff all over everything." Maggie laid out paper towels and drew Ellis's forearm onto them. The flesh chilled her fingers, but the rock-hard musculature felt far more remarkable. She forced her concentration to the first aid box and pawed through its contents until she found ointment and gauze. "And whatever's bleeding on your leg has to be checked, too."

"Later."

Maggie couldn't help but grin. "You could drop the pants so..."

"Thanks, Doc. It can wait."

Maggie dabbed at the wound until it was dry and opened a tube of ointment.

Ellis watched closely. "You really don't have to go to all this trouble. I can wrap it after I shower."

"I'm doing this now." She set gauze over the wound and proceeded to wrap it.

"You shouldn't be hanging out in wet clothes either. We should get you two home." Bandaging completed, Ellis stood and finished her drink.

Maggie looked under the table, found Retta sound asleep and breathing easily. Ellis looked, too, and Maggie whispered as they turned to each other.

"She's made herself at home."

Ellis nodded. "She's finally calmed down. Hell of a trauma for her."

"For all of us," Maggie said as they straightened. "Why don't you take that shower." Ellis squared her shoulders, as if ready to argue. "It's the least I can do, Ellis. And I don't care about my wet clothes, but you went swimming in yours."

Say yes. Let me do this for you. Besides, it feels good being here. Does it make you nervous?

Ellis lowered her eyes to the bloodstain around the rip in her pants and disappeared again. She emerged seconds later, carrying a set of light blue surgeon's scrubs with a pair of white cotton socks on top. "Ladies first." She pointed to the door with the rose wreath. "The head and shower are right there." She handed her the folded clothes. "You're not sitting around in a soggy sweatshirt and jeans. There are plenty of supplies inside and lots of hot water, so take your time."

Taken aback, Maggie slowly accepted the scrubs. "You know, I'm fine waiting. I don't mean to intrude, Ellis. God knows, we've—"

Ellis pointed to the head again like a parent. "Snap to it."

Maggie saluted and looked back before stepping into the bathroom. "There's no limit to your generosity, is there?"

Ellis turned with a frying pan in hand. "Grilled cheese and tomato soup okay with you?" She twirled the pan like a pro. "I'm guessing we're both hungry." She opened the refrigerator.

"Well...I-I suppose I am. I hadn't thought about it."

"Comfort food. I'll start and you can finish while I shower." She turned to Maggie and gestured with a butter dish. "Go."

And in a blur of time, Maggie was back at the table, surrendering to pleasures both inside her stomach and out. Blowing on a spoonful of soup, she gave up trying to analyze the reserved, captivating woman seated opposite her because Ellis Chilton simply was unlike any she'd known. And this, tucked into a boat on a rainy night eating soup and sandwiches with someone whose singular glance made her heart race, *just couldn't be real.*

"Amaretto, cheddar, and tomato work well together," she said, raising her glass to Ellis.

"I'm surprised, too. Think I'll try it more often."

"I can't thank you enough. This is just what we needed." She pondered how often Ellis prepared even this simple meal for herself. The compact galley certainly was fully stocked, had all the necessities, and she'd easily located everything she needed while Ellis showered and bandaged her thigh, but she couldn't deny the surreal feel of being in Ellis's world. "Have you lived on the *Rose* long?"

Ellis took her time chewing. If the question surprised her, it didn't show.

"More than ten years, but I didn't start renovations until about four years ago. Had to save serious money."

Having lost the house to foreclosure probably meant Ellis literally started this work from scratch. Maggie wondered if Ellis declared bankruptcy, and how much pain it must have wrought to fail at the family business, to lose her home, to renovate the *Rose* and erase memories. And to have endured it all without her mother or father. *God. How does a woman recover from so many losses?*

Maggie toyed with her spoon, trying to come up with the right words.

"The *Rose* certainly is gorgeous today, Ellis. I love it, so perfectly decorated and cleverly economical, efficient. There's a strength about it that makes you feel sheltered and safe, at peace." *Just like its owner.*

"That's kind of you. I appreciate that. I'm used to roughing it, so I just renovated to be comfortable, bit by bit. It's hard to know what people think when you don't have many visitors, but it's home."

"I'm very happy to be one of those rare guests," Maggie said and drew Ellis's direct attention. She hoped her sincerity, her pleasure were easily read. "Thank you for sharing such a big part of who you are."

"You make it easy, Maggie." She stacked their empty dishes, retreated to the sink, and appeared as finished with the topic as she was her meal.

Heavy silence settled between them. They listened to Retta's steady breathing and the blowing rain needle the rectangular windows on the boat's unprotected harbor side. Maggie wished Ellis would open up about the past, elaborate about the *Rose*'s remarkable transformation, say anything in her low, sultry voice to keep this extraordinarily improbable night from ending.

"Maggie?"

Bent to check on Retta, Maggie looked up over the table and saw Ellis quickly turn to the stove.

"Ah, would you like coffee?"

Maggie doubted that had been her original question. *Please say what's on your mind.*

"No, thank you. You've already done so much tonight." She brought her glass to the sink. "It's after two o'clock and we really should go. But first," she reached for the faucet, "I intend to do these dishes for you."

Ellis took her hand. "No," she murmured, so close, her breath warmed Maggie's ear. "You have no idea what you've already done for me."

"I've dug up your past and my dog has dragged you into the ocean. That's—"

Ellis cupped her face and Maggie's mind whirled at the tender touch. Her eyes fluttered closed and reality became the silkiness of Ellis's lips, the firm, possessive draw on her mouth that sent a bolt of fire to her core. Maggie slid an arm around Ellis's waist and held on, unsteady now, but yearning for more, and Ellis drew her closer with equal urgency.

The sure, expansive hand on her lower back weakened her hips, her knees, and Maggie nearly swooned when Ellis angled her head and deepened the kiss. *Dear God, I could do this all night.*

Ellis left a trail of kisses across her cheek, along her neck, and whispered into the crook of her shoulder. "I'm so sorry for not calling or…or stopping by."

"Sh." Maggie lifted Ellis's head in both hands. "It's all right." She kissed Ellis's lower lip.

"No, it's not." Ellis drew back slightly and scanned Maggie's face. "I *do* want to see you—in or out of that house. Or here. It…it feels right, special with you."

Maggie tugged her into a prolonged kiss, wrapped her arms around her shoulders when Ellis enclosed her fully. Kisses on her throat made Maggie sigh, and she ran a hand through Ellis's hair, relished its softness. "God, yes, this feels right. And I want to see you, too. Where doesn't matter."

Ellis squeezed her tighter, groaned against her collarbone, and slid her palms beneath the back of Maggie's scrub shirt. But a high-pitched whimper sounded from below, and they edged apart and looked down. Retta sat, watching curiously, tail wagging when they made eye contact.

Ellis scratched between Retta's ears.

"She doesn't want to be left out," she said, sliding her arm back around Maggie.

"She's feeling more like her old self, I'd say."

"So, she knows all about jealousy?"

"I beg your pardon. She does not." Maggie squirmed closer and pretended to bite the tip of Ellis's nose. "But she's an expert on hugs and kisses."

"Oh, really? Let's see." Ellis took a broad waltz step to the middle of the floor, dipped Maggie backward with a flourish, and held her there.

"Ellis!"

Retta swooped in and began licking Maggie's face and ear.

Ellis grinned down at them. "Hey, you were right. She *is* an expert."

"Ellis Chilton, let me up!"

"Wow, look at the size of that tongue!"

"Ellis! Retta, stop. Retta, please!" She flailed an arm to urge Retta away. "Jesus. Now I need a bath."

Ellis laughed as she lifted Maggie to her feet. "Yeah, you do. I'm not kissing all that dog slobber."

"Oh, you don't think so?" Maggie grabbed Ellis by the ears, kissed her firmly, and rubbed her wet face across Ellis's lips. "There, wise guy."

"Well, since you put it that way…" Ellis leaned in to kiss her, and Maggie pushed at her chest.

"Ew. I'm not kissing dog slobber on you from me."

Ellis wet a handful of paper towels for their faces. "I'd like to pick up where we left off."

"Uh-oh. Retta's nosing around now, Ellis. I'm sorry to tell you what that means."

"I can guess." She pretended to sulk. "Parenting can be damn inconvenient. I'll take her."

"No, I'll—"

"She's my goddog, remember?" She reached for a rain slicker.

"That's sweet of you, but it's almost three o'clock, time we—"
Ellis stepped up very close, ran a finger along Maggie's cheek, and then across and between her lips. She tipped her forehead against Maggie's and whispered.

"It's still raining. It's twelve minutes to three in the morning. Don't go."

CHAPTER NINETEEN

"I appreciate your attention to duty, Retta, but I doubt you've given much thought to my situation. Have you even been listening?" Wind blew her hood off and Ellis yanked it back on.

Retta stopped to reinvestigate the patch of grass she'd "watered" when they began their walk. The rain had dissolved into a heavy mist, but the wind hadn't abated and it whipped the mist inside Ellis's hood as she waited. She turned her shoulder to it, while Retta sniffed and snorted, oblivious to the conditions.

"Come on. You've done your business and now you're just being nosy. Your mom's waiting and we need to get back. *I* need to get back." With a little tug of encouragement, Retta finally moved on, and they started down the dock.

"So, was that invitation to stay the night too bold? Has Mom had sleepovers since you guys moved here?" Retta paused to sniff a coil of hose at an empty slip. "You wouldn't tell me, would you? You're loyal." Ellis turned away from another vicious spray, and Retta lifted her head, squinted through the mist at the *Tenn-acious*, and barked.

"Shh, Retta!" Ellis ran a reassuring hand along her wet back. "People are sleeping. That's just Hank's line blowing against a mast. Now, come. And pay attention." She urged her on. "So, your mom's not seeing anyone, is she? Do I risk thinking beyond tonight?"

The *Rose*'s soft light beckoned from the far end of the pier. *Are you comfortable there, Maggie? I hope so. Coming home hasn't felt like this in a long time.*

"I've never met anyone like her, Retta. Sure, she's really bright and thoughtful, and that just makes her even sexier, but, Jesus, she has me thinking an awful lot. And it feels good, like it's okay to be myself again."

Knowing the neighborhood now, Retta pulled Ellis to the *Rose* and set her front paws on the first step. She looked over her shoulder, waiting for the assist.

"God, you're smart." Ellis unhooked the leash and Retta squirmed in anticipation. A strong gust rocked them, but Retta's tail continued to swish like a windshield wiper. Ellis bent and scooped her up. "Now, no telling Mom what I said." She scaled the side and set Retta down. "Shake out here, please." Retta shimmied hard, fur fluffing from nose to tail.

Ellis laughed lightly and hung up her slicker in the saloon as Retta romped past her, first to reach the stairs. But seeing only darkness at the bottom, she stopped and sat.

"Door's shut, Retta." She started down. "There's lots to learn, you know, if you want to be a boating dog." The door swung open and light flooded the narrow stairs. "Aha! Here's Mom."

"And here you two are," Maggie said. "Did I hear Retta wants to be a boating dog?"

Retta cautiously maneuvered her way down and paused to receive the usual pats and praise. Then she basked in a cursory wipe-down, wiggling as Maggie ruffled paper towels across her head and torso.

"She'd take to boating like a champ, Maggie. She's so damn smart, it's scary."

"That's my best girl." Retta curled around and licked Maggie's chin. "Did you do your business or did you waste Ellis's time playing bloodhound again?"

"Nope. Once we got off the wharf, she got to work." Retta drew her paw away from Maggie's wiping, and ventured off to explore. "She's fine, Maggie. Thank you."

"We're not tracking water and dirt everywhere—especially after I just swept."

"You what?" Maggie's smirk dared Ellis to scold her.

"I did. Please leave your shoes right where you are."

Ellis took them off promptly. The galley looked tidy again, first aid kit gone, dishes and pans washed, and two fresh drinks waited on the table. No one except Ellis had tended to things on the *Rose* in many years, but remarkably, this felt quite the opposite of invasive.

"Maggie Jordan isn't one to sit idle, I see."

"I hope you don't mind. Besides, it's the least I—"

"I don't mind at all." She picked up her drink and handed Maggie hers. "I'm really glad you feel at home here. And, honestly? I don't think I've ever meant it more."

"I love it when you say exactly what you're thinking." She placed her palm on Ellis's cheek. "Being welcome here is all the more special to me because you mean it. I hope you'll feel that way about a certain *other* home, and *I* mean it just as much."

Maybe I will. Maybe sooner than later, if it means that much to you.

Maggie set a hand on her shoulder and leaned up to kiss her.

You know I'll consider it, don't you? You don't need me to answer.

Instinctively, Ellis slid an arm around Maggie's waist and drew her in. *I need you closer.* Body heat simmered through the thin scrub cotton between them, flared from Ellis's chest to her thighs, and as she fit her lips to Maggie's, she sensed combustion was imminent.

She grazed her tongue across Maggie's, drew on her lips, and Ellis's mind spun when Maggie indulged on hers. Maggie's desire prompted such emotional release, Ellis lost all sense of space and time. There was only Maggie, her graceful curves and toned muscles fitted perfectly against her body, as content in their union as their lips. Enlightenment, refuge, deliverance, all merged in her mind, and in a flicker of clarity, Ellis saw Maggie as *the* place to be. *Wherever she is?*

"Ellis." Maggie's whisper tickled her cheek. "We need to put our drinks down."

Ellis stepped back, took her hand, and led her to the bedroom at the bow. "In here," she said and put both their glasses on the shelf over the bed. She flicked on a small lantern nearby, went to Maggie, filtered a hand through her disarrayed hair, and let the silky waves envelop her fingers. "A little unruly and so soft. The first time I saw you, I knew I could get lost in this."

"And I remember the first time you took my breath away with these eyes." She trailed a fingertip over Ellis's eyebrow, around her ear, and linked her arms around her neck.

Ellis tugged her closer and kissed her as she drew Maggie down on top of her on the bed. Maggie fit against her so well this way, too, her slight weight just enough to press every arousal button that hadn't been pressed in far too long. Her hair lolled down around Ellis's face, shielding their kisses from the outside world, and Ellis reached for more.

She slid her hand beneath Maggie's shirt, across the satiny skin to her shoulders, and squeezed slowly, deeply. Maggie offered an encouraging hum against her lips, and Ellis gathered the shirt in both hands, drew it over Maggie's head, and tossed it aside. She rolled Maggie onto her back and ran her fingertips across a very pert nipple. Maggie groaned and pulled at her shirt. "I want this off."

Ellis rose to her knees, threw off her shirt, and her breath caught when Maggie's delicate hands took possession of her breasts. Ellis cupped Maggie's in return, buried her face between them, and kissed each one alternately.

"Mmm. Should I choose left or right?"

Maggie toyed with Ellis's hair, clutched her head closer. "A captain with no sense of direction? Ohhh." She writhed when Ellis nibbled her left nipple. "Oh, yes."

Ellis massaged her right breast, tugged the nipple, teased with her tongue before nipping it, and Maggie hissed at the sensation. Her playfulness, her vocal and physical responses were delightful surprises, and Ellis reveled in the opportunity to please her. That, in itself, magnified her arousal, as if it needed help.

She pushed Maggie's scrub pants down over her hips, and Maggie responded in kind. She yanked Ellis's down over her ass and smoothed a palm over her left cheek.

"Oh, nice butt."

"Show me yours."

"Check it out yourself."

Ellis gripped the bottom of Maggie's pant legs and pulled them completely off, turning Maggie over in the process. "Oh, sweetness." She hurried out of her own pants, knelt between Maggie's legs, and flexed her hands into Maggie's ass, made her moan into the pillow. Ellis kissed each cheek and then all the way up to the back of her neck. "I could do this for hours and hours."

She slipped onto her side and Maggie leaned in, hair disheveled, cheeks flushed, the most beautiful invitation Ellis had ever received. Maggie kissed her deeply and ran a splayed hand the length of Ellis's back, over her ribs to the side of her breast. Briefly, Ellis wondered if her own trembling nerves were noticeable. Their tongues collided, danced, and their kisses grew firm and hungry.

Ellis pulled Maggie's thigh over her own, and Maggie hiked it higher, a welcome that Ellis acknowledged immediately. She squeezed her way across Maggie's ass and reached between her legs, slid into a heated pool of readiness that made her swallow hard. She felt herself grow wetter.

Maggie broke their kiss to take a breath, and Ellis withdrew her fingers and urged Maggie to lie back. She shifted over her, lightly kissed her eyelids, nose, and mouth before lowering her head and scraping a nipple with her teeth. Maggie squirmed and gripped Ellis's hand. Eager to move lower, Ellis licked her chest, stomach, and hip, and Maggie captured her within her legs.

Ellis kissed the inside of her thigh, nuzzled into her hair, and looked up when Maggie called her name on a sigh. Grazing a palm over Maggie's abdomen, she absorbed the warmth all the way up to her breast. *Such supple swells and lush valleys, all the more beautiful in her vulnerability, her honesty.* Maggie squeezed her hand, eyes nearly closed, lips parted. *A vision stolen from fantasy.*

Ellis kissed her hair and slid her tongue the length of Maggie's sex, lapped her till she quivered. An arm around Maggie's hips, Ellis pressed deeper, sucked harder, and Maggie released Ellis's hand to grab fistfuls of the comforter. Ellis stroked down along her side and slid two fingers inside her.

Maggie gasped, her body contorted as Ellis nursed at her clit and drove steadily in and out of her. Ellis nibbled and Maggie twitched. Thrusting deeper, Ellis tugged at her clit with her teeth, and Maggie arched hard off the bed.

"Ellis!" Maggie trembled. Her legs, locked around Ellis's shoulders, hardened to steel. "Jesus, yes!"

Ellis pressed as far as she could reach inside, drew Maggie's clit as deeply into her mouth as possible, and drove Maggie into a swift, blinding orgasm. Maggie's racing heart pummeled at her fingertips, her lips and tongue, and Ellis watched as Maggie's body shuddered, stiffened, and slowly relaxed.

She inched back, gingerly withdrew her fingers, and rested her head on Maggie's thigh.

"Ellis Chilton." Maggie exhaled toward the ceiling. "You're a force of nature." She offered her arms and Ellis settled into them.

"And you're magnificent." She kissed each of Maggie's lips. "Everything okay?"

"Everything's perfect. The captain's not doubting herself, I hope, because I think *she's* perfect, too."

"Pleasing you means a lot to me."

Maggie pulled her closer and kissed her hard. "You make sweet sincerity look awfully sexy on a rugged sailor. It still baffles me, why some lucky woman hasn't snatched you up."

Ellis chuckled. "I don't know how lucky she'd be, Maggie. My heaping pile of baggage has stood in the way for years, and you've seen how that goes."

"That's right. You *did* disappear for two weeks. Hmm." She fondled Ellis's breast, plucked at a nipple, and Ellis shifted her hips to cope with the arousal. Maggie grinned. "I'd say we've pushed that baggage aside, wouldn't you?"

With you, it feels that way, yes.

"Absolutely."

Maggie urged Ellis onto her back. "You make me lose myself, forget myself. I've even forgotten the last time—God, see? Now, that's embarrassing."

"Tell me."

"I'll tell if you tell." Maggie kissed her nose. "It's been over a year for me, since Steph and I parted ways." She draped a leg over Ellis's hip and Ellis drew it higher until Maggie sat astride her. The heat and wetness on her abdomen made her blood race. Maggie leaned forward on her arms. "Your turn. Are you blushing?"

"What? No."

"You are." Maggie stroked her cheek. "God, you're irresistible. So, tell me. How long?" She rubbed her nose along Ellis's cheek, licked down her neck and whispered, "Trust me. Your artistry is phenomenal."

"About two years. I don't date much."

"The limited dating pool on an island doesn't help, I'm sure." She sat up and combed her fingers through Ellis's hair. The gentle touch tingled down Ellis's neck to her shoulders, and when Maggie spoke against her lips, Ellis nearly trembled. "Oh, Captain, I consider myself *very* fortunate to make your acquaintance."

CHAPTER TWENTY

The aroma of warm cinnamon greeted Maggie as she climbed the back stairs, and she wondered when Laura had learned to bake. Retta romped into the kitchen ahead of her, and Maggie stopped, speechless at the sight of Rachel at the oven.

"Let's see," Rachel began, as she plated a pile of scones. "Six fifty-two on a Saturday morning. Who could that be coming home?"

"What are you doing?" Maggie wandered closer.

"We used to make these with Grandma, remember? Okay, they don't look *exactly* like they used to, but—do not change the subject."

Maggie ran both hands through her hair and closed her eyes. Ellis's hands had done it much better, and she turned away and bit back a little smile. *You came just as fast as I did, so hard, so completely. You can hold on like that every time.*

Laura banged through the swinging door. "Let's get the fruit— Oh, Maggie!" Her wide eyes scanned Maggie's scrubs. "Oh, no! Were you in the hospital? Did something happen?" She wiped her hands nervously on her apron.

Rachel chortled. "Oh, something happened, all right." She crossed her arms and leaned against the counter.

"Thank you both so much for stepping up. I'm sorry I'm late."

"Late?" Rachel glanced at the clock. "Nah. We're just putting out breakfast for twelve in six minutes, that's all."

"Maggie, the coffee station is all set, and I just put out the juices, the caddies of preserves and jams, and the cereal canisters. Rachel got the fruit trays ready, and I—"

Maggie gripped her shoulder. "Please breathe. Sounds like you guys have things under control. Just let me wash up and I'll pitch in."

Rachel's inquiring gaze followed when she turned to the sink. "You both...I love you guys. You've done an amazing job. Everything's going to be fine. We just, well, we had an adventure last night."

"Never heard it called that before."

Maggie ignored her and dried her hands. "Retta took off at bedtime. She went all the way down to the docks and fell in." Laura gasped and Rachel straightened off the counter. "Yeah. Such miserable weather, and the harbor was nasty. It was a fright I never want to experience again. She would have drowned if Ellis hadn't swam out and saved her."

"Oh, my God. The poor thing." Laura hurried to Retta's empty dish and filled it. Retta trotted in at the sound.

"She's okay now?" Rachel asked.

"It took a while, but yes. She slept a lot."

Rachel raised an eyebrow. "Where? You two on Ellis's boat?" Maggie nodded, and opened the fridge for the fruit trays. "Ah. I guess that explains the scrubs."

Maggie pivoted with a tray in each hand and Laura took them away. Knowing Rachel watched her every move, Maggie focused on starting muffins.

"I'd tell you that we were soaking wet, but you'd take that wrong."

"Wrong? Tell me you two kissed and made up for lost time—all night."

"It was just so late..."

"Of course. Too late to come home, even when breakfast prep begins at six o'clock. I get it."

"I'm really sorry, Rach. I know you're leaving this afternoon and I should have been here, should have let you sleep late. I-I overslept."

Rachel pulled Maggie from the counter and hugged her. "Your hair's a sight and the scrubs are too big and you're glowing." She squeezed her hard and whispered. "You didn't sleep a wink and I'm thrilled for you."

Maggie felt her cheeks flush. "She actually takes my breath away."

"I'm guessing you stole hers, too."

"Stop. My face is burning."

"I forgive you for not calling. Sure, I could've done without Laura banging on my door in a panic at six a.m., but I understand."

"You're the best, you know." She kissed Rachel's cheek. "Poor Laura. She's never had to use her key to get in. God knows what she thought."

"And your car was here, but she got no response at the door to your suite, not even a bark from Retta. The lights were still on in your office and all of them in the common room. I think she thought you'd been abducted."

"When Ellis called and said she'd found her, I just flew."

"I was too buzzed to notice anything last night. Good thing for Laura I was upstairs this morning. Next time, she'll catch on."

"This won't happen again, Rach. I can't be irresponsible."

"You know what I mean. Y'think this could become a 'thing' between you? Or do you dare?"

Maggie sighed and backhanded a loose wave off her forehead. If only the answer to Rachel's question was automatic. But things weren't that simple, not if Jill McGee arrived in three weeks with purchase papers to sign. Long-distance relationships generally sucked, so a simple summer fling did seem like the logical resolution. *Since when did logic ever feel right?*

What felt right was speaking from the heart, sharing in their affection for Retta, standing together in the rain, taking a mutual pride in this house…

What felt right were those powerful arms around her, the ardent kisses that left her weak and willing, the strong, magical fingers so deep inside. And she could still feel Ellis tremble, still taste her surrender. They'd claimed each other, come together, vigorously enough to bring a concerned Retta to the bedside. No, they hadn't slept, just drifted through a dream, happily insatiable.

Maggie took a breath for composure. Just remembering their mutual orgasms started her heart racing all over again—until Rachel set a hand on her shoulder.

"Anything you want to talk about?"

Maggie forced a smile. "No, but I probably should." She poured batter into muffin tins and slid them into the oven.

"Let's do a late lunch downtown. My boat leaves at five thirty, so I'm spending my last day on the beach."

"How about we head to the ferry early, like three, and hang out? You'd like Dell's. And the steamship comes in right there, so no rushing required."

"It's a plan, but find a block of time to rest. If you're going to figure out how to finish what you've started, you'll need to grab some sleep."

❖

Ellis finished screwing hinges on a three-foot-square board she'd attached to the step box. Retta needed a landing of sorts, a way on and off the *Rose*, and being lifted over the side each time just wasn't practical. And it seemed likely that she and her mom would be visiting more often. *Funny that you're hoping for it.*

She swung the board up and it sat on the gunwale, nicely level, and she hooked the attached chains to the box on the deck. "Goddog." She grinned as she tested the arrangement, stepping up, then onto the little landing, and down the other side onto the pier. "Piece of cake, Retta."

"Who's Retta?" Tug Whitley asked.

Ellis hadn't noticed his approach and now wished he'd leave her to her musing. "A chocolate Lab."

"Ah. Pretty clever. You can fold that up and out of the way, huh?"

"Yeah." Ellis walked back up, over, and down onto the deck, and unhooked the chains. When she hauled the step box aboard, the miniature landing folded flat against it. *And no, you're not invited.* "I thought about buying ladders, but it was simpler to work with what I already had."

"Cheaper, too. Pinchin' pennies just like your old man." Conversation with Tug was always tedious, and she definitely wasn't in the mood to discuss money or her father. "So, I heard your saw running earlier and wondered what you were up to now. You thinking of taking on passengers? I know you scooped up that Tuck'r Inn cruise I couldn't do."

"You worried about competition?" She knew he was. *There's only one person I'd...* She straightened abruptly and stared out at the harbor. *Really? Would I?*

"Oh, hell no," he went on. "I got a pretty good deal going with them right now, big money for just a few hours every once in a while." He stuffed his hands into his pockets and rocked back on his heels, confident and cocky. "I'm telling you, folks come over, they set up shop, and they'll pay anything to keep their little pipe dreams afloat. Y'know what I'm sayin'?"

"I guess, sometimes." Maggie had hired him, but Ellis hated seeing her fit his scenario.

"You guess? Shit, Ellis. You know damn well what losing a business feels like. It's probably why you're always pinchin' those pennies. You know 'desperate' better than anybody." Ellis opened a can of sealant and began coating her project. If only the brushing would drown him out. The man never knew when to shut up. "I'm telling you, dealing with that newbie is paying off hook, line, and sinker, you could say." He laughed at his words.

"That so?"

"The Tuck'r Inn." He held up a meaty hand and signaled money by rubbing his fingertips with his thumb. "Tuck'r right here, baby. Four runs already and the woman doesn't have a clue. And she's about due to come calling again. By October, I'll be ready to book that Vegas vacation I've wanted for so long. Pretty sweet, huh?"

Ellis concentrated on the toxicity of the sealant, the coverage of each brush stroke, and tried not to explode. "You *really* are taking her for a ride."

Tug laughed roundly. "A ride. That's a good one." He tossed a hand at her. "But, eh, y'know everything's a write-off in that business, anyway. Lots of ways to pinch pennies, right?" Finally, he stopped staring at her work and stepped away. "Okay. Time to go. See you 'round."

"See you." She watched him saunter down the dock and almost hurled her brush at him. "Such a dick."

She couldn't finish the sealant job fast enough. She needed to walk. It was either that or head out to sea. Her mind, her stomach, her sex pulsed with thoughts of Maggie, and she needed space to function clearly. *Jesus, Tug. You're a total ass. At least her first cruise didn't go into your Vegas fund.*

The fact that Maggie had succumbed to Tug's price gouging four times did, indeed, attest to her desperation. It made Ellis question Tuck'r Inn's financial stability and how much of a battle Maggie currently fought behind her sunny disposition and her easy, infectious laugh. Maggie agonizing over a crushed dream was painful to picture—even if it *did* involve the Captain Pratt House. But Tuck'r wasn't just a business. It also was Maggie's home, and defeat could cost her both at once. *At least I had the* Rose.

Her supplies stowed away, and showered and dressed presentably, Ellis strolled along the waterfront and, as usual, took in far more than what the tourists captured with their cell phone cameras. She saw more than what serious photographers shot, beyond what visionary painters stroked onto canvas near the docks. Somehow, thinking about Maggie, interacting with her, had become special unto itself, and thoughts of the Captain Jacob Pratt House had faded into minor status. She'd once thought that impossible, that she deserved the added shame should she ever relegate the loss of home and legacy to an afterthought.

However, Maggie had changed things. She'd given the Pratt House a new name, true, but more importantly, she'd restored its vigor and honored its character. She'd lent her irrepressible energy to make it happen, and Ellis knew just from her brief tour of Tuck'r that the energy inside was palpable. Through Tuck'r, the Pratt House would never be anyone's afterthought, as long as Maggie was at the helm.

Ellis pushed open the door to Dell's and shivered in the air-conditioning as she headed for a stool at the bar. A hearty sandwich and a beer would serve her well into the evening, and maybe she'd take the *Rose* out for a spin. *You've got me feeling pretty lighthearted, Maggie Jordan. Are you busy tonight?*

Across the room, Maggie put down her drink and touched Rachel's hand. "Hey."

Rachel followed Maggie's line of vision. "Whoa. No way. That's her?" She turned back and winked. "I *have* seen her on the ferry. *Very* nice, big sister. Go. What are you waiting for?"

"One of the first times we spoke was right here, back in the spring. We didn't even know each other's names then."

"Can't say that anymore."

Maggie took a large swallow of her drink and knew she was in trouble. Intense arousal less than twelve hours old had her shifting in her chair. "God. She rocks a tight T-shirt, doesn't she?"

"Jesus, Maggie. I'm straight, not blind. Now, get over there."

"I'd like her to join us. Do you mind? She's kind of the quiet, reserved type, though. Such an intrepid spirit, and I think being at sea is to blame. I can feel that with her."

"That's what you feel?"

"Cut that out. I'd like you to meet her." Maggie pushed back in her chair. "I want to introduce her to you. Would you like to meet her?"

Rachel giggled. "You're a babbling ditz. You have sex with a handsome dyke all night on a boat and you ask if I want to meet her? Too much."

Maggie lowered her voice to a hush. "We did *not* have sex all night. Just…all morning." She grinned and set off for the bar.

Walking up behind Ellis, Maggie struggled to keep tactile

memories at bay. Just the look of Ellis's shoulders, her arms, her hand on her glass, churned rousing sensations in her depths. She placed her fingers on the back of Ellis's neck, stroked the dark hair at her collar.

"Hi."

Ellis turned on her stool. "Maggie!" She shot to her feet and took Maggie's hand, her pleasure drawing Maggie closer. "It's so good to see you." She surveyed Maggie from head to toe, shook her head, and sent her a sly look. "Jesus, you're a wicked temptation."

Maggie had just regretted throwing on a halter top and cutoffs to go out with Rachel, but Ellis's unabashed appreciation changed all that in an instant. The examination intensified a hunger for contact that she found hard to resist. Earlier today, they'd resisted nothing and gloried in every second. She squeezed Ellis's hand and grew a little weak when Ellis entwined their fingers. *Your fingers are magical, you know.*

"And you clean up *so* well, Captain Chilton."

Still holding hands, Ellis rested on her stool. "I was just thinking about you, trying to decide when would be good to call—and not come off like some…"

Maggie stepped between her legs and combed her fingers through Ellis's hair. "Never worry about that. Please call anytime." Ellis reached to her face and Maggie's eyes closed at the tenderness in the strong hand on her jaw. She yielded without reservation when Ellis drew her in and kissed her.

The bustle of the bar, patrons nearby, even Rachel, who she knew watched from afar, vanished as she dissolved into Ellis's kiss. A full-body rush urged her to lean in, lose herself in Ellis's mouth, and if Ellis hadn't inched back, she would have.

Warm, hushed words feathered against her lips. "Maggie. I melt when we do this." She pressed a light kiss to Maggie's lips, and lingered *not long enough* before withdrawing.

"Your kisses make me crazy," Maggie whispered. "You…God, not here." The light in Ellis's eyes offered something Maggie didn't dare consider at the moment. Rational thought was abandoning her fast. "I'm here with my sister," she managed, and found herself tracing Ellis's jawline with a fingertip. "Say you'll join us."

Ellis thought she'd probably follow Maggie anywhere at that moment. She left cash on the bar and let Maggie lead her across the room. The bright-eyed younger woman at the table set down her drink as they arrived and extended a hand.

"Hi, Ellis. I'm Rachel, the cute one."

"Hello, Rachel." Ellis shook her hand and took a seat next to Maggie. "I hope I'm not interrupting sister talk."

"We're just killing time before I catch the next boat."

Ellis checked her watch. "Just a half hour? I'm sorry you're leaving so soon."

"Oh, please. She's been here for *days*," Maggie said and rolled her eyes.

"You're going to miss me, you know. I even left you the recipe for Grandma's scones so your guests can have something *good*."

"You had no trouble devouring everything I made. Such a troublemaker."

Ellis enjoyed the jibing between them and saw the resemblance in more than just their rich auburn hair and athletic figures. Their lively, affectionate spirit created the same relaxed comfort she derived from Maggie's company.

"Ellis, have her make you cinnamon scones. They're to die for. I dug out the recipe this morning, and she wasn't through the door a second before she was swooning over them."

Maggie shook her head. "No telling tales, Rachel."

"Oh, wait," Rachel said and put a finger to her temple. "Come to think of it...Maybe it wasn't the scones that had her swooning when she got in." Ellis grinned. Maggie sat back and growled, but Rachel continued, undaunted. "Yeah, I guess coming home at seven in the morning after—"

"Will you shut up?" Maggie turned to Ellis. "How soon will the *Eagle* get here?"

Ellis shook her head and caught Rachel's eye. "I happen to know that your sister is a terrific cook." She looked directly at Maggie. "I'd eat your scones any day."

Rachel hooted.

Maggie playfully slapped Ellis's arm. "Do *not* encourage her."

Rachel shrugged. "Encourage what? I have to charge up on all this fun, take it home with me to spark up my humdrum life. The ferry rides," she winked at Ellis over the rim of her glass, "they're my wilderness adventures, and visits to Nantucket energize my creative juices. It's all good."

"Somehow, I doubt your life is boring."

"Hey, I sculpt in the nude for a reason."

Now Ellis laughed. "Isn't that a little dangerous?"

"Don't believe a word," Maggie said. "Rachel is an accomplished sculptress. She lives in Hyannis and her work is currently showing at galleries in Provincetown and Rockport. In fact, she's been invited back to P-town next summer."

Rachel waved away the praise, and Ellis liked her even more because of it. Much like her sister's, Rachel's direct manner was refreshing.

"How is it, working on the ferry? Have you done it long?"

"Ten years or so. Our crews are great, and there's really never a dull moment with the passengers. Nantucket Sound is a busy place for traffic and weather and keeps us on our toes."

"Do you meet famous people? Hey, I bet storms are scary. How about emergencies out on the ocean?"

"Yes, to all of that. But the best times are glassy waters on warm, sunny days, especially around Nantucket. When you can feel it all soothing your soul, you know you're in a good place."

Rachel seemed to consider that and grinned at Maggie. "I always knew real sailors were romantics."

Maggie threaded her fingers through Ellis's on the table. "This one is."

Maggie's eyes wandered over her profile, absorbing, touching. Ellis could feel their heat. *Or maybe I'm blushing.* She faced Maggie silently for an extra second, admired the delicate features, the naked honesty she had seen in last night's dim light. *I want you right now.* She squeezed Maggie's hand and Maggie squeezed back.

Ellis inhaled a steadying breath. "Let me buy us one more round. We have time."

She caught the quick, telling look between the sisters and wondered if she passed muster. Unquestionably, Maggie's opinion of her mattered more. After last night, there was no doubt of their physical compatibility, the pleasure each could provide, but here in the light of day, this had all the makings of "serious," and Ellis knew she'd have to face it head-on.

Maggie made her open up, think about heretofore risky things, like home, her life, her heart. Already, Ellis cared whether Maggie smiled, fulfilled her dream, and kept her dog happy. *No question, something in the universe has shifted.* She feared the quick decision, had learned the merits of thorough consideration the hard way. *It pays to put in the time.* Her father never would have imagined she'd apply his lesson to romance. *Yes, time will tell.* Something told her she couldn't afford to fail. Not again.

CHAPTER TWENTY-ONE

Maggie flung Retta's Frisbee back toward the house. Twenty minutes of this in the afternoon sun had brightened Retta's day, but not hers.

She could still see the number forty-eight burned into her mind from her bookings calendar and wished she had a mental screensaver to erase it. Or a magic wand to turn it into ninety-eight or eighty-eight. Sixty-eight, for that matter. And she hated losing a three-room booking referred to her from a satisfied guest. *I'm sorry, but Tuck'r no longer offers that sightseeing package.*

Retta dropped the disc at Maggie's feet and backed up, ready.

"Do you know your tongue's almost on the ground? Come on. We need water. Well, you do. I could use something stronger."

This emotional roller coaster is going to kill me. Finishing the weekend with a dinner date and then extracurricular activities on the *Rose* had been heavenly. God knows—and she had called that name several times—Ellis had been heavenly. But the first few days of the week had been a chore, lightened only by a few fog-impaired, scratchy minutes on the phone with Ellis yesterday. And today was the worst yet, losing that pricey referral. No matter how many hoops she offered to jump through, having no "Tuck'r Inn cruise package" had been a deal breaker.

The "newbie blues," she thought, weary of the ups and downs. *If Cavanaugh Resorts wants no part of them, then what?* She dreaded starting the peddling process all over again. Hooking Cavanaugh's interest in Tuck'r had taken five months and travel and materials money she no longer had. She considered seeking Ellis's opinion, laying all her cards on the table, and then cringed at the thought. They certainly had a good thing going, summer fling or whatever this was, and she didn't want to spoil it, not now that lone wolf Ellis Chilton had opened her big, soft heart. But was it too late to appear anything but some conniving opportunist who "doesn't have a clue and just fumbles around"? One of *them* who hits and runs—in *her* house, no less?

She looked past the red geraniums in the window boxes to the second floor and the new shutters, the attic and the re-pointed chimney, whose bricks had been purposefully selected. So much work, so much invested.

"Who wouldn't want a gorgeous place like this?" she asked as Retta drank from her bowl in the shade. "We've put everything into it." They walked out to the front yard, among the flowering shrubs. "Tuck'r really is pretty, isn't it, sweetie?" She patted Retta's head. "Thank you for not digging everything up."

Retta dashed back for her Frisbee, and Maggie bent to smell the roses at the corner of the porch.

You know there's still one alternative. The idea of keeping Tuck'r for herself had taken root in the back of her mind a month ago, but she hadn't had the nerve to banish *or* nurture it. The former could cost her dearly; staying the course with this flip project could mean crippling financial loss and starting anew with something simpler. The latter would mean the end of her career, and she'd struggled for years to be where she was now. *Which is...where?* She knew a life-changing event loomed. She just hoped she had the strength to handle it.

"Hey, Maggie." Laura held the screen door open and waved her inside.

Something had the common room alive with light chatter, and Maggie thought it a little odd that guests lingered inside on such a gorgeous afternoon. She stepped in, and the friendly activity, the homey atmosphere enveloped her. *It should feel this way all the time.*

Four guests stood in a semicircle, talking to someone near her office door. Several others sat with tourist brochures in hand, trading suggestions from one sitting area to another. Maggie sent Laura a curious look, but Laura simply nodded toward the office. When the semicircle opened, Maggie spotted what—who—had captured their attention, and her jaw dropped.

Ellis hung up the tintype of Captain Pratt by the doorway.

You're here. Here. And on a weekday?

Retta bounded across the room and Ellis crouched to receive her.

Maggie closed in on them. "Captain Ellis Chilton. Well, I'll be."

A young boy dropped to his knees to pat Retta. "Hi, Ms. Jordan. Me and Dad are going to the museum today. Captain Ellis's family has stuff there."

"Is that right?" She raised an eyebrow at Ellis. *Not so haunting now, is it?*

"Yeah," he answered. "Look at this." He yanked a battered Nantucket Whaling Museum brochure from his shorts pocket and pointed at the photos of artifacts.

"The museum is a blast, Jeremy," Maggie said. "They have tons of cool stuff. Too bad we can't take some home, huh?"

"I know." He turned to Ellis. "You had some right here, though."

Ellis grinned. "Yes, right here. When I was your age, I used to take things off the walls to play with—and got yelled at every time. They were antiques. Some were older than my grandfather, so they went to the museum for everyone to see and learn how life used to be in the old days."

Jeremy pivoted slowly to check out the common room's heavily beamed structure and its many decorations, the reprints of historic paintings, replicas of Nantucket's lightship baskets. At last, he turned back to the tintype. "That's real, right?"

"It is," Maggie said and sent Ellis a dubious look. "I suppose it should be in the museum, too."

Jeremy looked concerned. "Yeah, 'cause people who don't stay here won't see him."

"Good point," Maggie said. "I'll give it some thought, but I'd *really* hate to part with the picture. After all, this was Captain Pratt's home." She looked at Ellis. "And he should always have a place here."

"That's hard to choose, I guess." Jeremy stuffed the brochure back into his pocket and patted Retta's head again. "Bye, Retta. See you after supper. We're going to the museum now." He backed away, looking up at Ellis, wide-eyed and a bit enchanted. "Thanks, Captain Ellis." He grinned and saluted before running off.

Maggie shooed Ellis through her office into her bedroom and shut the door.

"To what do I owe the *extreme* pleasure of your visit? *Here*, of all places?"

Ellis took her hands and drew her in. "I traded a shift with someone who needed my Saturday off, and...I-I couldn't get you off my mind. Beautiful day, beautiful woman."

"I'm thrilled you're here. I hope it wasn't a tortuous decision."

"Valium helped."

"Right."

"Really, I *have* done a lot of thinking. It's been too long since I dealt with the past." She set her forehead to Maggie's. "You make so many things easier. Because of you, I now take more cold showers than ever. They keep me from overheating."

"God, you've made my day." Maggie slid her arms around Ellis's neck and settled against her chest. "I needed this badly." She brushed her lips across Ellis's mouth and welcomed a slow, languorous kiss.

"Hard day for you?" Ellis nuzzled Maggie's jaw.

"Mmm. Damn business numbers."

Ellis drew back just enough to study her face. "Business is slow?"

Maggie almost sighed at the compassionate look. "Could be a lot better, but you don't need to concern yourself with that. You're *here*. I'm so glad you even wanted to step inside again. I'd hoped you would."

"Coming up the front walk took a little courage, but I wanted to see you. Here. See you surrounded by pieces of my life and the magic you've performed on them. I hadn't been through the front door one minute before I noticed how good I felt inside. No sadness or regret, no…shame. Just an affection, a pride I hadn't expected."

"God, I love hearing you say that. It makes me so happy."

"You did it, Maggie, settling in here. You're responsible, and it feels *right*. I'm grateful."

Withholding her own intimate truths tightened Maggie's throat. She couldn't deny the pleasure of having Ellis in the house, in her arms. She could feel a rejuvenation in her that Maggie was proud to have invoked, but she couldn't match Ellis's signature honesty.

You think I've "settled in here," Ellis? Yes, it feels right to me, too, more so every day, but…If I leave you with anything when this summer ends, I hope it's the bright, positive outlook I see in you right now.

Ellis lifted Maggie's chin. "Those business numbers have gotten to you, haven't they?"

Retta barked at the door and Maggie stepped away to let her in. *Damn, this is hard. And it's starting to show.* Retta hurried to Ellis and dropped a stuffed duck at her feet.

"Oh, she's happy now." Maggie pecked Ellis's cheek. "Come on. There's fresh lemonade in the fridge."

Ellis gladly picked up the toy and followed, Retta, ever alert at her side.

To Ellis, Retta appeared more jovial than her owner today, and she thought it peculiar. Ellis always enjoyed observing Maggie in action, the lively, positive attitude and energy she put into doing the simplest things, but now, watching her take the pitcher from the fridge and fetch glasses from the cabinet, something seemed *off*. Maggie hadn't responded to her query about the business. She'd avoided it, in fact.

Is Tuck'r in trouble? It's impolite to ask.

Recalling Maggie's words about first-year struggles, she wondered how challenging things had become, and if the rest of the season looked as dark. *The foreboding pressure of defeat will eat you up.* Maggie didn't deserve to see all she'd invested go for naught. Neither did the house, and Ellis just *couldn't* picture it shuttered again, hoping yet another owner with equal passion would miraculously appear. *Too bad my credit history precedes me, even today. There's no way I could help.*

But Tug Whitley, of all people, sprang to mind, and through her irritation with him, she saw Maggie pouring vital funds into the harbor.

She accepted the lemonade with a distant smile. "Could we sit out back for a few? I know you're probably busy, and I shouldn't keep—"

"Not at all," Maggie said. "I have to whip up some goodies later, but the afternoon looks quiet." They sat beneath the patio umbrella and Retta stretched out in the shade. Maggie pressed a hand to Ellis's on the table. "Stay for dinner. Let me wow you with steak."

"You wow me, period," Ellis said, impressed by Maggie's noble attempt to lighten the mood.

"You're too charming for my own good. Stay, won't you? I've got you here and don't want you to go." She grinned at her own statement and quickly looked down into her glass.

"I'd like that very much. Thank you." *I don't want to go, either. We can do so much for each other.*

She pulled her chair closer and leaned on her knees. Retta scrambled from beneath the table, eager to play, and Ellis scratched the top of her head. "Not right now, pretty girl." Retta's perked ears flattened. Maggie looked on fondly, maternally, as Retta lay back down.

"Maggie, look at me." Ellis trailed a finger along the inside of her knee. "I know when something's wrong, when trouble's brewing. I've spent my life on the ocean, remember? And I'm used to the law of the sea, which is to offer help unconditionally. If you're in need, I hope you'll let me know."

Maggie took Ellis's hand and squeezed. "I don't know how or why fate threw us together…You're remarkable." She pressed forward and kissed her. "Yes, you might say the sea's a bit rough right now, but I refuse to burden you with business issues. I'm just embarrassed that my concern is showing, and I apologize for worrying you." She squeezed again. "You're so sweet to think of me."

"Could I make a friendly suggestion?"

"Feel free any time."

"Stay away from Tug Whitley."

Maggie chortled. "Oh, trust me. Already done. I'm through with that pirate. I might have nipped a hand that fed me, so to speak, because I think the cruises were catching on, but he's—"

"Yes, he is. Now…please listen. I've been thinking. What if *we* worked something out, you and I, the weekend cruises like you asked a while ago?" Maggie sat back as if shoved. "Not huge mobs of people, mind you, but…Would that help?"

Maggie shook her head. "The *Rose* is your little piece of paradise. You haven't thought it through, Ellis. I know there's a lot to it." She combed her fingers through Ellis's hair. "God, you're so kindhearted. I had no right to ask, back then, and I've always felt bad about it."

Ellis clasped Maggie's hands on her knees. "Look what you've done for me, where I am." She tipped her head toward the house. "I *never* thought I'd be here again, never thought I deserved to be. I've spent years feeling sorry for myself, getting by instead of climbing out of the damn hole I dug, and then you and Retta come along and shake me out of it. I know what the fight is like when a dream trembles: you do everything you possibly can. So please don't feel bad about asking. I get it."

Maggie's eyes watered. "Are you for real, Ellis Chilton?"

"If you're game, I'm willing to try the cruises. Just go easy on me." She cupped Maggie's cheek. "Let's see how it goes for the rest of the season. How about until the end of September?" Maggie's incredulous expression grew, eyebrows rising, furrows forming across her forehead, and Ellis loved surprising her. "Maybe it'll work out and be worth promoting for next year, and maybe then I could recruit another boat to help during the week. On the other hand, if, by the end of September, I've become a raving lunatic and you, a bitchy boss, Tuck'r might need an entirely different scheme for next season."

Maggie stood abruptly, the excited glow on her face making Ellis's heart pound. Just like the wedding party cruise, Ellis thought, this was the right thing to do. *We've got what it takes to make it work.*

Maggie drew Ellis's head down with both hands. "You really are precious to me, you know? Cruise or no cruise, just that you'd offer... You're some kind of special, and I'm just crazy about you."

Ellis lifted Maggie off her feet as they kissed. She wanted the moment to last for hours. *Yes, I'm crazy about you, too.*

CHAPTER TWENTY-TWO

As the *Rose* silently drifted into its slip, Ellis tossed the bow line to Hank and jumped onto the dock to secure the stern.

"Thanks for the assist," she yelled, doubting he'd heard her.

"You get all your gear?"

"I did." She nodded, sure this time that he hadn't caught her words. Thankful the usual collection of boaters wasn't around to listen in on such a quiet Sunday afternoon, Ellis resorted to the raised voice she usually called on with him. "Wasn't happy with those old vests, so now I can keep them as spares. Oh, by the way, I picked you up a new extinguisher. Hang on a second."

"You what?"

She held up a finger for him to wait as she went back aboard and returned with a shiny fire extinguisher. "Here," she said, holding it out. "Now get rid of your clunker in the galley."

"For me? I got one."

"It barely passes inspection, and I don't trust it. This one's easier to handle."

He hefted the steel cylinder and set it at his feet. "Yeah, you're right. Thanks. I owe you."

"No, you don't. How long have we been looking out for each other?"

"Since you was a little thing. Your pop would be proud of you, y'know, looking after this old-timer. And now you're looking after the house, too."

Ellis shrugged. "Indirectly. I think things are working out."

"How many cruises have you done now, five?"

She held up four fingers. "They're *joyrides*, Hank. Just taking folks for little *joyrides*. Just *friendly favors*."

Hank scratched at his wooly face. "Right. Keeps things unofficial."

"You got it." She ripped cellophane off new life vests and stowed them away.

"She's a very nice young lady, Ellis. I'd be inclined to help, too." She made a face at him. "Oh, like you support another B&B on Nantucket."

"Well, she's awful pretty. She comes by in her shorts and sandals, those long legs, that silky hair breezin' all over the place. Lord, like some girl off a magazine cover."

"Stop already. I'm trying to concentrate."

He snorted. "You think all this you're doin' will make a difference, keep her place running? What if she can't swing it and bails out like so many do? You considered that?"

Ellis stood up and squinted at him in the late afternoon sun. "I've had a great day. Knock it off." She went back to work.

"Well, have you thought about it? You're busting your ass, working every day and then here, too, making sure everything's perfect. She's special, isn't she?"

"She is. We've grown kind of close."

"What? Have you fallen for her?"

"I said we're close." *Jesus, Hank. The whole waterfront can probably hear us.*

"Bah." He spit over the edge of the dock. "Close, my ass. I've seen you two all lovey-dovey on the bow in the moonlight, seen you walking the dog in the middle of the night."

"Okay, so your eyesight hasn't failed you yet."

"Just make sure yours don't. Is she part of some big conglomeration, testin' our waters? This her first B&B? Where's she from, anyway? You know all this about her? Or are you two just sowin' your oats?"

She slammed her hands onto her hips and scowled. "Anybody but you, I'd tell to mind his own damn business. For your information, she incorporated like any smart businesswoman or man should. And she's from Albany, originally, and used to be in finance in Philadelphia. Anything else you need to know, *Dad?*"

"Fine."

"And *another* thing. She's put her heart and soul into that house, real sweat and every last cent. It's beautiful."

"It's not your house anymore."

"I *know* that!" She paced to the stern rail and back. "It matters to me that she succeeds. I want…I want her to be happy there."

The words echoed in her head as Hank stared at her. Finally, he readjusted his cap and hitched up his pants, clues he was about to heave his worn, wiry frame into motion.

"Well," he stated, too loudly for the sentiment, "glad we settled that. Just lookin' out for you, girl." He waved good-bye with a raised palm and ambled off toward his slip, extinguisher under his arm.

"See ya, Hank!" He probably hadn't heard her, but it didn't matter. Their salutations were understood. "Gotta love him," she muttered and gulped down half a bottle of water. "I should be as feisty at his age." Hank's cantankerous spirit served him well, wasn't about to quit any time soon, and she treasured his well-intentioned, albeit *loud* harping.

He certainly means well, she thought as she prepped for an evening at Maggie's. *I do want her to be happy there. He got me to admit it—out loud, even. And that I'm in deep…with Maggie* and *Tuck'r. And I like it. You're a clever old salt, Hank Tennon.*

She pulled on her black jeans and chose a mint green oxford from the closet, hoping to prove she owned more than uniforms, tees, and shorts, and, yes, hoping Maggie liked what she saw. Over the past few weeks, these occasional pizza-and-movie evenings on the couch had become something special. No longer a stranger at Tuck'r, Ellis visited regularly on weekends and had come knocking several times after work.

She loaded two bottles of Maggie's favorite merlot into her backpack and checked to see she was on schedule to pick up the pizza. *Even picking up a damn pizza has me buzzed. Yes, Hank, she's pretty special.*

She ran her schedule through her mind as she strolled up Main Street, pizza in hand. Next Sunday, the *Rose* would host three elderly couples for a two-hour jaunt around the island. She grinned, remembering Maggie's delight at the little "landing" attached to the step box. It served more than Retta now, and guests certainly appreciated it.

Granted, the weather had cooperated to date, but the cruises had gone remarkably well, and Ellis actually discovered herself looking forward to them. They'd been relatively stress-free, easygoing sails, especially enjoyable with Maggie aboard, supplying refreshments. Ellis accepted little more in payment than what covered her expenses, but Maggie had insisted they revisit the issue if the package deals increased in popularity. That *was* the point, after all, and Ellis truly hoped the promotion would push Tuck'r into the black and keep it there.

"The alternative's not great," she muttered, turning the corner at Davis Street. *We've never talked about the "what if," Maggie. Would you throw in the towel like Hank said? After all this? I bet you'd stay, find work on the island. Hell, you'd be in demand as an interior decorator, that's for sure.*

She studied the house as she walked around to the back steps, and a guest she met on yesterday's cruise waved from a front window. She waved back, taken by the smile on the woman's face. *You've brought "home" back to the place, Maggie. As it should be. You wouldn't leave, would you?*

❖

The following week, Maggie sat on the back steps in the dappled mid-August sun and watched Retta retrieve the ball. Rachel's well-meaning interrogation continued in her ear.

"Rachel. I'm not detailing my sex life to you, so stop hinting." She threw the ball again, and Retta darted away.

"Well, I can tell you're happy."

"We're seeing a lot of each other these days, and my numbers are climbing."

"Number of orgasms?"

"Reservations, you twit. The seventh cruise is already booked, so I'm breathing a lot easier. I'm so proud of Tuck'r. Guests rave about it. I signed my third referral yesterday—for September. And this morning, I even booked a repeat from June. That one's for the Christmas Stroll. Can you picture that? Main Street, the shops, the sidewalks all decorated? Maybe even a touch of snow? How perfect does that sound?"

"Listen to you, rattling on. I'm happy for you, Mags. I guess Cavanaugh will be impressed."

"I-I think so. The package deal has made the difference. Ellis may have caught us in the nick of time. She handles the *Rose* as easily as a car, like it's second nature, never a flinch. And my guests just love her. She's a natural with them, so generous and helpful. She really is amazing."

"Uh-huh. You haven't told her, have you?"

Maggie's heart skipped. "We're taking things one day at a time."

"Margaret Jordan, my dear older, wiser, blind sister."

"Don't. I know." She took a ragged breath. Retta sat and leaned against her side. "It's hard to think about, let alone find the right moment, the right mood. Every time it comes to mind, I choke. I don't know which of us would be more unhappy."

"So what does that tell you? Your one-day-at-a-time thing isn't fooling anyone, you know. Ellis is doing this because she *really* cares—"

"She cares about seeing Tuck'r succeed. She wants to see the house—"

"Jesus Christ. Stop. You're being selectively stupid. The house is all *you*. She cares about *you*, and you better open your eyes—and your mouth—soon. Hell, I saw the sparks between you weeks ago at Dell's. Now, hearing about all this 'progress' you're making *together*, how happy you sound...You're nuts about each other."

Maggie put an arm around Retta's shoulders and hugged her closer.

"Mags, I know you. Ellis just might be a keeper and you know it and you're nervous. Running off to some new project isn't the way to handle this. You don't have to flip Tuck'r so fast. You don't have to flip it *period*, if you don't want to."

"I love Tuck'r," she whispered. She lowered her cheek to Retta's head, and Retta caught her chin with a quick lick. "We love it here, don't we, Retta?"

"I know you do. I'd give you a hug right now if I could."

"I've tried to imagine living here as the permanent innkeeper, but it's mind-boggling."

"Valentin Enterprises could hire someone to continue the flip projects while you turn Tuck'r into a full-fledged inn. You could cook to your heart's content. At the very least, becoming an innkeeper would be a long-term adventure, but you're bold enough to tackle it."

"As the innkeeper, I probably wouldn't have time for all the traveling or the design challenges. There'd be no more Philly."

"Nope. Just cobblestones, higher prices, and raw, wet winters."

"And beaches, tourists, and everybody knowing your name."

"And salt air, ferries, and Nantucket roses."

Maggie had to smile at that. "I'd miss one Nantucket rose in particular."

"You don't *have* to miss her."

"Already, there's so much I'd miss, Rach, and Ellis—"

"Answer me this: If there were no Ellis, would you still want to stay?"

"Jesus. You don't just throw your life up in the air because of a few dates. I know that." The word "but" almost came out. Maggie closed her eyes and tried to sort emotion out of rational thought. "Okay, so my first impulse was to say yes, I'd want to stay even without her. Nantucket's grown on me. I'm adapting to life here and I like it."

"Nantucket's grown on you in, what, about four months? A summer's worth of romance? Will you outgrow it just as quickly if the winter months are quiet, dark, and miserable—and you're single? Personally, I think you go for what matters most. If flipping Tuck'r will maintain that financial comfort and achievement that completes you, then that's the way to go. What Ellis could bring to your life is something only you can say. Either way, it's a risk. The time's come to weigh the pluses and minuses."

"This is all so new. Life here, a house that feels so much like home, growing so attached to someone. I'd leave so much behind."

"Then break it all down to the bottom line. Staying would require a significant career change, rooting yourself into a completely different lifestyle, and a woman you're nuts about as part of your daily life. Moving on from Tuck'r means continued professional challenge, an ever-changing environment, no roots, no house, no *one* tying you down. Freedom."

"How ridiculous is it to *want* to be tied down after building an exciting career? Is that the most immature thing ever?"

"No, not if that's what you want."

"I just don't know, Rach. God, I can't believe it's come to this. I never dreamed it would. But it all feels so…"

"Honey, hear yourself. The fact that we've been hammering at this subject and you're on the verge of tears should tell you that leaving Nantucket, Tuck'r, and Ellis isn't in your heart."

"I don't know if she'd want any part of me if I left."

"It may not be wise to base such a huge decision on a new romance."

"I know. You're right, but…but Ellis is special."

"Mags. Ms. High-and-Mighty is coming in a week or so. Whether you sign and move on now, or four years from now…or never, you have to get your head straight and make a decision."

"I will. Somehow." Her stomach coiled at the thought.

"Want me to come over? Just to be there with you? We could drink wine and repeat ourselves and you could cry and we could drink more wine."

"Sounds productive."

"She's due next Saturday morning, right? Pencil me into my favorite little room as of Friday. I'll be there."

CHAPTER TWENTY-THREE

Ellis stopped on the gravel walk, appreciating the view. A stiff Atlantic breeze crested the bluff and lofted Maggie's ponytail off her back, staggering her as she scanned the height of Sankaty Head Light through her expensive Nikon. This was probably her sixth or seventh shot, Ellis had lost track, but the tightest so far, and judging by Maggie's enthusiasm, it wouldn't be the last on this glorious Sunday afternoon.

Couldn't have chosen a finer day, Ellis mused, *even though we didn't sleep much last night.* Maggie had grilled an amazing salmon dinner on the *Rose* and they'd spent hours in bed before Ellis walked her and Retta home. And this morning, she woke wanting more, unable to resist calling with an invitation to brunch and an afternoon "out."

Ever the tour guide, Ellis pointed out historic landmarks and recounted legendary tales as they meandered around the island in her truck. Playing tourist from Dionis to Madaket to Cisco beaches had never felt this good, and Maggie's rapt attention, her desire for details, her hand on Ellis's thigh, made all the difference in the world.

Their visit to the intimate village of Siasconset, the island's most eastern point, included a swim and impromptu picnic on Low Beach, Retta's exploration of yet another shoreline, and ogling multi-million-dollar beachfront estates. Taking Maggie up to Sankaty Light stirred an odd pride, as if she were about to introduce her to a respected tribal elder.

Maggie set a palm on the brick base and looked straight up. "See these?" She suddenly turned to Ellis, face bright with excitement, and thrust out her arm. "Goose bumps. How can a lighthouse give you goose bumps?" She stared up at the lantern. "I'm in awe."

"They tend to do that, especially when you're close enough to touch them. From a distance at sea, they move you for different reasons."

Maggie surveyed the horizon, the seemingly endless ocean, vast and foreboding, from far left to far right. "I'm sure they do."

"One of a sailor's best friends, especially with those shoals." Ellis gestured offshore. "Tricky water. And Sankaty has been around since eighteen fifty, so it's seen serious service. If only it could tell the tales." She led Maggie by the hand to a permanent marker in the ground, and Retta bounded out of the sea grass and sat on it. "Hey, you." Ellis waved her off. "Not too long ago, Sankaty stood here, but erosion took over. Imagine moving that thing? It was quite a show."

"I can't imagine. It's so classic with its red waistband. Hope I can hang a really good picture of it at home."

Home. Once upon a time, I couldn't say the word, and now it sounds so perfect coming from you. Ellis slid an arm around her hips, a thrilling reflex every time.

Maggie frowned at the camera. "I hope I timed it right and captured the beacon when it rotated toward us." She flipped through images on the screen. "It's hard to see in daylight."

A burst of sandy wind roared up from the beach, and Ellis tucked Maggie in closer and turned them away from it. She looked back, over Maggie's head, and spotted Retta nosing along the fence.

"Retta, come! Away from the edge."

They watched Retta amble closer, in no hurry to obey.

"How bad is the drop on the other side?" Maggie asked. "If she got through—"

"You don't want to think about it." Retta strolled by, nose to the ground, and Ellis bent to peer at the camera images. Nearly cheek to cheek, she hummed with approval. "It *is* hard to be sure, but I think I see the beacon. This shot is the one."

"If not," Maggie began, and her voice dropped, "we can always try again."

Anytime, any place, Maggie.

"As often as you like."

Maggie rose onto her toes and kissed her. "I'd like often."

Ellis enclosed her within both arms, brought her mouth to Maggie's.

"I think you're an amazing woman. And so beautiful. Have I told you that?" She kissed each lip deliberately. "Your energy and spirit are such a joy, and the light in your eyes…it's as honest as your touch."

Maggie threaded her arms around her neck and returned the kiss with a fervor Ellis wasn't sure she could handle. At least not while standing. Maggie spoke against her mouth. "Kissing you, way up here, so exposed to all the elements...what a high. Just us on top of the world."

"You deserve that feeling, Maggie. You put so much care in everything you do, and I love that."

"You are just as special and I hope you know that. I see it so clearly. You deserve to be on top of the world, too."

Ellis flashed a look to the ocean before drawing Maggie into a hug. "I just might belong out there."

"Part of you, maybe, but the other part belongs here." She kissed Ellis's ear. "I love this feeling, up here with you."

Ellis squeezed her tighter. "You're a treasure to hold, Maggie, a treasure I take to heart."

Maggie kissed her neck and nuzzled into her chest. "God, Ellis, you...This is just perfect."

Distantly, Ellis heard the excited chatter of children, and then Retta barked, confirming they were no longer alone.

Back in the truck, Maggie sat closer as they rambled southward on Low Beach Road toward the village of Tom Nevers, and listened attentively to Ellis's tales of the Wampanoag tribe and early settlers of the area. Maggie commented often about the lay of the open land, its rolling hills and proximity to the shore, and seemed a bit disappointed to come upon modern subdivisions of homes. An "intrusion," she called it, and Ellis warmed at Maggie's protective reaction.

"I suppose we're lucky that zoning codes are so restrictive," Maggie observed, studying the array of pretty Cape Cod homes, clustered neatly so far from the bustle of downtown. "They could be everywhere on the island, and that would spoil it."

"Makes me smile," Ellis said, "that you appreciate the open spaces. Yes, *we* are very fortunate that so much foresight goes into Nantucket's development." She grinned as she turned westward and drove in the direction of Surfside.

The road soon turned to dirt and now offered only brush and pines, all naturally muted by the Atlantic's wind and salt. The sea was most temperamental here, on the island's south side, and mist wafted over them in sporadic puffs, forcing Ellis to clear the windshield intermittently. Fog would likely settle in, and she hoped to hold Maggie's interest on this long, deserted straightaway until the road opened to more rolling meadows. As a new islander, Maggie needed to experience the mystical, surreal beauty that fog lent Nantucket's varied landscape.

Maggie surprised her by edging away and leaning out the window. She inhaled with purpose, eyes closed against the mist. "The salt is heavy in the air." She took another deep breath. "But it's invigorating. There really is nothing like it."

Ellis drove onto a small patch of sand and shut off the truck. Only the occasional call of birds and the whirl of the wind could be heard, but she knew Maggie would soon pick up on another telling sound.

"It's close, isn't it?" Maggie asked, delight in her eyes.

Ellis pointed to the brush alongside the truck. "Very."

"Can we go look?" She draped her camera around her neck. "Is it safe?"

"Come on. Retta, you stay, pretty girl. We won't be long." Ellis went to the front of the truck and took Maggie's hand. "There's a narrow path of sorts over here."

She led them up the slight rise, along a vine-covered strip of sand, and around several pines not much taller than them. In less than a minute, she stopped and drew Maggie to her side, gripping her firmly around the waist.

Maggie's jaw dropped at the sight of the ocean below. Waves several feet high broke relentlessly, crashing with a steady cadence merely a hundred yards out on the beach. Thickening fog lessened the view somewhat, but there was no denying that Maggie felt the impact, the breadth of ocean to the east, south, and west.

"Wow. It's magnificent. To drive along that road and suddenly be hit with this is…powerful."

She wiped the salty mist off her face and took a half dozen photos before sliding an arm around Ellis and taking hold of her belt.

Ellis watched her marvel at the sea, and suddenly saw her in a much different setting, searching for a sighting, waiting. *You would stand on a widow's walk, scanning the horizon for the Rose. I know you would. And I would come home to you.*

Maggie jerked in surprise. "Look! A surfer!" She raised her camera and snapped several shots. "I'd heard about…I mean, I know we're close to Surfside, but—"

"Surfers go out all the time, even in hurricanes, which I think is courageous, maybe even brave, but not always too bright."

"This is just so breathtaking." She kissed Ellis quickly. "Thank you so much for bringing me here."

"Let's get back inside. It's getting wetter by the minute." She urged Maggie away from the edge and back to the truck.

Retta bounced on the front seat at their return, and Maggie coaxed her into the back and lowered the window halfway for her. Immediately, Retta stuck her head out.

"The fog comes in so quickly," Maggie said as Ellis drove on. "It must catch boaters by surprise."

"The recreational boaters it does, and that can be really bad news. If you make a living on the ocean, you're always on guard."

"Has it ever caught you?"

Ellis nodded. She had a very healthy respect for fog, but there was a magic about it that she'd never trust. It created impressionistic images that captured the imagination, and as long as you were on land, the fascination was innocent, enjoyable enough. At sea, however, fog rendered you helpless, and disregard of its potential could prove fatal.

"I've been caught many times," she said. "I used to like it when I was a kid. You have no worries because the grown-ups take care of things, but I eventually learned about the concern and the fear." She glanced at Maggie and found her looking on with great interest. "Confidentially, whether I'm on the *Eagle* or the *Rose*, this grown-up hates fog."

"Sounds scary."

"When it's like pea soup, it is. Worse than driving your car with your eyes closed. The traffic's not the same, granted, and you do have gauges to go by, but a mistake can be far more deadly. And collisions aren't the only fear. Out there, fog is a sea monster. You can be doing everything right and it'll…claim you."

Maggie stared forward and Ellis wondered what images were running through her mind. An all-too-familiar one ran through hers, and she considered speaking of it for the first time in years. *Because I can. She listens…and she cares.*

Maggie turned to her. "The most time I spent on a boat was getting Tuck'r established, all those trips here. A few of those crossings were awful." She laughed lightly. "One was so bad, I remember thinking of the *Titanic*—which was a very stupid thing to do. I worked myself up into a pathetic mess and spent most of the ride with my eyes closed and my phone's music blasting in my ears."

"Same Atlantic Ocean. We've had some wild rides on the *Eagle*, and the other ferries, but no icebergs, thank God. Only the occasional iced-in harbor, and, of course, the fog. It can take shape suddenly, from out of nowhere, especially out in the Sound, and can suck you out of blue sky and sunshine before you know what hits you."

She stopped the truck at an old split-rail fence, and they looked out over acres of sprawling meadow, more like moors in the heavy mist than rolling farmland. Ellis let Retta out to run around and slid back in behind the wheel.

"Nantucketters once had a great reputation as farmers. I'm no expert, by any means, but the fog also helps our growing seasons. Today, quite a few folks are bringing farming back. We have some outstanding growers on-island now, and it's heartwarming to see that happen."

"It did surprise me to see so much local produce for sale." Maggie lowered her window and shifted into position. "I've bought local right from the start, for the goodies Tuck'r offers and myself, of course, but if Tuck'r served meals, I'd go one hundred percent local. It's right *and* popular." She snapped pictures of scattered farm machinery, rusty and overgrown by tall grass, long since retired on the property. "Tuck'r needs at least one of these shots."

That's just part of what it's all about, Maggie.

"A far cry from the shops on Main, isn't it?"

"Oh, it is, yes," Maggie said, now gazing over her camera. "Far from the wharves, the souvenir stores, the traffic. It must be just extraordinary, living out here. An entirely different world."

"And the mist paints such an antiquated picture."

"An ethereal scene, through all this fog."

It pleased Ellis no end that Maggie shared her appreciation of this setting. They'd come back on a clearer day, she figured, when she could introduce Maggie to some of the landowners Ellis had known since childhood, and maybe get tours of these grounds.

Maggie raised her window and wiped the mist off her camera, while Ellis summoned Retta back to the truck. They drove on, Maggie settled in close, a hand again on Ellis's thigh.

"I never thought much about the role fog plays on an island," she said and cleared a lock of wet hair off Ellis's forehead with an attentive touch that made Ellis smile. "Silly to overlook it, because it affects everyone, everything. And when it's vital to stay connected to the mainland, I just can't imagine the challenge."

"It's rare that the Steamship suspends service. Smaller operators have it the hardest. They can't afford to *not* run, so sometimes they take risks."

"You and your father must have seen it all."

"Yes. My grandfather, and all the way back."

"Did you ever need a rescue?"

"Only once because of fog."

Maggie turned in her seat. "Really? Did you collide with someone?"

Ellis could feel the concerned look on her skin, and it made her heart pound. *Say it. You're in a good place, and strong enough to say it.* "No." She cleared her throat. "Not a collision, an accident. I lost my father overboard."

"Oh, Ellis!" Maggie's hand flinched on her leg.

"The boom broke free and hit his head. There...there was nothing I could do."

Maggie wrapped her fingers around Ellis's bicep and squeezed. "Jesus. I'm so sorry. I can't imagine..."

Ellis took a breath and drove by rote as the memory assaulted her. She was grateful for Maggie's touch, their connection. "He was knocked back just enough and he...he sort of crumbled over the side."

"Oh my God, hon." Maggie ran her other hand through Ellis's hair and cupped the back of her head. "And this was in the fog on a crossing?"

Ellis nodded. The direct question drew both image and emotion sharply to mind, but she found it easier to handle than couched queries of the past, and heard herself speak words that had choked her for years. "We were in some real soup and I was at the helm, trying to keep an eye on him." Her voice shook and she cleared her throat. "I wanted to go check that boom line, but he wouldn't let me. Stubborn old salt. He staggered just t-two steps, and I could tell there was blood all over his face. And...he was gone."

Maggie lightly touched Ellis's hand on the steering wheel. "Pull over. Right here."

Ellis did, glad to surrender control at this moment, and Maggie shifted the truck into park and released their seat belts. She pulled Ellis into a hug, and Ellis held on tightly, her throat clenched against tears that wouldn't come anymore.

Maggie's whisper warmed her cheek. "I want you in my arms, Ellis Chilton. You need this and I need to give it." She kissed Ellis's ear. "Thank you for sharing that with me. I'll bet you haven't voiced it in a long time." She pressed Ellis's head to hers. "Take a breath, please. It's okay. I've got you."

CHAPTER TWENTY-FOUR

Alone atop the Sankaty Head cliffs, Maggie knew this view could only be surpassed by that from the lighthouse towering over her shoulder. She took a companionable comfort in its presence, the red-banded sentinel just yards away, overseeing all, and she considered herself one of the luckiest people on earth at this moment. Everything she saw she received with humble gratitude and unexpected need.

Beyond the protective fence and the tall sea grass around her legs, land plunged away to a swath of cream-colored sand and miles of rolling ocean, gilded so brightly by morning sunshine, she squinted even through her sunglasses. A lone trawler, its color indiscernible in the shimmering light, crept forward in silence just offshore, and Maggie wondered how long it had been at sea, if it was coming home here or still had many miles to go. Wordlessly, she wished it safe travel. In a way, its journey felt like her own.

Morning errands had put her and Retta into motion early today, but something had drawn her back here, where Ellis had shown her the top of the world, and she'd answered the call without hesitation. She hadn't considered why or what her subconscious sought. This clear, infinite vision? The insistence of indomitable Atlantic wind? The fortitude and tenacity of the ocean itself? Maybe all of that, she thought, because already she could feel the empowerment in her spirit.

Retta barked from the car, impatient for a beach run, and Maggie obliged, still lost in thought, barely offering a word. She drove down to Low Beach Road and released Retta, and watched her romp from the parking area into the breaking waves. Leaning against the hood, Maggie closed her eyes to the sun and let the wind dot her cheeks with salty spray. Curious, she tried imagining this place, this pose in January. She almost shivered.

The ringing of her cell phone interrupted the moment, and Maggie scowled but knew better than to ignore a call from the house.

"Yes?"

"Sorry to bug you," Laura said, "but Ms. McGee just called to say she missed her flight and would be an hour late. Rachel said I should call you. I told her you'd check at the flight desk anyway, but she said you'd want to know right away."

Maggie grinned at the idea of Rachel making Laura deliver the news. Rachel had delivered enough last night, a lengthy and, for her, profound lecture about "the great decision," and they'd polished off two bottles of margarita mix in determining Maggie's future. That Rachel could lift her head before nine a.m. came as a surprise. *Love you, little sister.*

"Thank you both for the heads-up. I'll just run another errand, then, before heading to the airport."

"Okay. Oh, and remember you wanted to pick up those prints. They've been ready."

"I'm off to Straight Wharf now, Laura. Thanks. We should be in around eleven."

"Got it. Everything's under control here. All five parties are already out for the day, and Rachel just went to buy flowers. She's making centerpieces."

Maggie laughed. "Excellent. I'm glad she's assigned herself a project she doesn't have to think about. I'm sure she's nursing a headache."

"She made some green drink in the blender and says she's feeling better."

"Sounds like Rachel. Oh, please tell her not to move the centerpiece I made on the front table. I want those beach roses from the porch to make a statement. She's free to put others anywhere she wants."

"I'll tell her, but not to worry. We've already talked about them, and I told her how much Ellis loves them. Oh, my God. I almost forgot: she called right after you left, just to say good morning."

"I missed her?" Maggie checked and saw she'd missed the text to her cell. Automatically, she looked out at the ocean. *Damn. How far away did I drift?*

"Yeah. She's the sweetest. I reminded her that you have an important corporate lawyer-type coming. She said you told her you'd be busy, but I think she still sounded kind of disappointed. She may have said she'd stop by for a few minutes. She's got such a sexy morning voice, you know?" *It's sexy in the afternoon and evening, too, and in my head all the time. Especially now.* "Wait. Did you say she's coming by today?" She stood up and paced around the car. *I just need this weekend to send Jill on her way. Their paths never have to cross.*

"I think so, but she knows you're having company."

"Well, Ms. McGee has a full day scheduled for us, probably hours at the Atheneum, and then dinner tonight, so we'll be in and out. Plus, she mentioned beaching it tomorrow before she leaves, so—"

"Ellis will miss you all weekend. Maybe you could give Ms. McGee a tour of the waterfront and...sorta...go see the *Rose.*"

Maggie tried not to sigh into the phone. Laura meant well, and Maggie was moved by her determination to bring them together, but this weekend Laura needed to keep her scheming to herself.

"It's important that Ms. McGee gets a feel for Nantucket's history, Laura. As I've said before, her connections could serve Tuck'r well down the road."

"Sure, I get it. Like courting an ambassador."

"Exactly."

"Except I think *she's* courting *you.*"

Maggie chuckled for Laura's sake. "She can think what she wants." *Chances are good Jill McGee won't be courting me or Tuck'r or Nantucket, after our talk this afternoon.* "Going to run now. We'll be there soon."

A long piece of driftwood dangling from her jaws, Retta raced from the water to the edge of the parking lot and stomped in front of Maggie.

"Are you going to just pose or let me throw it?" Maggie grabbed the stick and hurled it back toward the wet sand. Retta dashed after it. "Ms. McGee may not fancy sharing a ride with a wet, sandy dog, Retta, even if you stay in the back. She's not really a dog person anyway."

Jill was all about high fashion, luxury accommodations, and profit. Maggie didn't dislike those things, except when the price was one's heart and soul, and she wasn't sure if Jill had either. She *was* sure, however, that her own heart and soul were quite content these days. They'd never been happier, in fact.

She'd blurted out that fact last night, after Rachel and the first pitcher of margaritas tore the admission from her subconscious. Yes,

Tuck'r was the house of her dreams. Yes, she'd nestled into the arms of this island. And yes, she'd found someone who mattered. And no, the sale of Tuck'r Inn was no longer on the table.

She'd tried to convince herself that Ellis wasn't the deciding factor, but when she thought long-term, and considered the possibility of failing at their relationship, she knew she'd ultimately sell Tuck'r and leave. An island offered a pretty shallow dating pool, as she'd once observed to Ellis, so her heart's chances at happiness here would be slim—especially if they ran into each other as often as they had months ago.

But this relationship *did* matter. They had potential and that excited the hell out of her, even more than converting Tuck'r into a full-fledged inn and becoming the resident innkeeper. She loved seeing Ellis at ease in a common room chair, loved falling asleep on the *Rose* with that mussed hair tucked into her shoulder, loved waking up to kisses on her neck and possessive hands on her body. She loved the combination of reserved strength and soft heart, and how Ellis had bravely let her in, past barricades built to keep emotions in as well as out.

She's invested in us, and I will do the same.

With four photographs from their island jaunt last weekend now matted and framed and situated where Retta wouldn't step on them, she parked at the airport and went in to greet Jill. One of only a dozen passengers, she would have been easy to spot without the custom sandals, capris, and gaudy dark glasses. Jill called Maggie's name from across the room and strode toward her with suitcase in tow and her purse and laptop case over her shoulder.

Maggie almost shook her head at the confident, rather smug air about her. *To think I nearly lost my mind, hoping to impress her.* She laughed inwardly at the comparison of clothing. She wore one of Ellis's sun-bleached blue T-shirts that read, "Ferries get you coming and going." *I'm a Nantucketter. I'm allowed.*

Arriving at Tuck'r, Maggie decided to deposit Jill at the front gate and not the driveway out back where, again, Jill would have to traipse through the kitchen. It was a purely selfish gesture, she thought, designed to leave Jill with a picturesque memory of the "profit center that got away," once this day was done.

Rachel looked up from the newspaper when Maggie entered the kitchen, headed for the fridge.

"I'm just going to put together a light lunch, some fruit, cheese."

"She's here, then."

"Laura's getting her settled upstairs."

"How'd she seem?"

"Upbeat as usual. She has every reason to be. I do feel bad about changing my mind so late in the game."

Rachel nodded, watching her assemble a platter of food. "Oh, it was late, all right. She'll probably be pissed that you've wasted her time, her entire weekend."

"It hasn't been easy. I've never made such a big decision."

"Well, don't burn the bridge, in case you want to tackle another project someday."

"I hear you. One step at a time, please."

"Take that step right away, Mags. Don't drag it out."

Laura joined them and took a glass from the cupboard. "Anyone else for iced tea? Ms. McGee would love to sit on the front porch with you."

Rachel sent Maggie an expectant look.

"Pour one for me too, then, please, Laura. I'll take all of this outside." She picked up the platter and drinks on a tray and found Jill lounging on the porch glider. "In case you felt like nibbling on something," she said, setting the tray down.

"How thoughtful. Thank you." Jill sipped her drink and leaned back in the glider. "So lovely, Maggie. Tuck'r is simply adorable. You've done wonders and should be very proud."

"Thank you. It's taken a lot of work, but all our guests love it. We already have quite a few bookings for next summer."

"Is that right? That bodes well, doesn't it?"

Maggie nodded. *Yes, it does*, she thought. *For me, not Cavanaugh Resorts.*

"I'd like to talk business sooner rather than later, Jill."

"Any time you're ready." She sat forward, smiling with anticipation.

They both turned as two guests entered the front gate talking brightly about last night's dinner date. They greeted Maggie when they reached the porch and took seats nearby. Losing the opportunity for business talk, Maggie assumed her role of hostess.

"Good morning, ladies. This is our newest arrival, Jill McGee of Baltimore. Jill, this is Lisa and Mellie Sanborne of Washington DC, just married in June."

They exchanged handshakes and Mellie snared Jill into a conversation about neighborhoods they had in common. Minutes ticked away as Maggie's anxiety grew, knowing she needed to take Jill aside for some serious discussion.

"Sorry to interrupt, ladies." Rachel spoke through the screen door. "Maggie, you have a call in your office."

"Excuse me," Maggie said. "My sister, Rachel. What would we do without sisters, hmm?" She stepped inside and found Rachel waiting at her desk. "What call?"

"No call. You've got to get on with it, not shoot the shit all day."

"Rachel. I'm working on it."

"Right. Take her for a walk. Go to Dell's, the beach, somewhere, but start talking."

"Please stop eavesdropping and back off." She spun away, her mind a jumble of half-formed ideas. Outside, Jill sat alone, gliding gently in the warm breeze. *Thank God they moved on.* "Sorry about that. Listen, I'm bound to get more interruptions if we stay here, so let's take this someplace else. I'll treat you to a real lunch at the Met. It's not far from here at all. Well, actually, very few things are."

Jill laughed lightly as she rose. "Hey, anyplace you want, count me in." She winked and went back inside. "Just let me get my purse."

"Laura?" Maggie called as she entered the kitchen. "Ms. McGee and I are taking off for the afternoon. We're all set for the rest of today, aren't we?"

"Yup. You're good to go. And Rachel said she'd be around if I need an extra hand."

"Okay, thank you. And about tonight…Rachel might have plans, and Ms. McGee and I will be going to dinner—"

Laura leaned close and whispered, "Is she taking you out?"

"Treating me to dinner, yes," Maggie whispered in kind. "She has her heart set on the Brant Point Grill, so I'm *not* complaining."

"No way? At the White Elephant? That's serious *date* dining."

"Strictly business dining." Maggie jabbed Laura's arm playfully. "So tonight, if you want, you're welcome to come back and mind the store—on me, of course. I'm sure it will be just another quiet night, but if Rachel's going to be out, too…I'll leave it up to you."

Retta rocketed into the kitchen, barking at the rhythmic knock on the door. Laura followed sleepily, cursing Retta's not-so-subtle approach. Rachel hurried in behind her.

"By the looks of you all, I woke up the house." Ellis bent and patted Retta, who ran off in search of a toy. "Do you always answer the door so fast?" She laughed. "I saw you through the window."

"Come in," Rachel said. "I was just on my way out. Saturday night bands at the RC draw great crowds, too hot to miss. Laura and Retta were out front, reading. They're babysitting Tuck'r."

Retta ran back with the toy seagull and Ellis ruffled her ears. "What were you reading, pretty girl? *How to Master Humans?*" She looked from Laura to Rachel. "Maggie's out, I take it."

"Sorry, Ellis," Laura said. "That Jill McGee woman took her out to dinner."

"Ah. Hey, you do what you've got to do for business, right? Duty calls."

Rachel smirked as she slipped into a cropped leather jacket. "So they say. Listen, I've got to fly. Maybe I'll catch you tomorrow afternoon before I leave." She surprised Ellis with a quick hug. "Maybe *I'll* get a tour of your *Rose* sometime."

"Anytime, Rachel. Have fun tonight."

Bringing over the cookie jar, Laura wore a hapless look that Ellis didn't understand.

"Would you like some? I mean, you're welcome to stay a while, if you like." Retta nudged Ellis's thigh with the toy gull. "See? She wants you to stay."

"Thanks, Laura, but none for me this time." She kissed the top of Retta's head and threw the seagull into the laundry room. "I will steal a glass of water, though."

"Sure." She had a tall glass, complete with ice cubes, in Ellis's hand in seconds.

"Everything okay here tonight? Nice and quiet?" *Is it my imagination or are you severely distracted?*

"Ah, yeah. Everybody's out."

Ellis sat at the table and ran a palm over the familiar surface. "So...Jill McGee, huh? Do you like her?"

"She's all right. A bit stuffy, I think, kind of stuck on herself."

"Sounds like big-league business."

"Yeah. She's a corporate lawyer from Baltimore. And she's well-to-do, as they say."

"I see."

"She was here in July, too." Laura leaned against a chair and fumbled with a button on her blouse. "I guess she couldn't wait to come back, considering she originally planned to be here in September."

"Well, I imagine Tuck'r has that effect on guests, right? They hate leaving, so it's no surprise they hurry back. That's good to hear."

"She took her to the White Elephant tonight."

Laura's rambling took Ellis back. "Well, well. Nice dinner." Looking rather constrained, Laura only nodded. Ellis struggled to read between the lines. "Well, I hope Maggie orders the most expensive thing on the menu. I would."

"They have al fresco dining...under the stars."

"Yes, I know. *Very* pretty setting. Great ambience."

"Aren't you even a little upset?"

"That some businesswoman took Maggie to dinner? Wouldn't be too fair of me, now would it? Is there some reason I should be?"

"Well...I'm really not sure."

"Does Maggie like this woman?"

"You mean *like* like? Well, Maggie's all about promoting the business, but Jill likes her a lot. Rachel thinks so, too, and...and we don't like it."

Ellis smiled into her glass as she drank. *Devoted allies.*

"I'm sure Maggie will tell us all about her glamorous dinner tomorrow."

"That woman's not leaving until the last boat." Laura drifted to the counter, mumbling. "I hope she doesn't extend her stay." As if she finally heard herself, she looked over at Ellis and offered a sheepish smile. "I'm not being very mature. I'm sorry."

"Not to worry," Ellis said and fluffed Retta's ears. "Mom has things under control, doesn't she, pretty girl?"

Laura paced to the common room door and back. "No, I really am sorry. It's none of my business. Maggie's my boss and I have no right to butt in." She stopped and turned to Ellis. "You two are just perfect for each other."

Ellis wandered to the back door and patted Retta good-bye. "Thank you. I think so, too. I'm heading home now, but if you ever need anything here, don't hesitate to call. Okay?"

Laura nodded. She took a noticeable breath to calm herself. "Thanks, Ellis. You're the best."

For the beginning of the walk home, Ellis took a little amusement in Laura's fluster and tried to appreciate the emotional roller coaster of being nineteen. But by the time Ellis reached the waterfront, her thoughts had advanced beyond amusement to curiosity, with hints of envy and jealousy thrown in just to drive her crazy.

She settled into her computer nook, now determined to learn more about this Baltimore woman. She must have *something* that appealed, because Maggie didn't date Tuck'r guests. Wouldn't. And although neither she nor Maggie had used the word "exclusive," each had made it quite clear they had no interest in dating anyone else.

A flattering photograph of a smiling Jill McGee, dressed in a classic black business suit, appeared on the screen. "Well, hello, Ms. McGee. Aren't you the fox. Cavanaugh Resorts of Florida since two thousand six—in the Baltimore office of corporate acquisitions?"

She sat back in deep thought. *Maggie wouldn't date a guest, so are you an old business acquaintance? Did you once work with Maggie? Maybe you helped her incorporate her Valentin Enterprises or maybe you're just a former classmate.*

"No. Maggie went to Syracuse and it says here that you went to Wharton. Probably just an old friend, period, who knows her from… childhood, a neighborhood, friend of the family." She rubbed her face hard. "What's the big deal, anyway?"

Shaking her head at herself, Ellis went to the galley for a beer. "This snooping is ridiculous. I never checked up on Maggie, for Christ's sake." And she returned to stare at Jill's bright green eyes, the thin rosy lips, and perfect pearly whites. "Hmm. You're a very pretty lady, Ms. McGee. What do you want with Maggie?" *My Maggie.*

Without thinking, she found Maggie's information, scant as it was. She knew all the details that came up, the Albany childhood, the education, the years of experience in real estate finance, like her father as Maggie had said. As expected, no personal information was available, yet Ellis couldn't help but wonder how Maggie's Valentin Enterprises originated—and if Jill McGee had been involved. She'd never Googled Valentin.

So when the basic details of the one-woman corporation materialized on the screen, Ellis froze in her seat.

"Myrtle Beach, Daytona, Key Largo, Tahoe, Beacon Hill…Jesus, Maggie. You're a damn flipper. And now you've scored Nantucket. The house is just another notch on the belt, isn't it?" She fell back into her chair. "Son of a bitch."

A numbing buzz traveled through her chest and down her arms.

She nearly dropped the beer bottle. Staring blankly at the words, she began piecing together a very disturbing picture.

"Of course you want your business numbers up. Some big shot like McGee wouldn't give Tuck'r a second look otherwise. And that's why she came back. To see how things have progressed." She stood and climbed the stairs in a daze. "She came back to see if your latest numbers show Tuck'r is worth buying. And the sightseeing cruises did the job, didn't they?"

Now on the bow, Ellis took a long swig of beer and sat. "Is that why you've been happy lately? Because you know Cavanaugh will be impressed? Bet they can't wait to post another win, add that house—*my house*—to their list of assets. It's a victory dinner tonight, isn't it? So when do you shove off? Where will you go next?"

She snickered as she leaned back on her elbows. "Guess you were right, Hank." She drank heavily. "All that care and interest in this place, the 'top of the world' bullshit, all of it served a purpose." *Was any of it real?* "Find the fool in this picture."

CHAPTER TWENTY-FIVE

Jill placed her palm over Maggie's on the table, and the silver Tiffany band on her middle finger flickered suggestively in the restaurant's soft lighting. She leaned forward slightly, eyes rising off Maggie's lips to caress her face so intensely, Maggie straightened in her seat. When Maggie withdrew her hand onto her lap, Jill arched an eyebrow, probably more out of dissatisfaction than disappointment.

"Maggie. We need to do that serious talking tonight."

"It must seem as if I'm avoiding it, but truly, I'm not. Tuck'r just would have had too many interruptions, and the Met earlier was so busy. Yes, of course, I want to do some serious talking."

She moved her empty plate aside and drew her wine closer, intent on getting down to business. Jill's posture indicated she had other business in mind, however, and Maggie's irritation grew to a distracting level.

"I'm so glad to hear it," Jill stated. "I've had my hopes up for weeks now." She cleared her place setting as well, and leaned forward again. "You know, this Tuck'r business has brightened my days. Coming here, having you as a guide, getting to know you, has opened a whole new realm of possibilities, and I hope you're as open to them as I am." She touched her glass to Maggie's. "We'd make a powerful team, you and I, explosive, I dare say. And I'm not just talking about Cavanaugh."

Maggie sipped her wine and wondered what it would look like all over Jill's Donna Karan suit. *Oh, I can give you explosive. Getting a little ticked off should make things easier.*

"If I'm hearing you correctly, I want you to know that I'm only interested in business. I'm flattered—and happily involved with a woman." The image of Ellis at their table, so dashing in her outrage, nearly threw her off track. "And 'this Tuck'r business,' as you put it, has become something special to me, far from being just another in a string of projects. It's opened a whole new realm of possibilities for me as well. And I'm not just talking about Cavanaugh either. I'm talking about career, Nantucket, and permanent residency. I've changed my mind, Jill. Tuck'r is no longer for sale. It's my home."

Jill blinked, then glanced around at the other diners as if everyone had heard.

"Well, that certainly was momentous."

Maggie sipped again, as casually as she could considering her hand shook and her chest had tightened into rock. But she'd said it, all of it, and without missing a beat. "Momentous?" she repeated, and tipped her head to ponder the word. *Not so frightening when it's said out loud.* "Yes, I suppose it is. Appropriate, however, because this has been a summer of momentous achievements, and I'm proud to say they've brought me more happiness than I ever expected."

"Has this new person in your life influenced your decision to take up island life?"

"Oh, I'd be crazy to deny that. She most definitely has, but the decision, ultimately, was mine to make. No one makes them for me."

"I have to say, I'm disappointed, Maggie. Cavanaugh had big plans for Tuck'r Inn."

"And I appreciate all the time, attention, and resources Cavanaugh has lent the idea, your efforts especially, but this is the right decision."

"You would have been pleasantly surprised by our offer."

"I considered the possibility of a lucrative offer. And I admit to a lot of soul searching."

"It's not too late, of course. You would be financially free to produce any number of fine properties anywhere in the world—and Cavanaugh would be there for you—if you so wanted."

"I've been jumping around the country for quite a few years, Jill, and I've found a place now that offers a new range of challenges, not to mention the woman who innocently opened my eyes."

"You're actually serious about staying? You're miles and miles offshore. What about family, shopping, career opportunities, the winters, all the things—"

"My career will be here with Tuck'r. As for everything else, yes, there will be challenges, adventures, but I've always loved them. Being here, even for these few months, has shown me what I've been missing, and I'm really excited about what the off-season has to offer as well."

"You mustn't be afraid to change your mind, you know. I'm sure Cavanaugh will always be interested in taking Tuck'r off your hands, should that time come. In fact, before you slip away from us completely, you should know that we'd love to have you join our team. You're exactly the talent we need for the new properties we're acquiring off the coast in Galveston. So I hope you'll give that some consideration."

"Galveston?" Maggie stifled a chuckle. *The woman is impossible.* "That's quite a generous offer and I'm flattered, but I won't be changing my mind. Nantucket has come to mean a great deal to me."

"Well, I'm sure time will tell."

"The time is right for me, Jill. Right now."

Jill patted Maggie's hand. "Why don't we just leave that door open? How's that?" Maggie started to repeat her position, but Jill rolled on eagerly. "I have to say, your determination in choosing a remote island in *New England*, of all places, is, well, fascinating, but there's a wealth of more temperate, bucolic islands that could have captured your fancy."

Maggie leaned back in her chair, glass in both hands as she considered Jill's point. *Like every off-islander I've talked to since Tuck'r began. Feeling compelled to enlighten her makes me what, if not a Nantucketter?*

"Comparing a Barbados to Nantucket is like...apples to... to pinecones." She laughed at herself. "Every aspect of *this* island is so irreplaceable. Its history is reverent. Your coexistence with the isolation, the cost, the weather, the ocean is something you have to *earn* every day. And that hard work nets you an opportunity for a future here. An opportunity you cherish. How islanders put all that into their daily routines is remarkable, and their pride is justified. It's easy to see how it makes them happy, and I want some of that. I want to contribute, become a part of it. Right now."

"You're amazing." Jill shook her head. "This is why you're so successful. It's not in your nature to quit."

Maggie laughed lightly. "Like a dog with a bone, that's me."

"Okay, so I have to admit, this woman you've found is pretty damn lucky. I apologize for the...the..."

"The come-on?"

Amazing. She didn't even flinch, let alone blush.

"You're incredibly charming, Maggie, and in that dress, simply ravishing, and I'm sure you'd much rather be sitting here with your new love tonight."

My new love. Yes, I miss her tonight. She should be right here with me. She should have heard all this from me already.

"Apology accepted. I haven't had the heart to tell her about Cavanaugh. She's a native islander, and to them, flippers on Nantucket are…well, the word 'outcast' applies in a big way, so I've wrestled with keeping all this a secret. To make matters even more complicated, Tuck'r used to be her family homestead."

"Oh, good Lord. How ironic."

"It makes her *and* Tuck'r twice as special. And I'm hoping she'll forgive me when I explain it all—and be happy for us."

Maggie huffed out the window at the dismal-looking day and turned at the counter. Laura folded pillowcases in the laundry room, while Rachel sat immersed in the *New York Times*, working on her third cup of coffee.

"I've left two messages already." She checked the clock on the wall. "I want to hear from her before I leave. Jill will be down in an hour."

"You don't have to take her to brunch," Rachel mumbled from behind the newspaper.

"No, I don't, but it's the right thing to do."

Rachel turned the page and spoke without looking up. "You two covered all the bases last night, didn't you?"

Laura eyed them curiously, and Maggie wondered how she interpreted that.

"Thoroughly. And dinner was fabulous."

"Must've been. I heard you guys come in. It was after one."

"We talked about all sorts of things. She got her start working for a Trump company."

"Oh, well, that says a lot."

"Actually, once we dropped the shoptalk, she was very forthcoming and I enjoyed our conversation. I assured her she's more than welcome at Tuck'r, and she said she'll be back."

Laura took a quick step out of the laundry room. "She's coming back?"

"Whenever she'd like, yes. She's only leaving early today because of this crappy weather." Maggie checked the clock again. "I just wish Ellis would call me back." Laura returned to the laundry and Rachel turned to another page. "You two are practically sulking. Is something going on I don't know about?"

"Ellis stopped in last night," Rachel said.

"We told her you'd gone out to dinner," Laura added.

Rachel put the paper down and cleared her throat loudly. "*We* told her that corporate lawyer Jill McGee took you to the White Elephant for dinner." Laura ducked inside the laundry room.

"So…did she get upset or something?" Maggie frowned at their silence and set her hands on her hips. "Did she?"

Laura stepped back out. "I-I may have said I didn't like Ms. McGee…and—"

"And," Rachel finished, "Laura *may* have led Ellis to suspect Ms. McGee had ulterior motives."

"What?"

"Well, I-I just said that I thought she *really* liked you."

"Jesus, Laura." Maggie dropped her arms and spun to the window. "Jill *did* have more on her mind than business, but I quashed that stuff immediately. There's nothing—" She turned around and glared at Laura. "You know better than to—"

"I know. I know." Laura hurried forward. She dropped some of the linens and quickly scooped them up. "I'm sorry. I should never have opened my mouth. It wasn't my place."

"You're absolutely right. It's none of your business."

"I'm so sorry, Maggie. But-but Ellis was so great. She said, 'You do what you've got to do for business,' and sounded eager to hear how your night went. I mean, she wasn't jealous or anything. I-I told her—"

"What else?"

"That I thought you two are great together."

Maggie shook her head and turned to Rachel for input.

"Don't look at me. I was long gone." She brought her cup to the sink and hip-bumped Maggie. "She'll call. Don't worry."

"What's she supposed to think, Rachel?"

"Hey, stop. Don't blow this out of proportion. She's all yours and she's loving it. Too bad you missed her. She looked pretty hot, too. I love those tailored shirts she wears, nice and snug."

Maggie slapped her arm. "Shut up. I *did* miss her. I should have invited her along."

Rachel chuckled as she rinsed her cup. "Sure. Wouldn't that have gone over big, considering the business you had to discuss."

"Eh, you're right." She pointed at Laura, who still stood in the middle of the kitchen, seemingly afraid to take a step. "And you. You've got my head spinning." The phone on her desk rang and Maggie cursed. "I have to take this." She stalked into her office, only to return a minute later.

"That was quick," Rachel said.

"The elderly couple due on the late ferry…Mrs. Olden would like an assist with all their luggage." She took a light jacket off the hook in the mudroom. "Meanwhile, I have errands and a ton of shopping to do, and I want to get some of it done before Jill and I go to brunch."

"Helping with the luggage is awfully neighborly."

"That's part of the Tuck'r Inn hospitality, dear sister. Do me a favor and call the airport, see if flights are still on schedule for Jill? I don't trust this weather."

"I'll do it," Laura said, all too eager to please.

"Fine. Then get back to work. You're on my shit list, missy."

"Yes, ma'am."

Maggie grabbed her keys off the counter and Retta ran in at the sound, ready to ride. "Sorry, sweetie. You have to stay. I won't have room for you when I'm done." She gave her a little hug and spotted Rachel grinning as she turned to leave. "What?"

"You don't trust the weather."

"Well, I'm taking Jill to the airport after brunch, so it matters. Have you looked at the mist rolling in? It'll be pea soup fog in a couple of hours, the way it's building."

"Spoken like a sailor."

Maggie stopped short and smiled at the thought. "She's rubbing off."

"And rubbing never felt so good."

Maggie gave her a shove and headed for the door. Rachel caught her by the arm in the mudroom.

"One sec. With Laura around, we haven't had a chance to talk about last night's business. How'd it go? Did Ms. Tits freak out?"

"You're awful. No, she didn't, and I was kind of surprised. She actually offered me a job with them. Hopefully, I got my point across, that I wasn't interested. But she said Cavanaugh would welcome business in the future, if I wanted to pursue it—Tuck'r included. She wanted to leave it open for something more, but I declined and kept things professional. You would've been proud of me."

"I've always been proud of you." Rachel hugged her. "And I'm *so* happy for you."

Maggie kissed her cheek. "Let's hope my sailor is, too."

CHAPTER TWENTY-SIX

Ellis stopped at a trash bin on Main and threw the soggy paper bag away. The stuffed toy frog that had been in it went inside her jacket for safekeeping. Heavy fog had soaked through everything, and she grumbled about it as she continued toward the corner she couldn't see.

She counted on having a few minutes alone with Maggie and didn't want to rely on phone messages. They needed to talk about what had shown up online. Rationality had taken hours to arrive last night, and despite tossing and turning, she'd managed to stop jumping to conclusions and subdue a lot of that unbridled emotion. Unanswered questions would make her lose her mind, and that didn't need to happen. Not when a normal conversation could resolve things so easily between two people who cared so much for one another.

She refused to think she'd overextended herself with this relationship. They'd been connecting and giving, sharing in the most profound ways for almost two months, and showed no signs of slowing down. *Life wouldn't be the same now without you in it.* And she wondered if she'd been smart to fall this quickly. *Maggie. I know you feel it, too. So give us a moment today and help settle this mess in my head.*

The Tuck'r front yard was still, serene, as she stepped up to the screen door, and the common room's golden lamplight beckoned through the gloomy pall of fog outside. She slid off her dripping windbreaker and shook it, jammed the stuffed frog into her pants pocket, and took a refreshing breath of rose-tinted air. She picked a blossom from the vine that covered the nearest post and went inside.

A guest sat reading on the couch, undisturbed by Ellis's arrival or the sixties tune that played faintly from the portable radio in the corner. But the cozy room filled her with as much trepidation as nostalgic affection now, and she ground her teeth, wanting to feel only sheltered and surrounded by an atmosphere she loved. Above the fireplace, Maggie had hung a large framed print of the Tom Nevers farm scene, surreal and ageless with its old machinery in the fog. That moment in the truck returned vividly, and Ellis felt her heart wobble. To her right, a majestic print of Sankaty Light with its red waistband now hung between the windows. *"On top of the world," you said.*

"Hi," the woman on the couch offered. "Turned into a miserable day, hasn't it?"

Ellis thought she'd probably recognize Jill McGee anywhere now, that Internet photo burned into her memory. She was just as striking in person, even in an expensive purple running suit.

"Ah, warm, but yeah. Sure has." She hung her jacket by the door and crossed the room and peeked into Maggie's empty office. A shallow but wide print of the beach off New South Road, complete with distant surfer in the breaking waves, hung above the desk, and a gift-wrapped package of the same dimensions sat nearby. *I want more of these memories with you, Maggie.*

She left the rose on the keyboard and listened to the silence from the kitchen. Retta and/or Laura were bound to turn up any second.

"If you're looking for Maggie, she went to do errands. She had a list as long as her arm."

"Maggie's nonstop." *So what's your interest in her? Did you have a good time last night—with my lady?* The significance of that thought weighed her down into a chair. She set the toy frog on her leg and ran a palm across her face, wiping away the remnants of fog. *Feels like fog, all right.*

"You're a dog lover, I see."

Ellis nodded at the frog. "Retta's irresistible."

"Quite energetic. I think she's upstairs with Laura." She set her Kindle aside and made no attempt to soften her inquisitive gaze. Ellis didn't appreciate being evaluated or whatever this woman was doing, and was tempted to call her on it. "I'm Jill," she declared suddenly, "far from home in Baltimore." Legs tucked beneath her, she extended her hand.

"Ellis." They shook hands, and the expensive manicure didn't escape Ellis's notice. "Good day for a good book."

"So true. I'm passing time, though. I've been forced to wait out the fog, and this is torture, because I hate leaving Tuck'r."

"You've been grounded?"

"Socked in, was how the airport put it."

Ellis nodded, knowing the conditions so well that the very notion of flying had never entered her mind. "This will lift by suppertime."

Jill's smile flashed over the coffee table between them. "'Suppertime.' I love the feel of old Yankee words." Ellis was tempted to offer her "old Yankee" opinion of swanky shyster lawyers, but she let Jill speak. It seemed as if she enjoyed hearing herself, anyway. "The airport likewise assured me the fog would be gone in a few hours, but you say it with such conviction. You're a local?"

"Lifer."

"Ahh. Fascinating. Never a desire to live elsewhere?"

"No."

"Hmm. I'm a city girl, born and bred. My condo is fifteen stories up, just blocks from the ocean, and with a wall of glass, thankfully. In the spring, the sunrise angles right into my living room."

Ellis sympathized—a bit. *You could have sunrise anywhere at any time of year, if you really wanted.*

"Nantucket must be quite an adjustment for you."

"I'm in property acquisitions, so I'm used to changing locales. It keeps me well rounded, shall we say."

"Property acquisitions. Any properties here on your radar?"

She sent Ellis an incredulous smile. "Seriously? I'd snatch up a dozen, at least, if I could. I'm so taken by the meticulous care, the idyllic settings, the quaint charm."

"Like Tuck'r."

"Definitely Tuck'r. Maggie struck gold, landing this place. It has such hardy bones, such character, not to mention the history. What a bonus. History has incredible appeal, a great selling point. She's captured the essence of the era, preserved it to share, and I believe the potential here is limitless."

No doubt you know potential, but do you really know anything about bones and character, let alone that era? Please, God, tell me they didn't strike a deal.

"It's a beautiful place," Ellis said. "These Nantucket roots are as deep as they get."

"Oh, when Maggie told me about Captain Pratt, I couldn't wait to get here. I'm immeasurably grateful we connected. And I'm confident Maggie feels the same." She leaned forward and whispered confidentially. "I'm crossing my fingers for the opportunity to work with her in the future."

"Is that right?"

"I'll be back in due time," she said. "By then, Maggie might be ready to review our Galveston property."

"Texas?"

"Lovely property, but with Maggie's touch? She has such a creative eye. She could do wonders turning it around."

A cell phone sounded upstairs and Laura's voice carried down, but only half of Ellis's brain registered the conversation. The other half struggled to cope with Jill's.

Was I stupid or blind, believing Tuck'r means as much to you, Maggie, as it does to me? Future work with her? And Texas? Tuck'r wasn't your first flip, I know that now, and it's pretty clear it won't be your last. But, Jesus, you never said you'd be moving on. Quite the opposite. Does that make me a flip project, too?

She ran a hand back through her hair and pinched her eyes. They burned from lack of sleep and, now, from searching for warning signs she'd missed. *Enough already. Find your feet.*

"We're all set," Laura was saying. "Yes, they told her probably around five o'clock, so no hurry. No, Rachel said she'd catch the eight o'clock boat so you two could go out for dinner first. Okay, see you then."

Retta preceded Laura down the stairs, and they spotted Ellis simultaneously. Racing to where she sat, Retta dodged an easy chair, an ottoman, and a side table to wiggle against Ellis's knees. Ellis quickly hid the frog at her back, and her heart twisted a bit at Retta's blatant affection.

"Ellis, hi." Laura stopped at the kitchen door, bucket of cleaning supplies in hand, and flashed a nervous glance at Jill. "So...you're here."

"I was hoping to catch Maggie for a while this afternoon. There are some things I wanted to talk about." Retta stomped from one foot to the other, impatient for attention. Ellis hugged her and found it hard to let go. "Hey, my pretty girl. Would you like a surprise?" Ears perked, Retta backed up into the coffee table. Oblivious, she bounced on her front paws and barked, and Ellis whipped out the toy. "Froggie for you." Retta snatched it out of her hand and dashed off.

"I just had Maggie on the phone," Laura said and sagged onto one leg dejectedly. "I didn't know you were down here. She won't be back for a few hours now, till around five, when Ms. McGee's flight leaves."

"Well, she's busy. I understand." Ellis headed for the door, sensing *Ms. McGee* watched with great interest. *Got to get out.*

"I could call her back," Laura said. "You could—"

She stopped when Ellis shook her head.

"Don't bother her." *She knows where to find me.* She zipped her windbreaker and watched Retta trot by with the frog. "If you would, just tell her I stopped in?"

Rachel came through from the kitchen and knocked Laura sideways with the door. "Whoa! Sorry, Laura. Hi there, Ellis. I just get here and you're leaving? Like last night in reverse." Her mischievous look reminded Ellis too much of Maggie. *Shove off, damn it.* "Come on," Rachel said, holding the door open. "Join me. I was just going to raid Maggie's brownie stash, and we have to plan my tour of the *Rose*. Next time I come over, for sure." She narrowed her eyes. "You don't have to go, do you?"

"Sorry, yeah. I've got stuff to do, too. Work tomorrow. Early call, you know?" Rachel frowned and Ellis knew she hadn't been convincing, but there were only so many words she could muster at the moment. "Thanks, though."

Retta ran up to her and Ellis kissed the top of her head, then tossed the frog past Rachel into the kitchen.

"Maggie's really going to be upset that she missed you," Rachel said, her look now serious.

"Please…just…We'll catch up with each other eventually." She turned to Jill as she swung open the screen door and was surprised when Jill hurried to her feet.

"Ellis, you said? So I gather you're Maggie's…Well, her…"

Ellis took a breath and rejected the snide response that came to mind. "Good luck with everything."

❖

Rachel had relinquished the backseat to Retta and moved to the front by the time Maggie returned from seeing Jill off at the airport gate, and Maggie was glad to have her closer. Back behind the wheel, she closed her eyes briefly before starting the car.

"Do you believe her? All that time she had no idea who she was talking to?" She opened her eyes to see Rachel respond.

"I think I do. I saw the shock through all that makeup when it dawned on her. And I don't know how long they talked, but Laura was upstairs for almost an hour, so there's that."

"An hour. God. I told Jill at dinner last night that I hadn't explained it all to Ellis yet. How dare she blurt out stuff to someone she doesn't even know?"

"Did you ever tell Jill her name?"

"I don't remember. I thought I did."

Rachel shook her head. "Couldn't have. She's sharp enough to remember a name like Ellis, and like I said, she looked pretty blown away when she realized *that woman* was your girlfriend."

"Who knows what Jill said about me, or her and me, or flipping Tuck'r."

"You don't *really* know anything either one of them said, and it's hard to judge the things Jill did admit to telling her. I mean, she said she praised Tuck'r and your work, and…and that she hoped you'd work together some time."

"And how does that sound?' Maggie asked. "Like I'll be leaving for another project? Shit."

Rachel blew out a hard breath. "Yeah, well, she said she did mention Galveston, and that's not good."

"*So* not good." Maggie bit her lower lip as she shook her head. "I bet she didn't tell Ellis that I turned down that offer. Twice!" She pounded the wheel. "God damn it. I need to talk to Ellis." Maggie stared through the faint mist on the windshield. "My calls go straight to voice mail now. I have to get to the *Rose*."

"Well, I'm not leaving tonight. No way. Not with this nightmare going on. So I'll be around when you need me."

"Don't you have to get back to prepare that presentation?"

"I can do that in my sleep. I've done it hungover, so…You're more important and this is a fucking mess. So I'm staying. Let me drive."

"I'm fine."

"Then let's go. I need food, and if this is going to be an all-nighter, which is what it's feeling like, we have to pick up more alcohol."

Maggie started back to town, the earlier fog now just an aggravating mist, and she was thankful. Things already were hard enough to see. "You can take the car once we get to the wharf."

"We're making sure her truck is there before you run off into the friggin' ocean."

"She'll be there."

"And if not?"

"Where else would she be? She has to work in the morning."

"I sure as hell don't know. She's *your* girlfriend. Does she hit any bar in particular?"

"No. Well, maybe Dell's. She's not much of—"

"Uh-uh. Thanks to you, lover girl, that 'not much of a people person' thing doesn't apply anymore. I have news for you, big sister. Based on all you've told me, you've restored one hell of a woman. Captain Ellis Chilton is warm and friendly, incredibly charming, and charismatic as hell. And her touch of shyness is just delicious. If she turns all that loose on the single women on this rock of yours, you'll lose her."

Maggie stopped the car on the side of the road. She didn't need to listen to Rachel yell from three feet away what she'd been telling herself for the past two hours.

"Are you fucking done?"

"No. You're not going to lose her because you're going to find her and tell her everything—including that you're in love with her—and then you're going to have makeup sex and be late for making me French toast in the morning."

"French toast? Really."

"Did I tell you I'm hungry?"

"I am in love with her, Rachel."

"Hell, I know that. Glad you do. And she's in love with you. And now she's out there, zombified because of whatever it was Ms. Big Tits said and what she thinks you didn't say. It was pretty goddamn evident when she left Tuck'r. You know, as handsome as Ellis is, when she's blue, it's written all over that perfect body. And this afternoon, there was a lot to read."

Maggie lowered her forehead onto the steering wheel, and tears started.

"If I'd only been up front with her. God, she must be crushed." She sniffed. "None of this would have happened if I hadn't been so afraid of what she'd think, afraid of another rejection like that devastation back in Tahoe. I'm such an ass." She sniffed again and turned to Rachel. "Who knows what she's thinking now?"

"No time for crying." Rachel handed her tissues from the console. "Drive to the waterfront and find her truck so I can go get food. I'm starving."

CHAPTER TWENTY-SEVEN

I'm getting a dog."

The statement came out of the blue, broke the silence in the galley like a balloon pop. Hank snorted as he refilled their shot glasses, and Ellis nodded, mesmerized by his precision. Not a drop spilled, he set the bottle down with a thud.

"Just shut up and drink." He inhaled the alcohol fumes off the liquid's surface.

"I'm going to do it. A medium-sized one—but a good swimmer. Maybe next weekend." She raised her glass to him and they downed the whiskey in unison.

"Sure you are. What're you going to do with two dogs? That Lab already runs the *Rose*. Hell, she patrols the finger piers like a harbormaster, for God's sake. She knows her way around pretty good. You don't need another dog."

"I will. She won't be around much longer."

He grumbled as he leaned back. "Jesus Christ. Quit your bellyachin'. You ain't even talked to the girl about this situation, and look atcha. You're sulkin' down here with an ol' man, getting sloshed and feelin' sorry for yourself."

"You were right, you know. I should've been smarter, asked more questions." She pushed her glass toward him for a refill. "Another newcomer out to make a buck."

"Hey, we all get our heads turned now 'n then. Human nature. At least she dragged you back into civilization after too many years by yourself. Do you remember the last time you and I did this?"

"Yeah. I do. Don't go there, Hank."

"We tied on a good one for your old man that night. You know what he'd do if he was here right now? He'd kick your sorry ass."

"Couldn't blame him, could I?"

Hank slapped the table and she jumped. "Fuck it all, Ellis! Smarten up!" He poured another round, shaking his head. "He'd kick some sense into you—and *not* 'cause you fell for her. She's got the looks and the smarts and she's sweet as can be. Shit, even *I* like her." He slid the glass back to her. "No, he'd boot your butt 'cause you're slumped on that bench, whinin'."

Ellis straightened. She didn't want to think about her father's opinion, what his reaction would be to this mess. Another failure on her part. She drank the shot and coughed at the burn.

"Well, I could've been smarter. I know that much." She slid the glass back to him.

"Eh. You're done." Hank pushed the glass aside. "There's no controlling love, kid. Happens to everyone and usually more than once. Can make you plenty stupid, too. And right now you're stupid *and* pretty much drunk." He stood and put the bottle back in its upper cabinet. "Go sleep it off and face tomorrow with a clearer head and your chin up."

More unsteady on her feet than she liked, Ellis guided herself up the narrow stairs with a palm on each facing wall. She sensed Hank behind her and briefly worried about toppling back down onto him. Finally out on the deck, she stopped at the rail and took time to breathe.

She welcomed the stillness of the *Tenn-acious* on the harbor's calm water, and that the withdrawal of the fog brought back the stars. Having lost its earlier humidity, the salty air whispered against her skin, and she filled her lungs again.

"Tide's in."

Hank chortled as he patted her back. "Good thing for you. Less far to fall."

"I'm good," she said with a chuckle and maneuvered over the side and onto the pier. The air had cleared some of the fog in her head, too, enough to let her appreciate that the walkway beneath her barely moved.

"It's still early, you know."

"Not for you, it ain't."

"Perfect night for a cruise. I could handle this."

"Probably, but don't waste the fuel. Hit the sack."

"Hey, Hank. Ah…"

"Yeah. You're welcome. Now, I'm watchin', so get aboard—and stay put."

She kept a guarded eye on the pier, glad when she finally dropped into a deck chair on the *Rose*. The evening mist had dampened everything and she squirmed when the wetness seeped through the seat of her pants.

"Aw shit." She leaned forward and rubbed her face with both hands, trying to revive more clarity in her senses. "You're right again, Hank. Stupid." She stood, pleased she didn't stagger, and took a moment to survey the world around her.

Many boats were absent, having gone out early this morning to beat the fog, and stayed out. Some would show up after sunrise; one or two might arrive tonight. If they were lucky, those arrivals made "last call" at the bars, but then would roust her out of a sound sleep, bumbling like drunken pirates back to their boats. With a fond smile, she remembered the first time they woke Maggie, startled her out of a warm embrace, and Retta announced what she'd heard. The pirates had barked back. But even when the breeze offered notes from a band at the RC, as it did just a moment ago, Ellis knew the occasional noise would never send her in search of quieter confines. *How can you just pack up and go?*

She turned and sighed. "Where else would you find this?" Gazing across the harbor, she saw the glistening blue of summer, the angry, churning gray of storms, and the blinding white of winter, frozen silent. And now a glossy black in the late-summer twilight, the expanse showcased the venerable Brant Point and Great Point watchdogs at their finest. With their brilliant, regulated reminders, safeguarding those who passed and those who harbored here, the lighthouses exemplified the staunch, unflappable nature of every islander.

She almost shuddered at how *un*like them she currently felt. *So much for unflappable.* Newcomers fascinated by the size, intrigued by the purpose, took photographs as souvenirs but never saw the lighthouses for the monuments they were. She'd drawn strength from them many times over the years, and realized how much she needed their reinforcement now.

Times like this, we lose sight of what matters, she thought, heading below to change. "Lose a little faith in ourselves, right along with it." Proud that she'd made it all the way to her bed without the slightest sidestep, she cast off a shiver and let the close, warm quarters embrace her.

"Newcomers never really get it," she muttered, changing into dry shorts, "but I believed in you, Maggie. I believed you would."

She took a bottle of water from the fridge and, out of habit, turned on the radio for the marine forecast. The prediction of a gorgeous Monday made her click the radio off with a hard twist. "Damn it." She started up the stairs. "Figures, weather improves for a workday." She pulled a towel from a cabinet in the upper saloon and dried her chair but then decided to dry the seat at the helm. She hadn't been on the bridge for one minute before impulse took control.

She turned the key, and both engines rumbled to life. Needles on her gauges climbed to their proper positions, and suddenly she was on the pier, tossing lines aboard. She gave the *Rose* a healthy shove and jumped on.

At the helm as the *Rose* drifted, she thought she heard Hank yelling. She'd heard enough from him, knew she wouldn't be pleasing him on this night and, stubbornly, didn't look back. But she'd just nosed the bow outward when she heard urgent barking, and for that she did glance over her shoulder. Retta shuffled restlessly on the walkway, panting, tail wagging, and snapped off another bark.

Yes, I see you, too, pretty girl. Do NOT dive in. Where's your pretty mom?

Maggie heard the engines before she saw the *Rose* some thirty feet out, and ran to Retta's side, waving a hand for Ellis to stop. It chilled her to think Ellis might not.

But her fear eased when the engines' volume lowered. They rose again to a moderate level as Ellis backed up, then angled toward the slip. Maggie called out over the noise.

"Permission to come aboard, Captain?"

She heard no response, but Ellis continued in reverse, steering deftly while looking back.

Retta stomped in place, then began pacing along the pier. Insistent, she barked repeatedly as the *Rose* neared, and Maggie had to give her credit. *Whatever the hell you think you're doing, Ellis, avoiding me like this, you deserve to be yelled at.*

The engines fell into an idle drone, and the moment the *Rose* bumped the dock, Ellis set the step-box onto the walkway. Retta didn't wait for the little landing to be unfolded. She ran up the two steps and leaped over the side.

"Jesus!" Ellis said.

Maggie gasped. "Retta! You'll be the death of me!"

Ellis offered her hand to Maggie. "Quick, before we drift," she said in a crisp tone. "Don't think. I've got you."

Maggie took a breath and, on Ellis's pull, made the little jump onto the deck. "Well! Hi."

"Hi," Ellis said and backed away a step. "This is a surprise. Have a seat." She busied herself drying another chair.

Maggie placed a hand on her shoulder. "Where are you going?"

Ellis straightened and eyed the dock warily. Maggie knew Ellis didn't approve of the *Rose* bobbing freely so close to the pier, and understood when Ellis only spared her a glance.

"Going? Just…out."

"Would you mind some company?"

Ellis's hesitation worried her. They both had a lot to discuss, and going off in separate directions wouldn't accomplish anything. Maggie made the decision for both of them.

"I'm not here to intrude on your privacy, Ellis. I'm here because… because I need to be. I want to be, and I think you want that, too." Ellis looked back at the dock, now some ten feet away, and Maggie turned her chin with a fingertip. "Please correct me if I'm wrong."

"You're not wrong. We have to talk."

"Oh, we certainly do."

❖

Ellis searched her eyes in the poor light and Maggie knew the all-too familiar, beseeching look. She remembered being held by it on the steps, right here during the wedding party cruise. As then, she wondered if Ellis saw the honesty and genuine affection being offered.

Ellis stepped toward the rail. "I should…ah…" She wavered in an uncharacteristic move, seemed to change her mind, and headed for the stairs. "Grab a seat." She went up to the bridge as Maggie watched from below.

Retta scrabbled up from Ellis's quarters carrying a half-mauled bone she'd obviously stowed away and settled at Maggie's feet. "You've made yourself quite at home, haven't you?" She reached down and stroked her side, then sat back heavily. "Guess that's the elephant in the room tonight. *Home.*"

On the bridge, Ellis appeared occupied as usual, but Maggie ached to engage her in conversation. She hoped Ellis had some particular patch of ocean in mind, and once there, they would get down to the business of "them."

With slips and moorings behind, the *Rose* picked up speed, and

Maggie retied her hair back. The warmth of the air rushing over her body seemed out of sync with the calendar, she mused, with daylight gone much sooner near the close of August. The striped sky and changing wind had made dusk one of her favorite times of day, but this fading twilight just might have stolen her heart. She thought it curious, relating to the elements like never before, and suddenly attributed it to being so close to them, literally, surrounded by water, wind, and sky, and being grounded by this island.

She looked back at the gaily lit wharves and Nantucket Town, and hoped tourists took the time to *really see it all*. Out here, as Ellis wove out of the harbor, vacationing traffic amounted only to a handful of small luxury craft—the *Rose* an imposing presence among them—and Maggie enjoyed having so much of this ocean to themselves.

She relished the close-up view of Brant Point Light, and remembered first seeing it more than a year ago from the *Eagle*. *You were probably on board that day, and no doubt our paths crossed. I want them entwined, Ellis. For good. But we have to get through this rough patch, this...fog of ours, first.*

Just as she rose, intent on persuading Ellis to stop, the engines slowed.

"I really wasn't going to Europe or anything," Ellis said from the controls, and the touch of humor had Maggie hoping an easy exchange lay ahead. *You are truly at ease out here, aren't you?*

Hands on the railings, Ellis slid down the steps again.

"I have to practice that," Maggie said, and prayed that by the end of their conversation, she'd still be welcome. "So much easier than taking one step at a time."

"The ladders are narrow and steep, you're right. The saloon stairs aren't quite so bad, but I'm still impressed by Retta's dexterity." She went into the saloon and rummaged through the cooler. "Sam Adams and water. Poor selection, I'm sorry. The serious alcohol is below, if you'd prefer."

"A beer sounds great. Thank you." Ellis handed her the Sam Adams and sat down with a bottle of water. "You're making me drink alone?"

"I-I had my share earlier. Stopped just in time."

"I see." *For you, drinking to that point so early in the evening says a lot.* "Ellis." Maggie covered Ellis's hand on the arm of her chair. "It feels as if we haven't spoken in days...and we're way behind."

"Very true." Ellis nodded. "I know things come up. You have a business to run, Maggie. I understand."

Maggie leaned forward and shook her head. "No, don't do that. Please don't. Don't be such a sweetheart if you're really pissed as hell. I-I think I would be, if I were in your shoes."

"Oh, I was just getting started, Maggie. I *do* understand the trials of business. What I *don't* understand has nothing to do with that. I'm confused by all the emotions in play, crashing together."

"I can only imagine, and I'm so sorry." Maggie gripped the neck of her beer bottle so hard she told herself to back off before it broke. *God, I asked for this.*

"Being confused just enflames anger, you know?" Ellis said. "But I'm beyond anger now. *Almost* beyond blaming myself…maybe. Two hours on the beach earlier helped." Ellis pulled her chair around to face her. "Now it's just the hurt I have to handle. So I'm sucking it up right now, ready and willing to hear what you have to say."

"Ellis, I should have leveled with you right from the start. It was *so* wrong not to, and I apologize, truly. It was a huge mistake, but at the time, I was afraid of how this island, how *you* would receive me, and selfishly, I thought it wise to stay under everyone's radar. I've experienced the consequences of being unwelcome, and it was a horrendous time for me. I wanted to be successful—"

"Before anyone found out you were just here for the money. Because that's what flippers do, don't they? They hit and run, don't give a—"

"You see? That's the automatic reaction I tried to avoid. My work is high-end, Ellis, not roughshod hit-and-run. Every establishment I've produced is a success today, a relevant member of its community, and that's years of diligence and honest, quality work. I wanted nothing less with Tuck'r. I learned," she met Ellis's keen look evenly, "that you islanders are a tough bunch, and that made me determined to succeed."

"I helped you."

"You did. I've shared all the numbers with you."

"And Jill McGee can't wait to hand over the cash so you can find her the next flip."

"Stop." Maggie got to her feet and took a long drink of her beer. "Christ." She turned back. "Please just listen? I don't want us harping at each other."

Ellis ran a hand through her hair, and Maggie dismissed a desperate urge to hug her. *Please don't rush to conclusions.*

"Okay. Listening," Ellis said, her look hardened with apprehension.

"My conversation with Jill was an eye-opener, Maggie, and that's being kind. How was I supposed to react to that?"

"Jesus, I know." She hurried back to her seat and put the bottle on the deck. "Look, she had no—"

"How am I supposed to feel when I find you've only come here to flip my house to some corporation—and now you're going to Tex—"

"Shh. I'm not." Maggie shook her head and took Ellis's hand. "Please let me explain." She rubbed her thumbs over the back of Ellis's hand. "I'm not going to Texas. I'm not working for or with Jill McGee or Cavanaugh."

"That's the exact opposite of what she led me to believe."

Maggie rolled her eyes. "God, I could frigging strangle that woman. Forget everything she said, Ellis. I'm telling you what I should have told you months ago, plus…some things that are…kind of new." She gathered her composure and offered Ellis a hopeful look. "Yes, I came here to turn the Captain Pratt House into a vital, successful B&B. Yes, people who are unfamiliar with the difference call my turnarounds 'flips,' but I believe mine are higher-end. Nevertheless, locals don't always welcome outsiders. Sometimes they run you out of town. They'll even burn you out, and I encountered that in Nevada. So when I learned how…territorial Nantucketters really were, I was afraid, and decided to keep everything quiet."

She combed Ellis's hair back from her forehead. "But I never expected to end up with the house of my dreams. Or in a place out of a storybook. Or so in love, I'd give her my heart if she'd have it."

The tension in Ellis's face softened, replaced by a look of disbelief.

"You're serious?" She stood and drew Maggie up close. "Something this big can happen so fast and still be real?" Maggie dared believe she'd been forgiven. "I love you, Maggie. And I know it's real for me."

Maggie pressed her lips to Ellis's, lost herself in the feel of her mouth, the hands and arms holding her, the chest and torso melded to hers. *This is exactly where I need to be.*

"And I love you. It *is* wildly fast, isn't it? But *so* real for me, too. I want you, only you."

Ellis lowered her face to Maggie's neck. "Jesus, Maggie. I want to be good enough for you. I'll never fail you, I swear. Say you'll stay."

Maggie raised Ellis's head in both hands and kissed her lips lightly.

"I want to be here with you, every day, so yes, of course I'm staying."

"You really are staying?"

"Yes. Really."

"No flips?"

"No, Ellis. I want Tuck'r to grow up and be the full-fledged inn it's capable of, and I intend to run it. I'm not going anywhere for another turnaround project." She paused when Ellis kissed her deeply. "Wow," she whispered on a breath. "We need to do this lying down. Another one of those and my knees will give out."

Ellis gathered her closer and kissed her ear. "Come with me." She took Maggie's hand and led her below to the bedroom. Retta followed with her bone. "Sit right here," Ellis said and directed Maggie by the shoulders to sit on the side of the bed. Retta sat as well and dropped the bone with a clunk.

Unable to stop smiling, Maggie watched, fascinated, as Ellis cleared everything off a side shelf. Retta looked up at her, as if just as curious, and Maggie whispered, "I don't know what she's up to."

"You'll see," Ellis said, and finally, she lifted the shelf and revealed a long, narrow storage bin. She pulled out a slender box and the cloth-wrapped object inside it.

"This," she said, hurrying back to Maggie, "this is for you." She knelt and placed it across her lap.

"Ellis? What's this?" She looked down at the burlap covering and back to Ellis as Retta sniffed the fabric. "You know, I have a gift for you, too. A special picture already wrapped you were supposed to get yesterday. It's right where you left me the ro—"

Ellis touched Maggie's lips. "No talk of yesterday or, God forbid, earlier today." She stroked a finger along Maggie's cheek. "Unwrap this."

Maggie swiped away a tear and unwound the burlap. The back side of a long piece of wood appeared first, and she delicately turned it over.

"Oh, God! Ellis!" She flashed her a look that led to a stream of tears. "The quarter board! The-the Captain Joshua Pratt House quarter board." Her fingers trembled as she caressed the aged lettering. "Oh, my…It's the real thing, isn't it?"

"Hand carved in eighteen fifty-five."

"Ellis, I-I don't know what to say. Oh, my God." She stared at the lettering, the paint blasted away in many places by generations of

Nantucket's blowing sand and salty wind. Hefting the dry and cracked pine board, now light as driftwood, she shook her head in wonder. "This…this is history. *Your* history. God, I love you for this gesture, but it belongs to you."

"No, Maggie. I failed my family, failed our house."

"Damn it, Ellis. It kills me when you say that. You can't think that way. You're an amazing woman and you deserve this."

Ellis shook her head and pressed a fingertip to Maggie's chest. "*You* resurrected that house and restored its dignity. It's your house now and this needs to come back home, hang inside somewhere it can be protected for another hundred years."

"Now listen to me, Ellis Chilton." She dabbed a tear from Ellis's eye. "In a very special way, the Captain Pratt House belongs to us both." She cupped her chin, leaned closer, and kissed her. "*You* need to come back home, too. Think about it—then say yes."

CHAPTER TWENTY-EIGHT

Ellis stepped out into the foggy September morning with a cup of coffee and let the gauzy sunshine warm her face and arms. She knew that, soon enough, the rising sun and tide would burn away the mist and withdraw the salt, right on time for a Sunday cruise to nowhere. The best kind of cruise. Maggie loved them as much as she did and delighted in scheduling a weekend morning or afternoon of boating as often as possible.

Ellis marveled at their fate as she sipped her coffee. Already based on Ellis's workweek, the boating getaways required Maggie's clever maneuvering around guest arrivals and "minding the store," and Ellis took immense pleasure in helping wherever and whenever she could. Today was another of those days when they'd *made* time for each other.

The screen door shut softly and Maggie's arms locked around Ellis's waist from behind. Ellis squeezed them to her as Maggie kissed her ear.

"I knew I'd find you out here," she whispered, "getting all damp in the fog."

"It's going to burn off just in time for us." Ellis turned, set her cup aside, and kissed her. "Good morning, Ms. Jordan."

Retta arrived from the backyard and barked for her share of the action.

"Hush," Maggie said, and they patted her until she ran off to continue her morning inspection of the bushes.

Ellis massaged Maggie's supple form, flexed her fingers into her back. *I love how we fit, the feel of you, how right this is for each of us.*

Maggie snuggled deeper into her arms. "Mmm. Good morning, my captain. Thank you for helping with advance work again last night.

I probably should get you an apron if you're going to be slicing and dicing with me in the kitchen."

"No apron," she said and kissed her softly. "Although if I don't master that juicer pretty soon, I'll need one."

"I thought I heard you grumbling earlier." Maggie tugged her closer. "Does the sailor in you always slip out of bed so early? I'm not sure I want to get used to that."

"Only when I hear the *Rose* calling us."

"Oh, well, maybe *that's* what I heard. We should be on our way in a couple of hours. There're just five for breakfast this morning. Can you wait that long?"

"No. Let's go wake them all up."

Maggie laughed and led her back inside, excitedly detailing the treats she'd already packed for their outing.

Your enthusiasm is just one of the reasons I love you.

Maggie's devotion to her and the *Rose* seemed to grow by the day, equaled only by her determination to succeed with Tuck'r and its future. Ellis couldn't have been happier or more proud. Her own desire to help Maggie's effort grew steadily as well, and often left Ellis a bit amazed that she now appreciated her old home as Maggie's achievement, not as a painful personal loss.

It's all about love and respect. And optimistic vision. A long way from avoiding Davis Street, Ms. Jordan.

"They're all down in the living room now," Ellis said, adding two little butter dishes to Maggie's tray. "The couple from Boston asked for espressos."

Maggie looked up. "I'll make them if you take this out."

"To the parlor. Sure."

Ellis turned toward the door with the tray as Maggie watched over her shoulder.

"Ellis? I like that, you know. Parlor."

"Guess I fell back a few years. I meant—"

"No. Parlor, it is. From now on. *This* inn needs a parlor."

Ellis thought better of simply tossing the tray aside to sweep Maggie off her feet. *You've known how to reach me from the start.* Instead, she crossed the kitchen and kissed her. "After this, I'll load our stuff into the truck. If you're winding down here, I'll take off to prep the *Rose*."

"Ah…" Maggie's pregnant pause caught Ellis at the door again.

"That couple, the two women from Kansas City?" She grabbed Ellis by the belt. "Watch out for them."

Ellis feigned a pout. "Aw, must I? Midwest women are—" Maggie flicked Ellis's hip with a dish towel. "Okay! Actually, I was going to check out the hot blonde from Providence, the one who sits in the corner all the time."

Maggie lashed out again as Ellis escaped.

Little more than an hour later, Maggie stood at the helm of the *Rose*, motoring through harbor traffic guided by Ellis's hands on hers. Below, on the stern deck, Retta lay stretched out, basking in the sun, only rising when a passing craft required her review. The level of everyone's contentment reinforced Maggie's faith in her judgment, although she did regret the months lost prior to making the "momentous" decision.

The warm breeze carried an occasional chilly wisp, and Maggie fervently wished it was May and she had the entire summer to enjoy just like this.

"I can feel the change coming."

She leaned back against Ellis, welcomed the warmth of her chest and arms, and Ellis lowered her head to speak against her cheek.

"Very good. I'm impressed." Her warm breath tickled Maggie's neck. "Yes, today you can feel it in the air. Unfortunately, it won't always feel this warm."

Maggie disagreed. She'd enjoy this warmth every day, no matter where they were or what time of year.

Ellis indicated the proper course for leaving the harbor, and Maggie steered past Brant Point, tempted to throw pennies. The realization that she didn't have to, that her return was virtually guaranteed, lifted her heart, and she smiled at the lighthouse as if it had known her fate all along.

The *Eagle* approached as they exited the channel, larger than life it seemed, from a vantage point Maggie had never experienced. Ellis reached for the radio just as it crackled to life, and, with the huge ship bearing down on them, Maggie immediately missed the security of her presence. About to pull Ellis back against her, she flashed her a wary look but then relished the wink she won in return. She took a breath and maintained course as calmly as she could.

"Top o' the mornin' to ya, *Nantucket Rose*," the radio voice chimed, and Retta sat up, barking at the sound.

"And to you, Master Doyle." Ellis covered the mic and whispered

to Maggie. "Shamus Doyle. All five foot one of him. A salty leprechaun."
Maggie stifled a laugh.

"Beauty of a day y'picked, Captain Chilton."

"That it is. You drew Sunday duty."

"Indeed I did. No complaints, all's well. Y'headed out or just about?"

"Just about."

"This your lovely Maggie? Greetings, darlin'. And do I see you have a sea dog now, too?"

"We do," Maggie said as Ellis held the mic for her. "She and I are learning fast."

"You're in good hands."

Retta barked dutifully as the ships sailed abreast of each other, and Maggie joined Ellis in waving up at the *Eagle*'s wheelhouse. Doyle waved his cap out the window.

"Say, Ellis, just so you know, we swam through a bit o' soup a ways back, so keep an eye."

Maggie knew enough to interpret that as a fog warning, and she looked to Ellis in alarm.

Ellis kissed her forehead and whispered, "Fog happens, but we're having none of it." She sent Doyle a salute. "Roger that. No soup for us," she said with a chuckle. "Thanks for the warning."

"Steady as she goes, then, Ellis."

"Aye, sir. And to you." She hung up the mic and turned to Maggie with a grin. "Brace yourself."

Maggie didn't have a second to ask what she meant before the *Eagle*'s arrival horn nearly startled her off her feet. They laughed when Retta barked in response.

Ellis encircled Maggie's waist and tucked her fingertips inside the front of Maggie's shorts.

"I prefer you stay right there, Captain."

Ellis ground her hips against Maggie's and nuzzled her neck. "Do you?"

Her fingers inched lower and Maggie squirmed against her. "I'm concentrating, you know."

"So am I."

"Behave. I don't want to mess up. I like being at your controls."

"Helm. You're definitely at my helm, but I like being at your controls, too."

253

Maggie groaned as Ellis nibbled her ear. "Does this officially make me your first mate?"

"My only mate."

"Good, because I adore the *Rose*, you know, but I *love* you."

"Oh, and I love you, Maggie, my *true* Nantucket rose."

About the Author

A recent telecommunications retiree, CF Frizzell ("Friz") is the recipient of the Golden Crown Literary Society's 2015 Debut Author Award for her novel *Stick McLaughlin: The Prohibition Years*. Friz discovered her passion for writing in high school and went on to establish an award-winning twenty-two-year career in community newspapers that culminated in the role of founder/publisher.

She credits powerhouse authors Lee Lynch, Radclyffe, and the generous family that is Bold Strokes Books for inspiration. A life-long Massachusetts resident, Friz is into history, New England pro sports, and singing and acoustic guitar—and living on Cape Cod, just an hour from Provincetown, with her wife, Kathy.

Follow Friz on www.cffrizzell.com and on Facebook at CF Frizzell.

Books Available From Bold Strokes Books

Change in Time by Robyn Nyx. Working in the past is hell on your future. The Extractor series: Book Two. (978-162639-880-1)

Love After Hours by Radclyffe. When Gina Antonelli agrees to renovate Carrie Longmire's new house, she doesn't welcome Carrie's overtures at friendship or her own unexpected attraction. A Rivers Community Novel. (978-163555-090-0)

Nantucket Rose by CF Frizzell. Maggie Jordan can't wait to convert a historic Nantucket home into a B&B, but doesn't expect to fall for mariner Ellis Chilton, who has more claim to the house than Maggie realizes. (978-163555-056-6)

Picture Perfect by Lisa Moreau. Falling in love wasn't supposed to be part of the stakes for Olive and Gabby, rival photographers in the competition of a lifetime. (978-162639-975-4)

Set the Stage by Karis Walsh. Actress Emilie Danvers takes the stage again in Ashland, Oregon, little realizing that landscaper Arden Philips is about to offer her a very personal romantic lead role. (978-163555-087-0)

Strike a Match by Fiona Riley. When their attempts at matchmaking fizzle out, firefighter Sasha and reluctant millionairess Abby find themselves turning to each other to strike a perfect match. (978-162639-999-0)

The Price of Cash by Ashley Bartlett. Cash Braddock is doing her best to keep her business afloat, stay out of jail, and avoid Detective Kallen. It's not working. (978-162639-708-8)

Under Her Wing by Ronica Black. At Angel's Wings Rescue, dogs are usually the ones saved, but when quiet Kassandra Haden meets outspoken owner Jayden Beaumont, the two stubborn women just might end up saving each other. (978-163555-077-1)

Underwater Vibes by Mickey Brent. When Hélène, a translator in Brussels, Belgium, meets Sylvie, a young Greek photographer and swim coach, unsettling feelings hijack Hélène's mind and body—even her poems. (978-163555-002-3)

A Date to Die by Anne Laughlin. Someone is killing people close to Detective Kay Adler, who must look to her own troubled past for a suspect. There she finds more than one person seeking revenge against her. (978-163555-023-8)

Captured Soul by Laydin Michaels. Can Kadence Munroe save the woman she loves from a twisted killer, or will she lose her to a collector of souls? (978-162639-915-0)

Dawn's New Day by TJ Thomas. Can Dawn Oliver and Cam Cooper, two women who have loved and lost, open their hearts to love again? (978-163555-072-6)

Definite Possibility by Maggie Cummings. Sam Miller is just out for good times, but Lucy Weston makes her realize happily ever after is a definite possibility. (978-162639-909-9)

Eyes Like Those by Melissa Brayden. Isabel Chase and Taylor Andrews struggle between love and ambition from the writers' room on one of Hollywood's hottest TV shows. (978-163555-012-2)

Heart's Orders by Jaycie Morrison. Helen Tucker and Tee Owens escape hardscrabble lives to careers in the Women's Army Corps, but more than their hearts are at risk as friendship blossoms into love. (978-163555-073-3)

Hiding Out by Kay Bigelow. Treat Dandridge is unaware that her life is in danger from the murderer who is hunting the woman she's falling in love with, Mickey Heiden. (978-162639-983-9)

Omnipotence Enough by Sophia Kell Hagin. Can the tiny tool that abducted war veteran Jamie Gwynmorgan accidentally acquires help her escape an unknown enemy to reclaim her stolen life and the woman she deeply loves? (978-163555-037-5)

Summer's Cove by Aurora Rey. Emerson Lange moved to Provincetown to live in the moment, but when she meets Darcy Belo and her son Liam, her quest for summer romance becomes a family affair. (978-162639-971-6)

The Road to Wings by Julie Tizard. Lieutenant Casey Tompkins, Air Force student pilot, has to fly with the toughest instructor, Captain Kathryn "Hard Ass" Hardesty, fly a supersonic jet, and deal with a growing forbidden attraction. (978-162639-988-4)

Beauty and the Boss by Ali Vali. Ellis Renois is at the top of the fashion world, but she never expects her summer assistant Charlotte Hamner to tear her heart and her business apart like sharp scissors through cheap material. (978-162639-919-8)

Fury's Choice by Brey Willows. When gods walk amongst humans, can two women find a balance between love and faith? (978-162639-869-6)

Lessons in Desire by MJ Williamz. Can a summer love stand a four-month hiatus and still burn hot? (978-163555-019-1)

Lightning Chasers by Cass Sellars. For Sydney and Parker, being a couple was never what they had planned. Now they have to fight corruption, murder, and enemies hiding in plain sight just to hold on to each other. Lightning Series, Book Two. (978-162639-965-5)

Summer Fling by Jean Copeland. Still jaded from a breakup years earlier, Kate struggles to trust falling in love again when a summer fling with sexy young singer Jordan rocks her off her feet. (978-162639-981-5)

Take Me There by Julie Cannon. Adrienne and Sloan know it would be career suicide to mix business with pleasure, however tempting it is. But what's the harm? They're both consenting adults. Who would know? (978-162639-917-4)

Unchained Memories by Dena Blake. Can a woman give herself completely when she's left a piece of herself behind? (978-162639-993-8)